BROKEN
CONTRACT

BR⊘KEN CONTRACT

A Love Story

Martin Kraidin

SUNSTONE
PRESS

SANTA FE

Sunstone books may be purchased for educational, business, or sales promotional use.
For information please write: Special Markets Department, Sunstone Press,
P.O. Box 2321, Santa Fe, New Mexico 87504-2321.

Book and Cover design › Vicki Ahl
Body typeface › California FB
Printed on acid-free paper
∞
eBook 978-1-61139-294-4

———————————————————————————————

Library of Congress Cataloging-in-Publication Data

Kraidin, Martin, 1939-
  Broken contract : a love story / by Martin Kraidin.
    pages cm
  I. Title.
  PS3611.R345B76 2014
  813'.6--dc23

                        2014021965

———————————————————————————————

WWW.SUNSTONEPRESS.COM
SUNSTONE PRESS / POST OFFICE BOX 2321 / SANTA FE, NM 87504-2321 /USA
(505) 988-4418 / ORDERS ONLY (800) 243-5644 / FAX (505) 988-1025

Acknowledgements

I could never have written this book without the support of many people near and dear to my heart. My beloved late wife Lynn, of course, has been with me, in spirit, throughout the process, and I owe her everything. Lynn, one day I will indeed hold you in my arms, again. My four children—Stephen, Jonathan, Adam, and Elizabeth—have provided great support as well. Knowing that I am telling this tale has been hard on them, as the story of our lives has not been without its rocky parts, but in the end I received loving acceptance, courage, and encouragement from each and every one of them. Thank you for that. It means the world to me. Finally, I would like to thank my editor, Ruby Peru, for her invaluable help in condensing half a century of my life into a tale that I think is as romantic to read as it was to live. Thanks also to my many friends as well as my many doctors who, with their indefatigable support, have saved my life many times over.

1

May 2, 1984

"Good morning, Dr. Kraidin!" Sharon called out.

I stifled a smart-aleck comment as I slipped behind my desk, and she placed a stack of mail in my plastic inbox. "Are you sure you don't want me to just take these bills?"

I replied in the negative and my office assistant left me to enjoy my morning routine—sifting through every envelope, postcard, advertisement, and promotional coupon. As I did so, I noticed my jaundiced hands looked little better than they had eight months before, when the hospital released me. With a flick of the wrist, I flung the electric bill into the outbox on the desk's other corner, then a bill from a periodontal supplier. I tossed in an invoice from our cleaning company and another from our x-ray technician. Each morning, for the past twenty years, I had placed nearly every envelope directly into the outbox, sending it back to Sharon to deal with. The tradition of sifting through my mail each morning seemed silly and purposeless to her, but I felt a sacred bond to everything addressed to me, and for good reason, though I seldom remembered the reason anymore. These days, sorting through the envelopes, alone, served as a meditation.

I pitched a dry cleaning bill on top of the other envelopes, and then dropped some junk mail into the trash—an ad for cheap jewelry. That reminded me of something.

"Sharon," I said into the intercom, "could you do me a favor today? Go on down to Sak's and get my wife a Mother's Day gift? Have them wrap it."

"How much should I spend?"

"As little as possible!"

Sharon knew my sense of humor better than anyone. She laughed. "Should I tell you what it is or let it be a surprise to both of you?" she asked, with perfectly pitched sarcasm.

"Of course I want to know what it is," I lied.

The next envelope in the stack, neatly hand-addressed in ballpoint pen, didn't look like the others. When I glanced at the return address, I froze. The sender's name seemed to pop off the paper: Stephen Levenson. The return address cited Philadelphia, Pennsylvania.

I don't know how long I stared at that envelope, but Sharon's voice pulled me out of my reverie. She stood before me, again.

"Ready for me to take the outbox?" she asked.

I looked into her chocolate brown eyes and said, "I'm not ready."

In that moment, the world came into focus, as if for the first time. I noticed the slight crow's feet on either side of Sharon's eyes, the sound of her sleeves rubbing against the fabric of her white lab coat. She slipped her hands into the coat's front pockets and I faintly heard the rustle of paper in one, the jingle of paperclips in the other. For the first time, I smelled her hairspray, heard the sound of water in the pipes inside the walls, and detected a breeze on my left shoulder from the air conditioning vent. My senses were alert on a level I hadn't experienced in nearly two decades.

"Dr. Kraidin...Marty...are you okay?" Sharon asked, crinkling exactly three furrows into her brow. A strand of brunette hair, frosted blonde, fell over her tastefully rouged, left zygomatic bone.

I cleared my throat. "Yes. Yes, I'm fine. What did I say?"

"You said you weren't ready. For me to take the bills?"

"Oh, no, you go ahead. And...could you shut the door on your way out?" I asked, noticing Sharon's eyes peering at my hands, which flattened Stephen's letter to the desk, as if by touching every inch of it, I made it more real. Like most secretaries, Sharon snooped. I slid two fingers over the return address, though I knew the name Levenson would mean nothing to her.

"Sure," she replied. With her hand on the doorknob, Sharon looked back and said, "Don't forget about your surgery on Mr. Bodine at nine thirty. He's already prepped."

The door clicked shut behind her, and I relished my moment alone with this piece of paper I had waited two hundred and fifty-two months, three weeks, eight hours, and forty-five minutes to receive.

"I'm not ready," I said aloud again, thinking, I'm not well enough, I'm not strong enough.

I pulled a little-used, silver, letter opener out of my top desk drawer and slit the envelope as carefully as if it were ancient papyrus. From inside, I took two pieces of ordinary notebook paper, folded in thirds. My hands smoothed them flat while my eyes scanned the page, noticing the even, well-formed lines of cursive, the nicely indented paragraphs—nothing hasty here, a deliberate undertaking.

I closed the room's blinds to eliminate glare, leaned back in my leather chair, crossed one ankle over the other knee, and began to read.

5/2/84

Dear Marty,

For 21 years now, I have been wondering who my father is, and what he looks like. Unfortunately, there are no pictorial records of you. It's been during the past two years that my curiosity has come to a peak. To be honest with you, I really have heard very little about you from Mom and the rest of the family. What little I've heard, I dismiss because it's opinionated and biased. I want the truth, which only you can give me.

I have spent the past two summers in Palm Beach, which is where Mom's parents (Abner and Mary) live. Unfortunately, Mary died a year ago. Pop still has his boat, and consequently I work at a marina as a dock master. I also train with a swim team in Palm Beach.

Last summer I really started thinking about you. Being so near to you heightened my awareness of the large gap, which I have inside me. It isn't until now that I feel confident enough about my life and myself that I take the time and effort to contact you. I've made feeble attempts before, but they were quickly aborted for fear of being hurt. Now, I'm willing to take the risk, and would very much like to meet you in the upcoming weeks of the summer. I will bring no anger or ill-intentioned feelings to this meeting. I just want to meet, feel, and see you with my own eyes. I sincerely hope and pray that you are also willing to take the few hours out of your day to meet me, even if only this once.

Nobody knows about this letter. I ask you not to tell anyone either until we've met. Or, if we don't meet, please forget about this letter entirely. I'm the one who is putting his heart on the line; I hope that you are also willing to make this sacrifice.

Please Marty, let's meet soon.

Your son,
Stephen Levenson (Konick)

Tears flooded my eyes, as if they'd been waiting there, pushing to get out, for years. I lay my head on my arms and let my body go, shaking and heaving and sobbing until I thought I would throw up. I had never cried like that before, but I'd seen it. Lynn, Stephen's mother, had cried like that the last time I saw her. I remembered the shaking of her narrow shoulders, the sobbing, and the wailing like an animal in a trap.

The intercom buzzed, "Dr. Kraidin, Mr. Bodine is ready."

I pressed the button and said, "Reschedule him," trying unsuccessfully to keep my voice stable.

After a pause, Sharon buzzed me back, saying simply, "Yes, Doctor."

I pulled a legal pad out of a drawer and began writing in big, loopy letters. I told Stephen I would come to Philadelphia immediately. I wanted to see him without delay. I wanted to get to know him and tell him the truth about everything that had happened between his mother and me. I pointedly didn't mention Stephen's grandfather Abner, whom he called Pop in his letter. I thanked Stephen for writing me. Then I thanked him again. Looking again at Stephen's envelope, I reread the return address, which stated:

Stephen Levenson care of Je Vonna Moxley.

He wasn't writing from home. He wanted to receive my letter at a friend's house to keep this correspondence secret from Lynn. I wondered why.

After sealing the letter in an envelope, I slid both my letter and Stephen's into my inside sport coat pocket and slipped out of the office while Sharon was away, probably apologizing to Mr. Bodine. I figured a walk to the post office box on the corner would calm me, clear my head, and it did. But after dropping my letter in the box, I remembered Stephen had written his phone number beneath his name on the letter. Sending the letter seemed silly, now. After waiting 21 years, I saw no reason to subject myself further to the capriciousness of the U.S. mail. I wanted to talk to my son immediately.

I stepped into a phone booth, and then realized I carried no change. I couldn't call him from a phone booth, anyway. That wouldn't be right. I took a few steps toward my office. Then I found a quarter in my pocket, so I turned back to the phone. No, it's not enough money. I'll get cut off. I turned around again. Then I thought no, I should place the call without delay. I turned around again, back to the phone booth. I took a few steps and nearly bumped into a man on the street who gave me a look that said it all. My behavior appeared insane. I marched myself back to the office, where Sharon now sat at the reception desk.

"Cancel everything!" I said, waving my arm emphatically in a way that, I think, meant something like stop the world from spinning, please!

Inside my office, I shut and locked the door, then opened Stephen's letter to the last page, and put my hand on the telephone, a newly sacred object. My chest expanded with a deep, healthy breath, as I picked up the receiver and began to punch in the numbers.

Area code 215—I knew it well.

2

Bold footsteps and the banter of hundreds of students echoed throughout the campus' primary dental school building. Fred and I, like the others, fast-walked toward the square of glorious daylight at the end of the tunnel.

"Marty!" Fred said, suddenly stopping in his tracks, "Where's your cane?"

"I don't need it anymore!" I replied.

"Gee, that's great, Marty. Really great. I'm happy for you."

I had been wondering when someone would notice I had the old spring back in my step. After nine months either bedridden or propped up by a crutch or a cane, I finally felt like my old self again.

"It's a miracle!" hollered Fred playfully, jumping up to tap one of the University of Pennsylvania banners hanging from the hall's vaulted ceiling.

"What's a miracle is that I didn't lose the year over tearing my Achilles," I said.

"Oh Marty, Dean Lippard adores you. You're his fair-haired boy. If you'd fallen into the Black Hole of Calcutta, he would have dove in after you."

Tearing my Achilles tendon in a freak accident had, instead of setting me back a year in my schooling, caused the dean, teachers, and fellow students to rally around me like a team of triage nurses. Fellow students brought the class notes to my apartment, and my science lab teacher allowed me to set up my equipment at home, siphoning gas from the kitchen stove to power a Bunsen burner. If anything, I became more resourceful and independent as a result of the fiasco.

"Black Hole of Calcutta would have made a better story than a stupid supermarket display falling on me," I said, and laughed. I could afford to see the humor in it, after all. It was, if nothing else ironic, that I would get a sports injury for the only thing in school I did not excel in—sports. I was tall but no basketball player; lanky but no wrestler, swimmer or track star, too clumsy to be a gymnast; too skinny to be a football player and too uninterested to be anything else. Yet, only I could tear his Achilles tendon in a freak accident that left me crippled for the better part of the school term.

Even with the accident, it seemed nothing could bring me down; nothing could break the charmed bubble of my life. School was my refuge. It was here, even from my earliest days in elementary school and through high school and now into college life, school provided me the outlet to excel. It was in school where I realized my natural gregarious personality and the ability to not just fit it but to lead. None of these traits were encouraged at home where my parents believed mediocrity was both a standard and an achievement. And each time I did excel, my parents were right there to knock me right off my high horse. In one such example, my high school curriculum included art classes in which I was encourage to draw. My teacher was duly impressed with the artist Kraidin emerging in her midst and requested meeting my parents to talk about and art-based career in my future. Both my parents sat stone faced during the meeting while my teacher spewed high praise and encouragement. Later, when she had gone, and I said I would like to go into the arts, my father's only comment was a clenched-teeth deriding comment. "So you think you can make a living as an artist?"

Similarly, my music appreciation teacher saw promise in the naïve war-bling of young Kraidin and encouraged me to audition for the New York City All City Chorus—a prestigious group of young city wide young talent. To my utter delight and my parents complete disregard, I was accepted and was asked to perform at the world famous Carnegie Hall and then on none other than the Ed Sullivan Show where Mr. Sullivan himself—the maker of careers—served up high praise for our performance. But even that was not good enough for Helen and Al Kraidin who could only spit: "So what? Now you think you're going to be a singer?"

It wasn't so much that I could never please my parents. It was more like they could never see the practical value in these artistic flights of fancy and they were, if nothing else, practical people—devoid of praise or positive reinforce-ment. I don't remember ever a hug or kiss from my father. So when it came to school I don't believe I ran to it as much as I ran from my home life. And it was there where I found the chance to succeed and the support to do so.

It all started back in high school, when I won the title of class president, excelled as one of the most popular students. Then at Dartmouth, I cruised through my requirements in record time, transferred to U. Penn Dental School two years early, and became president of my class again. I had what they called a magnetism without being an egotist. I guess I could thank my parents for keeping that in check. Now, despite my injury, my grades still soared to the top of the class. There seemed to be no challenge I couldn't overcome and no election I couldn't win. I was Martin Kraidin, a man among men. Best yet, at six foot four inches, with my preppy clothes, stylish side-part, strong chin, and winning smile—I struck people as a dead ringer for a Kennedy. In 1959, a man couldn't ask God for more.

Fred and I joined the bottleneck of students surging through the front double doors and out into a perfect spring afternoon. The winter had dragged on miserably for me, what with hobbling around on my crutches, but this day felt like a rebirth. I walked like my old self again, and this first truly spring-like day of the season seemed to celebrate that fact with me. In fact, as I watched lively groups of students congregate on the grass, I noticed everyone on campus acted like something special was in the air. As we walked down a path toward our dorm, Fred waved furiously at two young ladies, a blonde and a brunette, approaching us.

"Who are they?" I asked.

"You know the one on the left, that's Lynn," he replied, "Remember? We met her a couple weeks ago at a mixer. I wonder what a couple of high school girls are doing here today?"

"No, not her," I said. "The brunette, the one on the right." I had a habit of noticing a girl from the ankles up, and I liked what I saw. Her long, gazelle-like legs seemed to dance down the path with an ebullient, carefree nature. The tight skirt she wore just covered her knees, and I could see the curve between her ankle and calf—delicious. Then the curve at the top of her knee—Wow! What a shape! Though she still hadn't come close enough for me to see her face, I already stood transfixed.

"That's Lynn," said Fred.

"No, the brunette," I repeated.

"Her name's Lynn, too!" Fred said, and laughed like a loon, throwing his head back. "I think the blonde's a real doll. What do you think?"

I didn't answer. I just concentrated on those legs, that beautiful bouncy hair, and pretty soon, when the girls' faces came into focus, I nearly fell into a trance when I got a good look at the brunette, with the ankles. Her face held a sweetness, but also a strong, handsome quality. Her pert chin held innocence, but her eyes gleamed with intelligence, meanwhile her whole being, to me, seemed radiant, magical, illuminated. And Lynn's smile, it hypnotized me. Every curve of it enticed, as if I'd never seen a mouth before, or teeth, or lips. In that smile, I saw her shyness, her goodness. I saw something else there, too—a playful wickedness, a penchant for surprises. In her smile, I saw all of Lynn. Stranger still, the sight of this woman seemed familiar. I hadn't met her before, but I felt about her as one would about a well-loved childhood toy or a favorite song.

Fred and I greeted the two girls with some casual banter, the usual thing. The two youngest guys in dental school, he and I usually struck out with most of the older, college ladies, so we always delighted in meeting girls closer to our age. Despite my fixation on her, I couldn't talk to the brunette. I opened my mouth, but my tongue lay there like a salted slug. My eyes just stared. I couldn't even blink.

The girls said hello and made idle comments about the weekend, the weather, whatever it was, and then they continued down the path. Watching Lynn go inspired me just as much as seeing her arrive. I could have watched her walk all night. Her legs moved like water, and her little round ass in that prim, gray skirt—the way it swayed effortlessly, the way it strained the fabric, just in the important places.

Once they'd gone, Fred resumed prattling on about his weekend plans—a party or something. We kept walking.

"Well?" he finally asked.

"Well, what?" I replied.

"I said, 'what time do you want to meet at the cafeteria?' Didn't you hear me?"

"Oh...I guess six or something."

"What's the matter with you, Marty? You feeling okay?"

"Fred? Do you have that girl's phone number?"

"Who, the blonde?"

"No, the other Lynn. The brunette."

"I can get it, I guess."

"Would you do that for me?"

"Gee, no problem, Marty. I'll probably run into the blonde at some point over the weekend. I can ask her..."

"Oh, no Fred! God, no. I need it right away. Immediately."

Fred stopped walking and looked me up and down, "What's got into you?"

"Lynn, the brunette..."

"Yeah, what about her?"

"That's the woman I'm going to marry."

"Marty? Buddy, I think you've finally gone around the bend."

"I'm serious, Fred. I'm going to marry that girl."

3

A true friend, Fred made some calls that evening and found Lynn's number for me. Drunk with expectation, I dialed her. When Lynn's mother answered the phone, I set a tone of absolute politeness.

"My name is Martin Kraidin. May I please speak with Lynn?"

When Lynn came to the phone, I reintroduced myself, and then stumbled through a request for a date. No sound came back over the line for a second. Two seconds. I even thought she might hang up on me, and it took all my strength to refrain from blurting out, "Never mind!" and slamming the phone down like some stupid kid on a prank. But then she spoke.

"Um...are you sure you have the right Lynn?" she asked.

The next evening, I jumped on a train at Reading Terminal and rode out to the city's affluent Main Line, where Lynn lived with her parents. Only eighteen, she honestly told me she didn't know why I, a college man, would ask her out. I don't think she had ever even been on a date before, but something about Lynn's insecurity reassured me. She spoke so honestly about it, while I had, for years, concealed my own self-doubt beneath layers of academic success, social propriety, irresistible charm, sparkling wit, and every other ruse known to man. I'd been good at it, too.

Lynn picked me up at the station in her parents' Chrysler then drove me back to her house—a mansion, really—where I met her mother and father who seemed both polite but almost as excited about this date as we were. Then she drove us to a local pizzeria for slices and sodas, all I could afford. That evening meant everything to me. Talking to Lynn felt so easy, and I lost myself in her shining blue eyes. We talked about school. She seemed so enamored about my "adult" college courses and I, in turn, was very interested in her high school experience and how different it was to mine—hers being a suburban education to my inner city upbringing. It seemed like such mature give and take. "No one has ever spoken to me like this," she said. And I knew we were connecting on a comfortable level as if we'd known each other for years. When she took me back to the station to catch the last train into town, we stood awkwardly beside the car, the sound of the approaching train in our ears.

The screeching of the train breaks said time was up and that was a blessing in disguise. I was nervous about giving her a kiss and if I had a lot of time to debate the 'should I or shouldn't I' I don't know what would have happened. But my train was about to leave and I had to move fast. I leaned in to kiss her but felt so nervous, the kiss turned out hesitant, boyish, unsure. I hadn't delivered such a pathetic kiss in years. The squeal of the train's brakes ended the moment. Not much of a moment, anyway. She looked at me and said, "I think you can do better than that." And with that, I did. This gal was no shrinking violet and I liked that. I summoned some courage, took her in my arms, pulled her close, and kissed her gently, sincerely, deeply. I kissed her until I felt nearly satisfied, but the conductor's "all aboard" and the rhythmic chug of the evening's last departing train called to me. I tore my arms from her slender frame and raced away, down the platform, onto the steps of the final car, and into a future where Lynn's lips would never be far from my mind.

"I'm going to marry that girl," I said aloud. "I'm going to marry Lynn Konick."

The following day, and the next, I called Lynn and she called me. We talked mostly of my studies the year before, at Dartmouth, where I had majored in art while fulfilling dental school's pre-med requirements. French art, literature, and philosophy fascinated me, and she enjoyed hearing me speak of it. I went on to talk about my current work in the school lab, my math classes, science classes, all my classes, really. Lynn didn't just listen politely. She asked questions and appreciated the infectious joy I took in learning. She talked about her high school, too, but it didn't fascinate her. Mostly, she wanted to know about my work, my interests, and all the new and exciting ideas far beyond the little world she inhabited in her parents' Main Line mansion.

All week, every week, I worked at odd jobs when time allowed and scrimped and saved to take Lynn out on a Saturday night. I skipped meals, sharpened my pencils down to nubs instead of buying more, and started writing smaller to conserve paper. Every way I could save a dime or a dollar, I did it, dreaming of my next chance to treat Lynn to something nicer than a slice of pizza.

Finally, on one of my obligatory Saturday phone calls home, I told my father, "I've met someone really special. I want you to meet her."

My father told me to hold on, then came back to the phone a few minutes later. Now Mother had her ear pressed to the kitchen phone as well.

"Marty, listen," said Father. "We've got an idea."

"We have tickets to the opera—Madame Butterfly," said Mother. "Why don't the two of you take the train up to New York, meet us at the Met, and we'll give you the tickets?"

"It would be our pleasure!" said Father, in a truly rare moment of generosity.

"We can meet the young lady there in the lobby!" added Mother.

When I told Lynn, she went white. "Opera?" she said. "I don't know anything about opera."

But the next time we spoke, Lynn prattled excitedly about the opera, suddenly full of knowledge. "I know the whole story," she said. "Lieutenant Pinkerton marries Cho Cho San, but then he leaves Japan. She gives birth to his son and she's sure he will return for her, but when he comes back, it's with another wife!" Then she added, "Guess what? My mom said we can drive the family car to New York instead of taking the train."

Lynn's mother, Mary, had taken her on a grand shopping spree that included a synopsis of the story as well as a gorgeous set of evening clothes. Lynn and I had been dating for a few weeks at this point, and Mary clearly adored me.

"The Chrysler? Can I drive?" I asked.

"Of course!" she replied.

"Wait a minute. You're telling me you didn't have any evening clothes, before?" I added, incredulous. Her home looked like something out of a glamour magazine—pillars on the front porch, an impeccable lawn, and a uniformed maid—the lifestyle screamed society, grand balls, and yes, frequent trips to the opera.

"No," she answered plainly. "Mom never bought me things before, really.

Just school clothes, you know. Now, she dresses me up like a doll. It's all because of you, Marty." I knew I had met my fairy tale of a woman but the more she spoke of how her parents did little for her, the more I believed this Cinderella would be my Princess and I her Prince Charming.

At the opera, in her elegant evening dress with her vivacious talk of Cho Cho San's plight, Lynn charmed my parents completely. "She's certainly the right height for you!" Mother commented in what passed for a compliment. Again, there was no pleasing my parents even when they seemed overtly satisfied. To my mind Lynn was the right everything for me. Throughout the evening, I made no attempt to conceal my adoration of Lynn—every part of her, every word she uttered.

When the opera ended, Lynn cried and I wiped away her tears. Later, we drove home down the New Jersey turnpike, and she reached out to touch my neck, my face, my hands on the steering wheel, like she could hardly believe we'd found each other.

I pulled over at the first exit and kissed her and kissed her. I remember the silky feel of that dress, the smoothness of her bare shoulders. While strangers' headlights whizzed past, the two of us necked, alone in dreamland. And when I pulled her father's car into the driveway late at night, no reprimand awaited us, just a note from her parents saying "Marty, why don't you sleep in Lynn's brother Howard's room tonight? You've missed the last train home."

For the record, sleeping in her brother's room was not a veiled invitation to prowl the halls. I was a perfect gentleman. That night, I lay my head on the pillow, thinking things could only get better. I dreamed of my future life with Lynn: our children, our home. I dreamed of touching her pearly, enchanting body for the rest of my life. The next morning, Mary made Lynn and me bacon and eggs, orange juice and coffee, toast with marmalade.

"Anything you want, Marty!" she chirped. Mary even sent Gussie, the maid, away, wanting to make our meal herself. She treated me like a prince, Mary did. Sitting at the breakfast table, the morning sunshine turned Lynn's chestnut hair into an angel's halo while I tried to keep from smiling until my face cracked, tried to converse with Mary and Lynn about important topics, like a man.

Abner was both a second-generation success story and his own Horatio Alger success story at the same time. His father had already made a name for himself in the garment industry when young Abner came to work for him in his Philadelphia factory. It was there, where Abner met his future bride Mary, a young and attractive seamstress working on the factory floor. Abner's father objected to the budding romance and a fistfight broke out between father and son right there on the factory floor. Abner walked out on his ornery father and never looked back and swore right there that a son had no loyalty to a father.

Vowing to make his own mark in the garment industry, a mark to rival the success of his father, Abner opened his own factory in Lewes, Delaware across from Cape May, New Jersey. There with his Mary in tow, Abner bought a second hand school bus, bussed his cheap labor, taught them to how sew and produced a line of basement store women's sportswear. He was on to something. An inexpensive wrap blouse known at the 'Capri' caught on and Abner Konick's success was truly a rags to riches story.

With his newfound wealth, Abner bought a series of bigger and better boats—yachts, if you will, all named "The Capri"—and kept his little water front house in Lewes from where he commuted to the Philadelphia Main Line mansion on the way to make weekly stock deliveries in the city. His was a life of hard work and routine. You had to hand it to Abner Konick because no one handed him anything.

4

"Marty, you have got to be kidding me!" exclaimed Ken, my fraternity brother, later that week, in the campus dining hall. He dropped his head into his hands. "You spent the night at her house? Her parents didn't mind?" He shook his head. "Marty, you really are lucky. You really are a lucky bastard. Did you get your hands on her, then?"

"That's none of your business."

"Why not? Come on. Tell me what happened for once."

"It's not like that. I spent the night in her brother's room."

"You're a kick in the pants, Marty. You never change."

"What's private is private. That's all."

"Sure, what's private is private. Like that night at Skidmore. Have you still not told anyone about that night?"

"Yeah, I told someone: my doctor! I thought I got a disease from that!"

Ken stood up from the cafeteria table, struck a pose, hand on bouncing hip, speaking in falsetto: "What are you boys looking for?"

"Ken, don't remind me, for God's sakes, and sit the hell down."

"And you said, cool as a cucumber, 'We're looking for what you've got,' an octave lower than your normal voice, I swear it. Like you were an old hand at picking up whores."

"Shut the hell up, Ken. I don't want to remember that night."

He whispered, "But what really happened? I mean, I saw you pay the prostitute. Are you still telling me you didn't do anything with her? You've got to tell me someday, Marty. Come on!"

I sighed. Ken had a way of pushing, pushing, pushing, and I knew he wouldn't stop until I gave him a bone to chew on. I pulled his shirttail and made him sit down again, then leaned in over my spaghetti.

"She said, 'wash yourself,'" I whispered. "Did yours say that?"

"Yeah, I had to wash myself in this basin," he replied. "I don't know how many other men had used that same water, but I did it."

"I didn't. I said, 'Look, I already took a shower.' Then the woman became exasperated and said, 'Oh, I'll do it.' It wasn't exactly the sexiest way to get started. I think she was annoyed."

Ken giggled and raised his eyebrows, encouraging me to continue the story.

"She was anxious to get the thing over with, but...you know."

"What?"

"You know. It wasn't exactly a turn-on."

"So?"

"Let me put it this way. I finally said, 'I'm not a submarine. I don't go up and down like a periscope.'" Ken laughed, nearly spewing his lunch, while I continued. "I need affection. Inspiration. I don't know about you."

"I did her," said Ken, "but honestly it was pretty awful. She could just as well have been reading a magazine."

"Exactly. So I said, 'I mean no offense to you, Ma'am. You're a nice lady and all.' Well, that really got her. She said 'Nobody calls me ma'am and a lady. You're really a nice boy, you know?' I just wanted to get out of there, but frankly, I was afraid some pimp was going to come in and rough me up if I didn't screw this woman. I had my eye on the door and looking for my pants the whole time."

"And that's it? You left?" asked Ken.

"No, then she wanted to adopt me. She said..." I cut myself off with a laugh. Looking back, and it had been months; I finally saw the humor in it. "She said, 'You know, I could teach you a lot. You're a real nice young man,' and I said, 'Oh, I'm sure you could, Ma'am. I'm sure you could.' Then she did her thing, you know. Orally."

"Oh, so that's what happened."

"And, you know, it went like that. And afterward she said, 'You should come back and see me. You're such a nice young man. I want to see you again.' I was just afraid of this pimp I imagined, like something from the movies, that this guy would come and beat the hell out of me if I left the room too soon or too late or said something wrong, so I kept saying, 'Yes, Ma'am, I sure will come and see you again. I sure will.'"

Ken's grin made me laugh again. In truth, I had spent hours at the campus infirmary during ensuing weeks, getting checked for every disease in the book, plus psychological counseling. The whole experience put me in a sexual tailspin. I found it so disgusting. And the way the prostitute wanted to be my auntie afterward really spooked me. At this point in the conversation, I'd finally given Ken enough juice to satisfy him, and surprisingly I actually felt glad he'd pressured me to talk. I enjoyed finally laughing about our little adventure, since I knew for certain I'd never go to a prostitute again. Plenty handsome, I didn't need to, after all. And anyway, I didn't want it like that. I wanted love.

"So, tell me about this Lynn," asked Ken.

"Oh no. I'm not telling you about her," I replied. "You'll start making crude remarks."

"I swear I won't. I swear."

"Well, she's tall, and she's a brunette."

"Yeah? Is she stacked?"

"Shut up. You're disgusting." I got up to leave.

"What's with you?" Ken asked. "It's just a girl!"

With my long legs, I outpaced him. Ken was just like a lot of other idiots in my fraternity. Completely devoid of sensitivity, they didn't know the difference between a typical college girl, and a "working girl," and an angel on this earth. Well, I didn't live in that world.

I knew the difference. Did I ever.

5

I cranked open a pane of the big, bay window in my studio apartment, trying to let some of the joy of spring inside while studying for final exams. Lynn and I had been dating less than a month, but my constant thoughts of her made it nearly impossible to concentrate. I noticed a happy couple walking along the sidewalk, down below, and felt heartsick that I couldn't see Lynn until the following weekend. True to form, just as I thought of her, the phone rang.

"I keep thinking about you, Marty. I want to come over," Lynn said.

"Sweetheart, don't tempt me. I have work to do."

"I'll only sit on the bed and read," she told me. "I just want to be near you."

I couldn't resist, so I said yes, and she came over. Indeed, she did sit and read silently while I enjoyed the simple comfort of having her near, even though I sunk my nose deep in the books.

The intensity of school was incredible and at times I wasn't sure I could get through it. Just knowing Lynn was emotionally supportive was a tremendous help. But the truth was, the only way to get through the mountain of work was to do the mountain of work. I poured through my books with aggression and tenacity as I was determined to keep my grades up. I loved the work and the closer I came to my goal the more I began to love my chosen career.

I chose dentistry the way many of my generation chose their respective careers—by finding a role model. Mine happened to live up the street from us on Long Island with the nicest house on the block. When I mentioned to my father that I wanted to live in a house like that, my father finally showed an inkling of encouragement in following in the good dentist footsteps—proclaiming the nobility of dentistry as a profession. Ironically, my father and Lynn's father were both in the garment industry with my father a modest success and the Abner Konick a Main Line Philadelphia true rags to riches story. I wonder if the Kraidins lived more like the Konicks just who my role model would have been.

Over those last few weeks of school, being silent together became a habit of ours. One time, I immersed myself so heavily into the work—writing, reading, memorizing, pacing the floor, checking my notes—I forgot she was there. When I looked up and found Lynn curled on the bed, engrossed in her book, just being there, it felt like heaven.

Eventually, Lynn's mother Mary started baking casseroles and sending them over to me with Lynn. They spoiled me rotten to the core, Lynn and her mother. I loved it.

Then one day, the very moment I let Lynn in the door, I knew something was different, just from the odd look on her face. I asked, but she said nothing had changed. I tried to hit the books as usual, but felt Lynn's eyes on me the whole time; so finally, I glanced over to where she sat, on the bed. Sure enough, Lynn's bright blue eyes looked into mine. I didn't dare linger, didn't dare get lost in those eyes.

"Behave," I told her.

"Sorry," she said, and I went back to work. But pretty soon, I felt it again. Her eyes. I glanced over, and she quickly looked down at her book, clearly not reading it.

I said, "I have so much work to do, Lynn. Really."

"I know," she said.

"Is there something you want to talk about?"

"No, nothing," she said.

An hour later, it happened again. "I can feel you looking at me," I said, without glancing up.

"I'm not bothering you. I'm just looking."

"It's bothering me. I can feel it."

"Come over here a minute," she finally said, and when I looked up, I caught her trying and failing to conceal a mischievous smile.

"Oh Lynn, don't distract me. Please, Darling!"

"Just for a minute. Come over here and sit on the bed with me."

I sat on the bed, thinking I'd take a five-minute break, but my willpower vanished instantly. Pretty soon we necked, then petted, hot and heavy. I lay next to her, held her body in my arms, and felt her breathing—my hands up her open blouse, first wrapped around her slender back, then cupping soft handfuls of her breasts. Homework forgotten, I rolled over on top of her and felt Lynn's long legs part beneath me.

"I've never done this before," she whispered, unhooking my belt.

"I know," I replied. "Are you sure you want to?"

She answered with a kiss—an unmistakable affirmative. We both knew we would get engaged, soon. Nothing needed to be said.

Sure, Lynn was a "nice girl," but too adventurous to be quite that nice. We didn't live in that world, anyway—the world of unrequited passions, awkward dates, and concern for our reputations. We lived in our own world, where we knew with total confidence that we were for each other. Nothing else mattered. We knew this in the way young people fall into knowing like an abyss. Not an ounce of caution existed between us.

After we made love, we cried, both of us. Just a couple tears shed in each other's arms—tears of joy, nothing maudlin. Our bodies fit together so beautifully. I never wanted to let her go, ever. Couldn't imagine making love to another woman. The moment we met, Lynn became the only woman in my world, and now I felt surer of that than ever. Others became little more than strange creatures on the periphery, going about dull and uninspired business. They could have been stray cats or lost luggage for all they meant to me.

After Lynn drove home, I called my father—not because I wanted to, but because I had to make my obligatory Saturday call. First, I heard a busy signal. I tried again a half hour later, but the line remained busy. Dutifully, I kept trying.

Neither of my parents would deign to call me on a Saturday, no matter how busy they kept the line. They expected me to make the weekend call—or preferably, come home for a visit—no matter what obstacles presented themselves. In much the same way, throughout my childhood, every weekend without fail, the whole family had driven to an old folks' home to visit the uncle that had raised my father and brought him to America to escape the pogroms. Respect for parents dominated my family's old-world culture. My parents were once a year Jews who celebrated the high holidays—barely—kept the house kosher out of deference to my grandmother and expected me to walk to synagogue with my father as a way to control me rather than observe any religious traditions. But it was their way and had always been.

When I finally got through, my head still spun with thoughts of Lynn, and I felt quiet, contemplative.

"Everything okay?" asked Father.

"Sure," I said. "Everything's just fine. Keeping my grades up. How are things at home?" I could hear my mother weeping in the background.

"Okay. Your mother just got off the line with Aunt Judith. I wish she wouldn't talk about your sister, but she can't help it. Now, she's crying again."

I didn't know what to say. It had been eight years since my sister Sheila married a man, Walter, who was both an unbelievable control freak and down-right disrespectful to our parents. In fact, he had already cut all ties with his own parents, insisting they were only 'biological factors'. At some point early in their relationship, my parents told Sheila she could "do better," and set about treating Walter with outright hostility. She foolishly relayed their bitter words to Walter and he exacted his revenge once they were married by forcing Sheila to cut all family ties, just as he himself had done. My parents still spoke of my sister's "betrayal" of the family as if it had happened yesterday. In fact, Sheila's presence, as the source of Mother's perpetual sorrow, seemed stronger now than before she left home.

To make matters worse, five years ago, when Sheila gave birth to my parents' first grandchild, mother, father and I tried to visit her in the hospital, but as soon as Walter saw us, he hollered, "What are they doing here?" and called security to escort us off the premises. We hadn't seen Sheila since.

None of us knew why Sheila first took up with Walter. A gorgeous young woman, she could have taken her pick of men. All I could figure was he must have been an ace in bed. Though I had once loved Sheila very deeply, I now hated her for disrespecting our parents the way she had—an inexcusable offense, in our verging-on-orthodox Jewish culture. I didn't even want to discuss her, but to Mother, The Sheila Situation offered a wound to pour salt in daily. It took some time to come to realize that both my parents and Walter were equally to blame for the initial steps in the conflict. He met them with an already jaundiced atti-tude toward parents and they proceeded to fulfill his worst fears by demanding the almost-servile demonstrations of respect they felt to be their due. However, I, on the other hand, was exactly the sycophant my parents had raised me to be. So I felt sure all the blame lay on Walter and Shelia's heads.

"That's too bad," I said to Father.

"Why did Sheila have to go and marry that Walter?" my father asked. "That man is awful to the core. I mean, he really is."

"Yes, he is. I know it."

"I just wish she would change her mind, come home sometime, or at least call. She could at least call. Don't you think she should?"

"Yes, she should, but she won't. Anyway, Lynn is fine. Lynn and I are doing fine."

"Who?"

I reminded him about my girlfriend, Lynn, and felt like I ought to mention my own name as well. Your son, Marty? Remember? The one that calls every Saturday? The one that skipped to dental school two years ahead in order to save you thousands of dollars in tuition? The one at the top of his class? That Marty Kraidin?

It didn't matter; I had long ago grown accustomed to the treatment. Just like in childhood, when Sheila came to mind, Marty disappeared. I gave Father a cursory report of my progress in dental school and said goodbye, eager to get back to thoughts of Lynn.

I hadn't planned to, but as soon as I hung up with Father, I called Lynn at home. She had only just come in the door. I couldn't stand to be away from her for even that long.

6

Mary led her husband, Abner, and daughter, Lynn, in a rousing chorus of Happy Birthday while I grinned from the seat of honor, Abner's usual place, at the head of the Konicks' dining table. The family maid, Gussie, entered, bearing a perfect, two-layer chocolate cake studded with the dancing lights of twenty-one candles. Before I blew them out, I wished, of course, to marry Lynn. A wasted wish, since that seemed inevitable, but nothing else in my life felt lacking. I eagerly unwrapped the pile of presents before me, the best of which turned out to be a 35 mm Nikon camera from my parents.

Lynn and I put on our boots and trudged out in the February snow to take photos. She pointed at icicles, snowmen, picturesque landscapes, and I pretended interest in them, but I only wanted to shoot photos of her. Lynn from the front—her gorgeous smile lighting up the snow. Lynn from the back—her angel's hair peeking out from under a wool cap. Lynn's radiant smile. Lynn's graceful gloved hands. I didn't care about acting like a fool for her. Being in love with Lynn felt powerful. Having this girl to care for focused my energies and strengthened my resolve to succeed in every way.

Flushed with the exertion of our photographic adventure, we came inside and I called my parents.

"I love the camera, Father. Thanks so much!"

"Happy twenty-first," my father said in a dry, cold voice.

Then my mother took the phone. "We would have liked it if you had come home for your birthday, Martin."

Father came on the line again, "We're very disappointed in you."

"I didn't know you two wanted to be with me," I replied. "You should have said something."

"It's not our duty to say anything, Martin," replied Father. "You should have come home. A son comes to his parents on his twenty-first birthday."

"It's awfully far up to Long Island. Lynn's parents invited me, so I just accepted. I didn't think."

"You certainly didn't."

"But you didn't invite us," I complained.

"We shouldn't have to invite you," my father replied. "Or is it you think now that you're a man, you don't need us?"

"I don't think that!"

I heard nothing else on the line for a few seconds. Finally, my father said, "I hear a lot of voices in the background. It sounds like you are having quite a time."

"We are," I replied.

"We are sitting home, alone. And your mother has been crying again, about Sheila."

"You could have come to Philadelphia and taken Lynn and me out to dinner," I replied. "We could still do that, in fact, perhaps tomorrow!"

In the background, I heard Father relay the idea to my mother, and then her voice coming from far away. "No, Al," she said. "It's too late. He's made his choice."

Didn't they know they were chasing me into the arms of the Konicks who were treating me more like a son then my own parents?

When I got off the phone, I wandered into the parlor, where Lynn's father Abner put his long, muscular arm around my shoulders and boomed, "The birthday boy!" Standing 6'4", just like me, Abner always looked the picture of wealth and prestige—perfect hair, perfect tan, perfectly creased trousers. He exuded masculine authority in a way that dwarfed every other personality in the room. Early on, I noticed the way Mary and Lynn scuttled out of his way and let him have the last word in every conversation, but I saw no reason to cow-tow to the man. I treated him with appropriate respect, that's all.

Mary and Lynn clapped and cheered and sang a couple more bars of Happy Birthday while Abner popped the cork on a bottle of champagne.

"To Marty!" toasted Abner, raising his glass high. "He's our man!"

I put on a smile and tried to forget my parents' words, but I couldn't enjoy the party any longer.

"What's the matter, Marty?" asked Mary, always a keen observer.

"Oh, nothing, it's just...my parents were upset I didn't go visit them today," I said.

"Of course," Mary said, "They miss you. That's a shame. Maybe we should invite them to the house next weekend? Make it up to them?"

"Nonsense!" boomed Abner. "Marty is a man, now. He doesn't need to be doing his parents' bidding. He's celebrating with us. That's his choice. Now, who needs a refill?"

Predictably, Mary dropped the subject. Lynn caught my eye and smiled in sympathy. I tried to smile back, but couldn't.

My parents' complaint brought up an old, familiar mixture of guilt and anger that left me deeply troubled. At 21, I still hadn't abandoned the hope that one day I could satisfy my parents by being the good son whose excellence and loyalty would erase Sheila from their minds.

Abner jolted me out of my melancholy with a series of hearty pats on the back and more congratulations. No one could stop and think in Abner's presence. You just had to roll along with his party, so I downed my champagne with a flourish.

"That's right, I'm celebrating!" I boomed right back at Abner. "More champagne all around!"

7

February 28, 1960

The tinkling of fine china and silver made my family home sound just like Abner's exclusive club. I enjoyed the sound as I descended the stairs in my formal dinner jacket. Mother fussed over selecting candlesticks, polishing glasses, repositioning the gravy boat. At her best that day—a little nervous, a little excited—she focused on showcasing our home and, for once, refrained from talking about Sheila. This will be one evening, I thought, that my sister, or the ghost of my sister, can't ruin.

Ironically, my father and Abner made their respective livings in the same business: the garment industry. Each man owned a factory, but his world couldn't have been more different. Abner's stately manor dazzled the eye with crystal chandeliers, marble statuettes, and a prideful tone of old money. By contrast, my father's wealth shone so new as to be a constant focus of discussion for my uncles and aunts.

My family's two-story, middle-class home, with its one telephone and tiny television, in its up-and-coming neighborhood, seemed, to our apartment-dwelling relatives, like a luxurious abode. Thus, a parade of relations descended upon my parents every Tuesday evening to watch Milton Berle, eat my mother's cooking, and generally reap the bounty of my father's relative wealth. Meanwhile, my grandmother would make a point of criticizing every aspect of Mother's decor she viewed as excess.

Judging by outward displays, it certainly seemed like Abner possessed a far better head for business than my father, but, for all I knew, my father could have hoarded millions, because no matter how much he had in the bank, he never spent money he didn't have to. For instance, back when Sheila and I were children, on the rare occasions that the family went out to dinner, Father taught us to look on the right side of a menu first, where the prices were printed. On our occasional summer vacations to the mountains or the beach, we took the car instead of flying and stayed in the cheapest hotels. Some parents could have made that fun—car games, stops at roadside attractions, perhaps an amusement park or two—but not mine. I loved my parents, but they weren't fun people. They were serious, cautious, anxious people.

I remember once in high school, proudly bringing home a test paper graded 98.

Father reacted, "Where are the other two points?"

Mother exclaimed, "You almost did it!"

High standards didn't drive their behavior. It was just that they simply didn't know how to be happy. If those two ever enjoyed anything, it was being miserable. I didn't understand this at the time, though. Like any kid, I thought my parents' dissatisfaction had something to do with me, so I worked as hard as I could to win their ever-elusive approval.

To say I liked Abner's devil-may-care attitude toward money would be an understatement. That's how I wanted to live once I had made it in life: fun loving and generous to a fault. Nevertheless, I felt guilty accepting Lynn's parents' invitations weekend after weekend and never making the trip up to see my own parents. Not as guilty as my folks would have liked me to feel, but guilty enough.

When Abner, Mary, and Lynn came to the door, I hung back and let my parents greet them. After the introductions, we sat down for cocktails and hors d'oeuvres. For months, although they had never met, the two sets of parents had been behaving like rival gang members, fighting over Lynn's and my time like it was currency. So, while Lynn and I snuggled on the sofa, we delighted in watching our parents chatter away, now, like school chums. What a relief. They talked shop about the garment industry, then, chatted about favorite restaurants. Abner and Mary brought up fashion and art and the symphony, and my father held forth on the subject of opera. The meeting remained congenial throughout, just as it should have been, because everybody but Lynn knew a secret.

Afternoon sun slanted through the window, lighting up the glasses, the silverware, the perfect shine my mother had personally polished into every utensil. The light showed off embroidered white linen napkins that Mother had, at my request, folded into squares and lay flat upon the plates. The scraping of chairs ceased as we all settled in, and then, with perfectly natural gestures, took our napkins off the plates.

Lynn gasped. On her plate, beneath the napkin, sat a velvet box.

"What's this?" she asked.

"I don't know," I replied. "Why don't you open it?"

Inside lay a gleaming gold ring with a pear-shaped diamond. When I told my father I was going to ask Lynn to marry me, he quickly called his friends in the city on 47th street in the diamond district. My father my have been frugal but he knew the value of an investment and he was going to insure that I get the best diamond for my money. Everyone seemed to be in on it. My father found the dealer, my mother helped me pick out the ring—a much nicer ring than any 21-year-old college student ought to be giving his girl—and Mary, Lynn's mother, surreptitiously found out Lynn's ring size without her knowing it. As usual, my most intimate of moments was another family affair.

When Lynn saw it, she cried. The mothers cried, too, and the fathers beamed.

I grinned like Howdy Doody when Lynn said, "Yes! Yes! Yes!"

Our engagement felt perfect, but even better, by carefully orchestrating the event, I had managed to please all the parents at once. I cared so much about that.

After dinner, my father the penny-pincher looked on in amazement, and possibly horror, as Abner announced he had made reservations for all of us to see Lena Horne that night at the Waldorf Astoria's intimate Empire Room. These were highly coveted tickets you had to know important people in order to get. My parents saw the gesture as nothing more than showing off and more of the Philadelphia ostentation. Of course that didn't stop them from enjoying every moment of the evening. Between the sighs and the rolling of the eyes there was plenty of laughter and applause.

There, in the most elegant theater I'd ever seen, Lena sang magnificently. We all danced the night away—three couples, all of us swooning with the ecstasy of the moment, the perfection of our love, the pure opulence of the room, and our magnificent dreams of the future.

The dinner and the show weren't enough for Mary and Abner. So excited were they about our engagement that, a few weeks later, they threw us a huge society party beneath a tent on the lawn at their mansion. Mary planned everything, and that woman knew how to do things right. She hired cooks and caterers and a live band. When it came to splendor, Mary didn't overlook a thing. Before the party, she and Abner even gave me a gift: a beautiful ring with a star sapphire.

"You know what they say Marty: you don't marry the girl, you marry the family. Consider this your engagement ring!" I wore that ring with so much pride and so much ignorance.

In the receiving line, Mary, in her infinite cleverness, had rigged it so that she stood on one side of me, Lynn, on the other. Mary whispered the names of each approaching couple in my ear, so I could surprise these strangers by greeting them by name. Meanwhile, Lynn kept an eye out for anyone sneaking up on us from the wrong direction. Boy, did I ever charm those people. As they walked away, I heard many a wife whisper to her husband, "How did he know our names?"

My parents attended the party, of course, but no amount of champagne could wash the sour expressions off their faces. All this excess, all this expenditure and showmanship, and to top it all off, the caterers weren't even kosher. My father didn't approve, and my mother resented what she considered the Konicks' attempt to buy me.

"They're just generous, Mother," I said. "It would be rude to say no to their gifts." But she grumbled all through the party.

Later, Father cornered me near the grand piano. "Nothing's free, Marty," he warned, looking pointedly at my ring. My father was never known to be prophetic but this was one time when I should have taken note and listened.

I smiled, aware of being constantly observed by the Konicks and their friends, and muttered through my teeth, "They're not exactly giving me a choice, though, are they?"

Later, Mary pulled me away from the crowd, too. She looked into my eyes and said, "Marty, we're so glad about this engagement. You know all our friends think you are the most wonderful thing imaginable, and so do Abner and I."

I gave her a big hug. I liked Mary. She did everything she could to make our engagement seem magical and special in every way. She even bought Lynn a striking, pink, Chanel suit for the occasion.

Lynn looked magnificent—not like an 18-year-old girl, but a woman. Even though she had just graduated high school, and had entered her life as first date, first crush, first everything, she looked every inch ready to be a society wife. I felt every inch ready to be the successful periodontist I had set out to become, with that profession's perfect marriage of artistic and technical sensibilities. I couldn't wait to become a professional, a husband, and a father. But of course, we children had never made a difficult decision in our lives. As in love as we were, Lynn and I probably knew each other better than we knew ourselves.

Fred, the friend who introduced us, elbowed me in the ribs and said, "Man, Kraidin, you hit pay-dirt! Look at this place!"

"It's not pay-dirt," I assured him. "I'm marrying into a wonderful family, and I'm in love. That's all the pay-dirt I care about."

He shook his head and gestured toward the Konicks' magnificent mansion and the pristine lawn all around us. "You really are charmed, Kraidin. Nothing ever goes wrong in your life."

"I know it, Fred. I'm lucky."

"You are one lucky bastard," he kept saying, over and over.

I didn't just have luck, though. I worked hard and used my smarts, too. But meeting Lynn that day on campus had been luck, pure and simple, and her family behaving so magnanimously also turned out lucky for me. Yes, in addition to bringing some natural gifts to the table, I relished being king of the lucky bastards and saw no reason to expect that luck to dry up.

Finally, Lynn and I had a chance to steal a moment alone. I followed her across the dance floor, as we made our way outside the tent. "Walk beside me and hold my hand, Marty," she insisted.

"But a loyal subject always walks behind his beloved queen," I replied.

"Don't be ridiculous, Marty. Why are you always walking behind me, anyway?"

"I'm watching your ass move when you walk. I can't get enough of it."

"Oh! You better stop that!"

"You love it," I replied saucily. She did. Lynn adored being adored. When we were finally on the terrace, I added, "That skirt's amazing. I mean, how do they get them to fit like that?"

"I don't know, but however they do it, it's expensive. Can you believe my mother bought me this suit?"

"Sure, why not?"

"You don't know my mother, Marty. Before you came along..."

"Never mind all that," I said. "I'm here now, and I'm never going away."

That's how we thought about life. The past didn't matter: our childhoods, our parents, and the things we had been taught to believe. We took it for granted that by getting married, we would somehow erase the past and start life with a fresh slate. But as I embraced my beautiful fiancé in the cool afternoon air, my father's dour words came back to me, "Nothing's free, Marty."

8

Abner and Mary bought Lynn a brand-new, white, Chevy Impala rag top so she could drive into town and see me more often. Chrome everywhere, red vinyl seats, and a rear deck treatment that looked just like an airplane's tail section. The car's roomy interior made it perfect for double dating or just parking and necking for hours. What a dream! Lynn always liked things to be elegant and graceful, like a Grecian goddess, and this car exemplified her style to a T.

When we went out together, Lynn let me drive. Whether we drove to the movies or all the way to the Main Line to visit her parents, it didn't matter. As the man, I drove. She liked it that way. In fact, Lynn even had a car detailer write my initials, M.K., on the driver's side door and hers, L.K., on the passenger side.

Lynn used to bound in and out of the car, slamming the door carelessly after herself, until one day I told her, "Get back in the car!"

"What are you talking about?" she replied, puzzled.

"I know you can open the door yourself, but I am a gentleman and I'm always going to open the door for you!"

Lynn liked that. I enjoyed being a gentleman and she reveled in being treated like a lady. We might have been a little young but we loved hanging on to old-fashioned traditions that weren't so old fashioned in the Main Line, but we saw ourselves that way: a couple through and through, each with respect for the other. No hesitation. No holding back. Neither of us looked for "greener grass" in other pastures. We enjoyed each other too much for that. After a while, Lynn let me keep the car so I could pick her up at home for dates. Driving around campus with the top down, I became the envy of all my classmates.

One weekend, while we cruised around town in the Impala, showing ourselves off, I reminded Lynn of our trip to the opera. "Let's go see my parents again," I suggested. "They miss us."

"All the way up in New York?" she complained. "But my dad bought us tickets to a show tomorrow."

Over the past ten months, Lynn and I had spent a great deal of time visiting her parents, going with them to their club, out to dinner, and out to shows. They paid. Who was I, I felt, to turn down Abner and Mary's incredible generosity? God knows, except for that trip to the opera, my own parents hadn't invited us to do anything other than visit the house and just like on my birthday, these sounded less like invitations and more like complaints of neglect, but I didn't expect anything else. My parents kept our home kosher and conservative and would never be fun, big spenders, like Abner and Mary, who only visited synagogue when the mood struck them.

"Come on, Lynn," I pleaded. "I haven't been home in months, and my parents need me. They need us. They've barely had a chance to get to know you!" I didn't add the fact that they had rarely expressed any interest in getting to know Lynn, so busy were they wailing and moaning over The Sheila Situation.

"Honestly, Marty," answered Lynn, her unfastened hair blowing in the wind as we cruised beneath the grand oaks of Riverside Drive. "You know what my dad says? He thinks you're too close to your parents."

"But I only see them once a month, as it is!"

"I know. But that's what he thinks."

"My family isn't easy-going like yours, Lynn. I have obligations."

"You think my father's easy-going?"

"Isn't he?"

Lynn didn't answer but looked off into the distance. Finally, she said,

"Never mind about that. I don't want to drive all the way to Long Island. Not today or tomorrow. Let's just laze around here," she added, provocatively. "Pull over."

I parked the car in a cozy spot beside the river and she reached for me. Soon my lips found hers and all thoughts of my parents disappeared.

During our call the following Saturday, Father took a short tone with me again on the phone. Then, he put my mother on.

"Marty, don't you think you're spending a lot of time with your girl-friend's family?" she asked.

"No," I answered.

"Well, it certainly appears that way to us."

I said, "Shouldn't I spend some time with them? They think I should."

"We're your parents. They're not. I don't see that there is any more to say on the subject."

"I'd rather spend time with you, Mother, but it's so far to go home. I wish you guys would come to Philadelphia."

"Nonsense. It's your duty to visit your parents. We're not going there."

"I have to keep my grades up. It's not easy to take a weekend away from school."

"You can study here. No reason why not."

Actually there was one very good reason why not—the Sabbath—but I didn't protest. The next weekend, I drove up to Long Island, sans Lynn, for a visit.

There, I listened to my mother moan and wail to every friend and relative in the local calling area, all about Sheila's "betrayal" of the family. Mother's cries of "Look what she did to us!" used to elicit sympathy from me. After all, I felt sad about The Sheila Situation, too. But after eight years of this, the whole melodrama grated on my nerves, especially hearing that constant refrain: "Look what she did to us!"

That weekend, I tried to act attentive while Mother sat at the cluttered kitchen table, sorted bills into piles, and recounted, point by point, every detail of Sheila's rejection of the family. That's when I recalled a memory of my own, from some time before Sheila and Walter got married. At thirteen years old, I sat at that very same kitchen table, doing homework, when Sheila came into the house after having been away with Walter for the weekend.

She threw her arms around me and said, "My baby brother! I've missed you so much!" and smothered me with hugs and kisses. Then Walter stepped into the room.

"Stop hugging your brother. Stop kissing him. That's disgusting. I never want to see you do that again!" he yelled. And she did stop.

I don't recall ever having received more than a perfunctory hug or kiss from either parent, so when Walter took Sheila's love away from me, that hit hard. But after watching my parents throw themselves on their bed, sobbing and wailing, day after day, I pushed my own pain to the side. It seemed unimportant by comparison.

That's why, way back then, at just thirteen, I resolved to make up for

Sheila's "betrayal" by becoming the best son anyone had ever seen and, unlike Sheila, making my parents proud. With my looks, brains, and decent acting skill, becoming "mister charisma" turned out to be pretty easy. Throughout high school, playing the role of exemplary son became a habit, and after a while, I forgot why I did it. Everyone came to expect that of popular, friendly, polite, hard-working Marty.

That Saturday morning, my father and I resumed our old tradition of walking the few miles to synagogue together—a father/son ritual we both enjoyed. The rest of the day we relaxed: no studying, no driving, no catching up on household chores. The busier my academic life became, the harder it was for me to relax into the traditional "day of rest," but I managed. After all, I'd done it all my life. On Saturdays at U. Penn, I attended Jewish services at the university's non-denominational chapel, and even acted as cantor, but I didn't go so far as to refrain from studying on the Sabbath. In my parents' home, however, I didn't dare touch a textbook. It was simply the right thing to do.

Sunday evening, riding the train back to Philadelphia, I realized that despite her plea for me to visit, my presence didn't comfort Mother at all. A shameful sense of being a bad son overwhelmed me, and I resolved, yet again, to treat my parents better.

During subsequent weeks, I nagged Lynn to go visit my parents with me. "It seems greedy," I told her, "Letting your parents take us golfing and out to dinner and out to the club and everything, when my own parents don't have a son or daughter at home at all. After all, you have two brothers. Your parents are hardly all alone."

"Yeah, but Dad doesn't even like Howard and David."

"How can you say that?"

"They're so wishy-washy and nerdy. You know how they are."

"David? He's just a little kid! How can you call an eight-year-old wishy-washy?"

"David's cute and I love him, but you just touch him and he cries, you know? That's why Dad doesn't take him anywhere. As far as Howard, you know how he is—artsy fartsy. Dad doesn't know how to act around people like that. He wants his sons to be big and tough and manly, which neither of my brothers is ever going to be."

"They're his sons, for God's sakes!"

"Yeah, but you're the son he always wanted. You have it all."

I looked at her a long while. "What do I have?"

"You have that Marty-ness!" she declared, poking me in the ribs.

"Well, my parents happen to like my Marty-ness, too. Did you ever think of that?"

Reluctantly, Lynn acquiesced to the idea of driving up to Long Island, and that Spring we spent two weekends in New York.. On Saturdays, she walked with my father and me to synagogue and somehow endured the rest of the boring Sabbath without complaint. I rewarded her on Sundays by driving her north on I-95, all the way up to Connecticut, where we'd sightsee around Greenwich, Stamford, and Norwalk. Once we attended a Shakespeare festival and always we cruised around looking at the rolling green hills and rustic old barns.

Even though she liked those drives, Lynn never expressed much enthusiasm for going to Long Island. Finally, one evening, we sat down to a casual dinner at a burger joint near campus, just the two of us, and I found out why.

"My parents don't want me to go to New York anymore," she said.

"You mean to visit my folks? Why on earth not?"

"I told you. My dad thinks you're too close to your parents."

"But they're my parents, Lynn. Why would he say that?"

"I don't know, but I'll tell you this: my dad isn't close to his parents. In fact, he used to fight with my grandfather," she said.

"Sometimes I fight with my father, too. It feels awful."

"No," she said. "Fight fight. Fist fight. My father's father beat him pretty badly as a child, and then when he became a teenager, too big for whipping, my grandfather just punched him in the face. Dad punched back, and they fought each other like a couple of street toughs. When my Dad married my mom, who was from a poor family, my grandfather didn't approve, so, after one particularly bad fight with his father, Dad left home forever and never looked back. We never see my grandparents on that side. They're just gone. They're bad people. So that's what Dad thinks men should do. Cut ties with their parents, like him."

"His father was awful. Of course he left. But my father's not that way."

"Doesn't matter to Dad. He says leaving his dad made him a man. Made him more self-reliant. So, he thinks all men should do that."

"Like Sheila."

"I guess so. Except Sheila's a girl. That's different."

"How?"

"He thinks a man should go over to his wife's family. My dad would say Walter and Sheila should have rejected Walter's parents, but not yours. I guess that's the tradition Dad was brought up in...or else he made it up. I don't really know."

"I'm not cutting my family ties, Lynn. No way in hell. You think I want to be like my bitch sister?"

Lynn paused, ate a bite of her burger, and smiled. "I guess not. I don't know. All I know is I love you," she said.

I kissed her, and we didn't discuss the issue further.

9

March 1960

The date for the wedding was set for June 17, 1960.

"See to it everything goes smoothly for my wife," Abner said with a wink, slipping the catering director a wad of bills as thick as a sandwich.

I had to admit, I liked Abner's style.

Having set her heart on throwing us the wedding to end all weddings, Mary brought Lynn, Abner, and me to the prestigious Warwick Hotel, in Philadelphia's Rittenhouse Square, for a walk-through of our chosen venue. While Mary and Abner chatted with hotel officials about color schemes and ballrooms, Lynn marveled at the ornate ceilings, chandeliers, and gilded ashtrays. I mostly stayed out of the way.

Throughout the three months between our engagement and the wedding, Mary and Lynn immersed themselves in wedding mania, while I worked hard to keep my grades up. Lynn frequently asked my opinion on scheduling and style issues, but I didn't care. I just wanted to marry her. That, and calm her down. The more decisions needed to be made about the wedding, the more stressed Lynn became. Some days she seemed absolutely beside herself.

One day, we visited the Konicks' house for lunch, where Abner posed a hypothetical question.

"Marty," he asked, "if you were on a sinking ship with your entire family, who would you save?" Not waiting for a reply, he answered himself. "Lynn! Your wife!" He poked a finger at Lynn's face like she was a sightseeing attraction.

"Of course," I replied.

"You save your wife and Leave. Your. Parents. Behind." He added, with unmistakable emphasis.

I cleared my throat. "Well, I love my parents," I said, "but I would certainly save Lynn first."

"You're a man now, Marty, and you have to think about your future, not your past," Abner added, and left it at that.

After lunch, Lynn and I took a walk around the estate, and I told her, "Lynn, Warwick Hotel or no Warwick Hotel, I'm not going to 'leave my parents behind' as your father said."

"What's the Warwick got to do with it?"

"Open your eyes, Lynn. Your dad is a generous guy, but then he turns around when I'm least expecting it and asks for something in return—something I'm not willing to give."

"My dad just wants the best for us, Marty," she said.

"For us? I don't know about that. I think what he really wants is to keep me for a pet," I replied.

"Don't be ridiculous. Not a pet, but a son."

"Lynn, I'm also my parents' son. And that's never going to change."

She didn't like that. "My father thinks you're a mama's boy. Are you, Marty? Well, are you?"

"I'm my own man, Lynn, but I have parents the same as you. I'm not going to hurt them."

"Oh my God, Marty. Think for yourself, for once. When are you going to become a man?"

"How dare you!"

"Dare nothing! It's the truth. Growing up means stop sucking on your mama's tit. That's the way it works. Don't you love me and want to start a new life with me?"

"Of course I love you, Lynn," I said, thoroughly confused. By now we had arrived on the lawn near a set of double French doors leading into the drawing room. Lawn furniture formed a semicircle on the fresh-cut grass. "Sit down, Darling," I said. "Let's talk here."

Lynn sat, but on the edge of a seat.

"I love you," I said, "but I'm not going to disrespect my parents to prove it. You should know that by now."

"You're not going to prove it?" she asked, incensed. From my perspective, she was suffering from a classic case of premarital jitters but the more irrational she became; the more I was running out of ways to calm her down.

"I'm marrying you, for Christ sakes. That proves it!"

"No, you're not!" she screamed, tugging violently at the ring on her finger.

"I'm not marrying you! I don't want to have anything to do with you!" She got the engagement ring off, and, to my horror, flung it across the lawn.

I dove into the grass, searching desperately for that diamond. "I can't believe you did that, Lynn. I can't believe you."

"I'm not marrying you!" she shrieked.

I stood up and looked her in the eye. "Fine. Have it your way, but don't you dare just stand there. Get down on your hands and knees and help me find that ring."

"I won't! I don't care!" she replied.

Mary poked her head through the French doors. "What in the world are you two doing?" she asked.

"Nothing," I replied, on my knees in the grass. "I just dropped something."

Mary shut the doors again and I turned to Lynn, saying, "I swear to God, I will get your mother out here to help me find that ring."

"You better not!" she replied, but that got her to help me look for it.

When we finally found the ring, the sense of relief was overwhelming. I felt as if I had just metaphorically saved my marriage without even realizing we were in any sort of trouble. I told her, "Don't you ever do that, again." I should have been more aware that the ring wasn't the issue...the words were.

Lynn put it on her finger and said she was sorry. By the end of the day, we returned to normal again.

That's how topsy-turvy things became in the build-up to the wedding. Abner dropped his strange hints; Lynn came completely unhinged; Mary remained blind to everything else as she obsessed over the guest list, wedding cake, bridesmaid's dresses, and whatnot. Meanwhile, my parents' resentment of the Konicks' generosity grew daily. As for me, I felt like a zebra carcass being fought over by a bunch of hyenas.

Throughout all of it, I carried a full course load in dental school. Each week brought new drama that distracted me from my schoolwork. Some bad, like the ring in the grass incident, but some incredibly good.

One day, Mary asked Lynn and me to sit down with her in the parlor.

"What are your plans for a honeymoon?" she asked.

Lynn and I looked at each other. "We don't really have any plans yet. Something simple, though," I replied.

Mary said, "I think you should go to Europe."

"I said something simple!" I exclaimed.

"Marty, I have some money saved away, and this is my gift to you: a dream honeymoon. I want you two to see Europe."

"Mom, I can't accept that!" I said, before Lynn could accept. By this point, I called Mary Mom, though my own mother remained, quite formally, Mother.

Lynn had already told me her mother grew up dirt poor and met Abner when she got a job working as a seamstress in Abner's father's garment factory. Then, when she and Abner fell in love, they eloped. The look on Mary's face when I tried to refuse her gift made her feelings clear: Mary never got to have her own dream wedding, and now she wanted to live vicariously through Lynn and me.

"I want you to learn something now, Marty," Mary said sternly. "When a gift is given to you, you accept it graciously. This is my gift. It's five thousand dollars, and I want you to spend it all."

That sum would have put me through an Ivy League college, including all living expenses, for two solid years.

I had no idea how to book a honeymoon, but with that kind of money in the balance, I felt I should start by finding a reputable travel agency. To me, the best of the best resided in Rockefeller Center, so I caught a ride with Abner on his weekly trip up to New York. He dropped me at 30 Rockefeller Plaza, on 5th Avenue, opposite St. Patrick's Cathedral, near the statue of Atlas holding up the globe. That seemed appropriate, except that instead of holding up the world, I stood on top of it.

I wandered around the bustling area, looked down at the famous ice skating rink, and finally walked into the lobby of 30 Rockefeller Center. Men zipped to and fro with their briefcases and business suits, elevator doors whooshed open and shut, and the echoing lobby gleamed with cold, steel efficiency. I felt completely out of place, but, in reading the building directory, soon found "Arthur Pope Travel Agency."

Dressed in my usual preppy suit and tie, I blended right in with the businessmen as I boarded the elevator and rode up. When I walked into the office, I assumed the same confidence I once used on those prostitutes Ken and I met in Skidmore, only instead of "We want what you've got," I said, "I'd like to book a trip to Europe." Interestingly, either phrase would have worked.

"What kind of trip?" the receptionist asked.

"Honeymoon," I replied.

With that, she raised her eyebrows and pushed a button on her phone.

"Mr. Pope will see you directly."

Mr. Pope emerged from his office and shook my hand. A tall, middle-aged man with graying hair, his conservative suit, tie, and glasses gave Mr. Pope a distinguished, no-nonsense air. On the wall, I saw Mr. Pope's degree from Harvard, so I told him I was a Dartmouth man. That went over well, and he invited me into his office. I told him Lynn and I wanted to see Rome and Paris, that we had a month to do it, and then I let drop how much I had to spend. Mr. Pope paused a moment, as if frozen by the figure.

He looked me up and down, surely noting my age, and tilted his head as if to say, are you sure? I gave him a subtle nod, as if to say, I certainly am. Then he smiled. Broadly.

Mr. Pope leaned back in his chair and seemed to sink into a reverie. He picked up a pencil, did a few calculations, and then walked over to a map of Europe on the wall. He slid his finger along it, tracing roads the map didn't even depict. I had expected him to pull out some brochures and advertisements, but he did none of that. He planned our entire honeymoon in his head.

"You will fly into Rome," he said, "And be picked up by a private car and driver, who will chauffeur the two of you throughout Italy, then France, right through the French Riviera. Only then will you drive to Paris, where you will enjoy front-row tickets to the best shows in the city and advance reservations at the finest restaurants. After your stay in Paris, you will board a train to Le Havre, where you will set sail upon the French ocean liner "Liberté" and steam your way home, all in luxury, first-class accommodations. Sound good?"

Without so much as a second thought to the decadence that had been proposed for the young Mr. and Mrs. Kraidin, I said, "Book it!".

10

May 1960

Through the classroom window, I watched Lynn pacing the campus walkway in a tight sweater and pair of pastel blue, Mr. Pants slacks. The Mr. Pants brand ruled the runways at the time, and boy did they ever show off Lynn's figure and her long, long legs. When Lynn told her mother I liked the look, Mary took Lynn straight to the store to buy a pair of Mr. Pants pants in every shade of the rainbow. Excess truly seemed to be the Konick family calling card, and I loved it.

I couldn't wait to get outside, and when I finally burst through the doors, I swept Lynn up in my arms. May, beautiful May in Pennsylvania, blessed us with its perfect weather. A year had flashed by since we first met, and I loved Lynn more than ever. I worshipped her.

"Dance with me, Lynn," I said, and took her hand in mine.

"Oh, you. Be serious."

"I am serious. I'll hum a tune," I said, and wrapped my arm around her slender waist.

"People are watching!" she complained.

I made her dance with me anyway. I could see anxiety about something lurking behind her eyes, but I wanted to play.

"Let's go for a walk," Lynn said.

"Let's go for a dance," I replied, humming a faster tune and twirling her around.

"I'm serious!" This time she pulled away with fire in her eyes.

We walked through campus, passing beneath the lovely maples, and she talked about this and that, mostly idle chit-chat, until finally she sighed, stopped walking, turned to me, and said, "Marty, I'm late."

I should have seen it coming, but I didn't. In fact, I rarely gave pregnancy a thought. I hated condoms, never used them, and Lynn, as young and innocent as she was, didn't insist.

"How late?" I asked, frozen to the spot.

"Four weeks," she replied. "I don't know what to do."

"Do you think you're pregnant?"

"I don't know."

"If you're pregnant, we can move up the date of the wedding." I said with a nonchalance belying my absolute panic. A pregnancy would ruin everything. It was the ultimate scandal. We could never possibly have a storybook wedding; that was for sure. But moreover, I wondered how I would even finish school with the obligations of a young family.

"No," she said. "We can't!"

Truly, we couldn't. Lynn and I had very little control over the wedding details. That is, unless we talked to Mary about our problem.

"I don't even know if I'm pregnant, Marty. I have to find out for certain, but if I go to Dr. Johnstone, our family doctor, he'll tell my mother."

A pregnancy test was a multiple day, anxiety filled, experience. Women had to see a doctor for a "rabbit test" and wait a couple of days for the results. We sat on a bench along the path. She put her head on my shoulder and hugged me tightly as I ran my fingers through her silky hair and kissed her head.

"I do think you should tell your mother, Lynnie. But that's up to you. As for me, I don't know what to do, but I do know a man who always knows what to do. I think we should go and see him."

Dr. Soltz agreed to see us immediately.

Way back before I met Lynn, my friend Ken and I had our little adventure with those prostitutes. For me, the experience led to an incredible amount of anxiety, so when I went home to Long Island that summer, long ago, I found a great psychiatrist to help me deal with it: Dr. Soltz. Among other things, Dr. S. assured me no pimp would waste his valuable time tracking me down because of my inability to perform with the hooker. But more importantly, Dr. S. played the role of the encouraging father I needed.

My parents never gave advice, only stern disapproval when something wasn't perfect, which seemed always to be the case. Instead, they raised me with tradition—something I respected, though it didn't help me with women, teachers, academics, my life goals, or anything else a young man needs advice on. I enjoyed my pious walks to temple with Father every Sabbath, and I even respected the frustrating frugality that ensured our family would never do without, but when it came to answering life's difficult questions, I couldn't find the answers in Judaism. I needed a psychiatrist.

Lynn and I drove the three hours to Dr. S's office in New York and told him the problem. Quickly and kindly, he managed to obtain an immediate appointment for us with a gynecologist friend of his.

The gynecologist sat us down and asked what we had been up to, so I told him outright that we engaged in sex without protection. No sense being coy at this stage of the game. He gave us a short lecture on the contraceptive methods of the day, which, starting that year, 1960, included The Pill. Though times being what they were, an as-yet-unmarried young woman like Lynn certainly wouldn't ask her doctor for that. No way.

"I better not be pregnant," Lynn snapped at me, in the middle of the conversation.

"I take that to mean this is all my fault?" I replied. "You were just hanging around on the bed?"

"Oh! I can always count on you for a smart-aleck comment," she said, and then laughed in spite of herself.

Lynn turned out not to be pregnant after all, but her hormones had gone out of whack because of stress. Preparing for the wedding, especially with Mary insisting on perfection in every detail, pushed Lynn to the brink, but our fighting made things worse. The fights always centered on Lynn's desire to see me separate myself from my parents, both emotionally and physically. Lynn's body responded to all of it by going berserk.

After our appointment, I begged the doctor not to send the bill to my father, but to let me make payments on it over time, which he did.

About a week after our secret trip to New York, Lynn and I stayed out late on a date, and I slept over in her brother Howard's room, as usual. Early the next morning, I awoke to find Howard gone and Mary sitting on the side of my bed with a face as pale and drawn as death. She reached over and grabbed my forearm, hard.

"Is Lynn pregnant?" she whispered. "Her period is late."

"No, she isn't," I replied.

"Because if she is, Abner will kill you," Mary hissed at me, really trying to impress me with the gravitas, like Abner might come after me with a revolver or something. At the time, I found the thought ridiculous.

"It doesn't matter. We're getting married soon!" I replied.

"That's no excuse," Mary said.

I truly saw Abner and Mary and Lynn and me as one big, happy family and didn't think anything could possibly go wrong between the three of us. I smiled broadly, sat up in bed, and wrapped my arms around Mary's petite shoulders, embracing her sleepily, but with gusto, and kissing her on the cheek.

"Don't worry, Mom. Everything's going to turn out great," I said. Pretty soon, thanks to that old Kraidin charm, I got Mary to smile again.

"What am I going to do with you?" Mary asked.

"Just keep on being as wonderful as you are!" I replied.

Oh yes, I smiled at her as broadly as the Cheshire Cat, but if I had actually listened to what Mary was trying to tell me, instead of laying on the charm, I might have learned something very important that morning. There was a side to Abner I was being cautioned about...if I had only listened.

11

May 1960

One Friday morning that May, I enjoyed the rare pleasure of crossing the threshold of Lynn's bedroom. I helped Lynn fold some shirts and place them in a suitcase while her mother, father, and two brothers scurried around the house, throwing last minute items in the car.

Over all the bustle, I could hear Mary arguing with a dressmaker on the phone, shouting, "I said lavender, not lilac! Lavender!"

Mary had invited me along on a family outing to their cottage in Lewes, Delaware. Of course, I said yes.

While I helped Lynn pack, she told me about the town, "There's a boardwalk—with the best burgers! And the waves are incredible. You'll love Dad's house. Finally, the weather's good enough to go."

"Dad's house? I thought it was a vacation place."

"Well, sort of. Dad's factory is in Delaware, so during the week he stays there."

"But Delaware must be...what?...five hours away?"

"Six if you drive respectably. That's why he has the cottage. Dad only comes home on weekends. It's always been that way, ever since I was a kid."

"Don't you miss him?" I asked.

Lynn shrugged her shoulders, "Not really. Honestly, sometimes it's better when he's gone."

"Why?"

"Oh, no reason." She paused, and then added. "He's pretty disappointed in my brothers, I think. They didn't turn out to be like him at all."

"But he dotes on you," I said. "I've seen it."

"Oh, that's just when you're around," she replied, "Normally, we don't see much of him except at dinner. If he nudges me and says, 'Hey there skinny Lynnie,' that's the only way I know he's in a good mood."

"Skinny Lynnie?"

Lynn laughed and shrugged. "Well, I guess I'm pretty skinny,"

"You're svelte. You're hot. You're gorgeous!" I folded one of her bikinis into her suitcase, my hands nearly trembling with the desire to see her wear it.

Lynn laughed and said, "When I was born Dad was disappointed I wasn't a boy."

"I'm sure that's not true!"

"Oh, it's true alright. He was so sure I'd be a son he painted the room blue and bought a bunch of fire-truck toys and baseball mitts. Then, when I was born, surprise! He went out that very night and got drunk. In fact, when my mother gets mad at me, she always reminds me of the fact my father never wanted a girl."

"Lynn...why would she say such a thing?"

"I don't know," Lynn replied.

I could only respond by holding Lynn in my arms and telling her all that would change now. Maybe that is our mission: to be the best parents ever to our children. I know it my sound a little 'Pollyanna' but we are in charge of breaking the cycle, to learn from what we've seen and what we have been exposed to and bring up our children in a world of love, acceptance and support. Maybe we had to go through our world to make the world a better place. I wanted her more than anything in the world.

"Sure, it already has changed," she said. "I'm the center of attention now that I'm engaged to a periodontist who looks like a Kennedy."

I poked her in the ribs, and she giggled. "I'm just a college student," I said.

"For now."

Embarrassed, I silenced her with a kiss.

Out in Lewes Lynn and I played in the sand all weekend. Watching her splash around in a bathing suit pretty much defined my idea of heaven, so I never wanted to go inside.

On Sunday afternoon, as we walked along the beach one final time, holding hands, Lynn said, "Hey Marty, wait here a minute, okay?"

"Where are you going?"

"Just wait here. I want to walk ahead by myself."

I stayed there, looking out over the waves, while Lynn walked along the beach. She look around, perhaps searching for shells, and I watched her gorgeous ass in a rather decadent bikini, starting to think hanging back turned out to be a pretty good idea, after all. Then Lynn turned around, grinning fit to burst, and sprinted toward me.

"Lynn, what are you doing?" I yelled in panic. One second later, she leaped into my arms, wrapped her long legs around me, and whooped with joy. I caught her around the waist, held fast, and kissed her. My Lynn...always full of surprises.

We returned to the cottage that afternoon and bounded up the porch steps from the beach, vibrant with love and adventure, and hungry for dinner. Abner sat on the porch, looking out at the waves, and didn't return our greeting. Mary brought him a cocktail, for which he didn't thank her, and then she went inside and bustled around, tidying an already tidy house.

Lynn and I changed for dinner, then chatted with Lynn's brothers about all the fun we'd had that day. Abner ignored us all, staring out to sea. I tried to bring him into the conversation a couple of times, but no one else did.

Before long, Gussie announced dinner and we sat at the rectangular table in the usual formation: Abner at one end, Mary at the other, Lynn and I side by side, and David and Howard on the other side.

As we took our seats, Abner grumbled, "I sure hope the pasta isn't overcooked."

A moment later, Gussie came out of the kitchen with a big bowl of spaghetti. She served Abner first, according to family tradition, but before she could serve the next person, who happened to be Lynn, Abner picked up his fork and tried a bite. Immediately, he spit out the noodles and slammed his fists down on either side of the plate.

"How many times have I told you? I hate overcooked pasta!" He stood, snatched the bowl, and hurled it straight across the table at Mary. She ducked, and the ceramic bowl crashed to the floor. Pasta, meatballs, red sauce, and potshards flew all over the room.

"How many times do I have to tell you?" Abner yelled, not actually at Gussie, but seemingly at the room in general, spittle flying from his mouth. His face turned bright red and his clenched fists pounded the table again, this time hard enough to knock over several empty glasses. Then he stalked from the room, through the front door, down the porch steps, and away in the gloaming.

Lynn had grabbed my leg under the table and squeezed tightly enough I was sure to stop the blood flow.

Gussie vanished into the kitchen and the five of us sat in silence for several minutes, avoiding eye contact. Lynn's face went red, but I saw more embarrassment there than surprise. In fact, of the five faces present, only mine registered genuine surprise at Abner's outburst. Finally, Mary looked up from her plate, dabbed the sauce off her blouse as best she could with a napkin, and called Gussie out of the kitchen.

"Gussie, are there more meatballs?"

"Yes, ma'am."

"Then please make some more spaghetti, Gussie," she said with a calmness in her voice and looking at the assembled family as if nothing much had happened. "There is no sense skipping our dinner."

After dinner, I asked Lynn to walk on the beach with me, where I encouraged her to talk to me about Abner's behavior.

She sighed. "Dad has a temper. He's a violent man, Marty, and he drinks way too much. I didn't want you to know. I hoped he'd behave himself, but...I knew it was just a matter of time. He acts like this a lot more often than you know. You saw how composed my mom was, afterward? Well, she's used to it, that's all."

"He threw the bowl right at your mom's head!"

"Yeah. He throws things a lot. She usually ducks in time."

I didn't like the sound of that. "Why does she put up with it?" I asked.

Lynn fell silent and looked up at the starlit sky. "I don't know." A star fell. Lynn pressed her body against mine, and I took her in my arms. "She's afraid of him, I guess. We all are. I try so hard to please him, Marty. I try, but he's never happy. You just don't know when he's going to go off."

"I need to get you away from him," I said. "He could kill someone, acting like that." And then it occurred to me what Mary had told me back on the edge of the bed when she thought Lynn was pregnant. Fearing she was, she warned me that Abner would kill me. Now, I believe she wasn't joking but warning me of the violence of which the man was capable. Clearly when Abner didn't get what he wanted there were consequences and I suddenly worried how that would factor into my and Lynn's lives. I looked at my much cherished star sapphire ring on my finger and thought about my father's prophecy. "Nothing comes free." And I shuttered.

12

On a Friday afternoon, Lynn knocked on my door unexpectedly.

"Marty, I've got to get away from my mom!" she said. "The wedding is making her crazy. Every day she's on the phone, yelling at someone for God knows what." Lynn threw her purse on my bed as if it had offended her. "She sits and goes over fabric swatches like it's life and death. And when she asks my opinion about flowers or something, whatever I say is the wrong thing. She throws her hands up and screams, 'I don't know what to do with you!'" Lynn threw her hands in the air to demonstrate, nearly knocking a book off a shelf.

"I can't believe how much work it is to put on a wedding," I said. "Poor Mary."

Lynn wheeled to face me, scorn in her eyes. "Poor Mary? You're crazy. We didn't need to have the biggest society wedding Philadelphia has ever seen, you know, but we are."

"We are?"

"Oh my God, Marty! People all over town are vying for invitations. People you and I don't even know. People my parents don't even know."

Somewhere in the midst of all this planning Mary had also managed to go shopping for Lynn's and my honeymoon, returning home with exactly the type of clothes we would need to fit in in Europe's grandest hotels. These included a tuxedo and seersucker suit for me, both specially tailored to accommodate my extra-long arms.

My parents, of course, seethed over the extravagant gifts.

"Why don't you let me buy you what you need?" my father asked.

"I don't even know what I need," I told him. "Besides, Father, you wouldn't buy me those things—not in a million years."

Silence came over the line. Of course, I spoke the truth, but he didn't want to admit it, so Father became permanently angry with me. Meanwhile, Mother cried a lot more than usual. Her grief over Sheila had become, more than ever, a kind of performance art. I suspected her fear that I, too, would abandon her fueled this grief. So, Lynn's request to get away from her parents filled my heart with gladness. Now I could show my parents that, despite the Konicks' generosity, I remained their loyal son. A Kraidin.

"So you wouldn't mind visiting my parents for a weekend?" I asked Lynn. "They really need me right now."

"Oh God, Marty, I'd love to! I've got to get away from my house for a while."

While we drove north, Lynn and I talked about how the wedding had taken on a life of its own. In fact, our entire romance, as handled by Mary and Abner, had become a public spectacle.

"You know, there's something else that's been bothering me, too," she said. "It's about your sister, Sheila. I know it's hard for you, but I really feel like I ought to meet her before the wedding."

I wasn't crazy about the idea, but figured Lynn had a right to meet my sister if she wanted to. So, later, from my parents' house, I called Sheila. On the phone, Sheila sounded genuinely happy for me and proud of all my accomplishments in dental school. In fact, she sounded like the old Sheila, the big sister, who used to be my best cheerleader, my biggest fan, but I didn't trust her friendliness for a minute.

Sheila and Walter didn't live far from my parents' place, so we agreed I could bring Lynn to their house the next day. I made it perfectly clear, however, how I planned to conduct the visit.

When we arrived at my sister's little split-level place in Queens, I opened the car door for Lynn, gave her a kiss, and said, "Good luck." She walked to the front door while I took a walk around the block.

An hour later, Lynn and I met back at the car.

"So?" I asked.

"She was nice," Lynn said. "We had a lovely conversation, and it's a nice, clean home. Her little girl played in the background while we talked. Sweet little girl."

"No drama? What a relief."

"Well...everything went fine until I asked her to be my matron of honor."

"You what?" I yelled, horrified.

Lynn stuck her nose right up in the air and said, "It's my right to ask who I want. I don't have to ask your permission." As Judaism was to my family, so were the "rules of polite society" to Lynn's. She knew them backwards and forwards.

"Oh my God! You're crazy!"

"Don't worry," she said. "Right after I asked her, Walter walked in."

"That jerk."

"Sheila introduced us, then she told him about my request. She actually asked his permission to be my matron of honor! Well, Walter very calmly looked at her, like they were talking about the price of peas or something, and he said, 'Sheila, you know you have always had a choice. It's your family or me.' Then he walked out of the room."

I shook my head. "What an ass.."

"An ass indeed!" Lynn replied with wide, horrified eyes. "And he looks like a little gnome!"

"Didn't I tell you?"

"Yes, you did, but wow. Anyway, Sheila apologized for not being able to attend the wedding at all and saw me to the door. That was that."

I called Sheila and Walter every name in the book. Crazy as it might have been, I really had expected the two of them to put their hatred on hold for Lynn.

"Those two couldn't for one hour be civil. Not for one hour," I finally said, adding, "If that had been me, I would have given Walter a kick in the ass. No way would I let anyone separate me from the people I love. No one has a right to do that."

"What an awful man," she said.

"He is, but Lynn, I hold Sheila just as responsible. She knew perfectly well the agreement she made when she married him. Oh God, this visit was a huge mistake."

Despite the fact I'd stayed outside, the visit had still managed to open up old wounds. I seethed as I drove, and Lynn knew it. She stayed quiet.

Back at the house, I called Sheila. "I don't ever want anything to do with you again. Do you understand? You are out of my life forever."

At that, Sheila cried a bit too loudly, I thought, for it to be real. I hung up and washed my hands of her.

13

With all the caterers and florists buzzing around, no one noticed me sneak down the hallway at the Warwick. I couldn't help my curiosity. Before getting dressed for the wedding, I just had to peek at the ballroom. One step inside, and the view transported me. The walls dripped with live Wisteria boughs so hung as if they'd grown there. It could have been the garden of an English manor house or some a French castle. The gentle lavender cascade of flowers, like handfuls of pearl strands, softened every surface, caressed every corner. Somehow the florists had even adorned the two-story ceiling with a grand, arced trellis that overhung the entire room, enveloping it in the charm of a decades-old sanctuary. The intoxicating honey-sweetness of the flowers made me lightheaded. Here and there, broad-leafed trees, dotted with tiny sparkling lights, shaded quaint sitting areas all around the central court, itself surrounded with so many even rows of chairs they seemed to stretch to the horizon. At the center of it all, Lynn and I would marry on a simple grassy mound. I had to hand it to Mary. That woman had a sense of design so gorgeous it could barely be believed. And Lynn took after her—elegant, always elegant.

I called Lynn from the hotel room I would share with her that very night, wanting to tell her about the miraculous ballroom and express my joy. Lynn, breathless as I, admitted she had peeked, too. I felt so much gratitude to Mary, not just for her financial and time contributions, but also for putting her whole heart into our wedding.

As I shaved in the hotel bathroom, I was glad all the parents finally seemed happy. I even fantasized my parents would become friends with Abner and Mary. Maybe, I thought, the association would loosen Mother and Father up a little, and maybe being around my parents and their values would bring out the best in Abner. I envisioned a kind of grand enlightenment of all parties.

Putting on my pants and tuxedo shirt, I realized I didn't have a single butterfly in my stomach, jitters, or anything like that. I wanted to marry Lynn, and the sooner the better. Donning my tailcoat, I congratulated myself on my good choice of top hat and tails for all the men in the wedding party. I chuckled at the memory of Abner's objection—"I don't wear things like that!"—followed immediately by Mary's defense of my choice—"Abner! It's his wedding!" I had specifically requested only this one detail, so Mary made sure I got it.

I straightened my bow tie, put that top hat on my head, took a moment to admire my handsome reflection in the mirror, and thought, let's get this show on the road!

That's when the phone rang and my parents summoned me to their hotel room. I prepared for a touching, possibly embarrassing, father-son talk, perhaps with an addendum from Mother on what traits make for a good husband. I resolved to listen thoughtfully, no matter how corny their advice.

Perched on the edge of the bed, Father fastened his cufflinks; meanwhile, Mother applied mascara in front of the vanity. "Well, Marty...you turned out to be some son," began Father.

"After all we've sacrificed for you, you treat us like this," added Mother. "It's almost impossible to believe."

"All the gifts you take from the Konicks, all the time you spend with them, I should think we raised you better than that," continued Father. "I would never have believed lightning would strike twice. First your sister, and now you!"

"It's unseemly the way you carry on with them," said Mother. "And how many days have you spent in Long Island in the past six months? Ten, that's how many. What am I supposed to tell everyone? I don't have Sheila anymore, and now I feel like I don't even have a son."

"We've sacrificed everything for you. Do you even know how much your dental school tuition costs? It's unbelievable, and all for a son who never comes to see us."

"We've given you everything."

"And you, Martin. What have you given us?"

"I'm getting married in two hours, and this is what you have to say to me?" I asked, incredulous.

"You're probably going to move away and never see us," replied Father. "Never let us see our grandchildren, either, just like Sheila."

"Your grandmother would roll over in her grave if she knew about this," added Mother. This barb cut me to the quick, since my grandmother had died just a couple of weeks before.

"You're gadding about town like some big shot," snapped Father.

"Shoving us to the side like so much garbage," added Mother.

"That's not how a man behaves, abandoning his parents," said Father.

The harangue continued until finally, I stormed out of the room. Without thinking, I tore the top hat from my head, dashed down the hallway and five flights of stairs, and ran through the hotel lobby. I felt like running down the street, just getting away from there, but in the lobby I bumped into Fred, my best man.

"Marty, what's wrong?"

Pacing the plush carpet of the Warwick lobby, hat in hand, I told him.

Fred grabbed my shoulders. "Listen to me. Don't be like your parents, Marty. Don't let your negative thoughts ruin it for everyone else. Think of Lynn, and man up. Get in the there, and smile, and enjoy your wedding."

"You're right," I replied. "I don't want to be like them."

In the end, our beautiful garden wedding went off without a hitch, just as planned.

Some three hundred guests danced to the orchestra—no, a simple band would never have been good enough. It was all over the top and the Konicks beamed with pride as every dollar spent shown brightly and beautifully while the Kraidins smiled barely through clenched teeth as the ostentatious show was all too much for Helen and Al. The only touch of humility was when Abner got up and announced to the crowd that he had yet one more gift for the young couple and proceeded to hand them a box of thousands and thousands of S&H Green Stamps—redeemable for merchandise from a bargain catalogue. The gesture brought the house down.

The tradition of the "going away outfit" required the newlyweds to change clothes and bid goodbye to the guests with a big bon voyage, as if we were leaving on our honeymoon right there and then. In reality, our plane didn't leave until the next day, but that's how you did it. Lynn put on a green silk suit, I changed out of my tails and into a suit and tie, and we waved goodbye to all our adoring fans.

That night, up in our hotel room, Lynn and I had the most incredible fun. Almost all our wedding gifts were checks, so we added them up on hotel stationary. Despite the royal treatment we'd been getting from her parents, up until that moment, my bank account barely contained enough for the next month's rent. As for Lynn, she had never held a job nor received an allowance in her life. She ate, dressed, and was entertained at her parents' whim.

Watching the numbers tally up, we giggled and gasped, until finally I grabbed the stack of checks and said, "Lynn, lay down on the bed!" I threw them up in the air, and as the checks fluttered down around her, she rolled around in them like a puppy in the grass. I leaped onto the bed, rolled onto my back, kicked my legs in the air, and cried out, "We're rolling in dough!"

14

June 18, 1960

After guiding us through Idlewild airport and helping us settle into our first class seats on the plane, Mary leaned over my aisle seat to give Lynn a hug. She said goodbye with moist eyes full of pride. Lynn's father stood sandwiched between Mary and another passenger trying to load his suitcase into the over-head bin, but somehow Abner managed to reach over the armrest to shake my hand.

"Have a great honeymoon!" he said.

"We will, Daddy," Lynn replied, and Abner bent down so his daughter could lean over me and give him a peck on the cheek.

My father, who seemed to have recovered from his wedding-day sour grapes, squeezed into the aisle, too, reached over the head of the man seated in front of me, shook my hand, and said "Bon Voyage, Marty! Send us a postcard if you find the time."

Then my mother, stuck way down at the end of the aisle, sidled past a boarding passenger, shoved my father to the other side of the aisle, and tripped over the man in front of me in her attempt to throw herself into my arms.

I stood to catch her and mother wept and planted kisses all over my face. Seeing this, Mary seemed to think she hadn't been effusive enough, so she reached behind me, grabbed Lynn's face, and did the same. Then, while my mother clung to my neck as if I were going off to war, Mary released Lynn, stood on tip-toe, reached right over my mother's clinging form, grabbed my head, pulled it down to her level, and kissed me full on the mouth.

"This is disgusting!" yelled Abner. "Mary, come away from them!"

"Helen, that's enough," hollered my father. "That is quite enough!"

"My son is leaving! He's leaving us!" whined Mother.

"Oh Marty, I'll miss you!" cried Mary.

At that point, a cabin steward approached and asked all the parents to leave the airplane. In fact, he threatened to call airport security if they didn't.

"I'm only saying goodbye to my son!" cried Mother

"I can't bear to see them go!" moaned Mary.

"Stop this disgusting display!" yelled Abner, loud enough to wake a baby in coach, who sent up a wail of a protest.

This cacophony continued for several minutes, until the steward did indeed call airport security and a team of uniformed men bodily removed our four parents from the plane.

After a moment of stunned silence, Lynn asked me, "What was that all about?"

"Hell if I know," I said, meanwhile trying to erase the memory of Mary's gigantic smacker.

For hours after the plane took off, we sat quietly, not even holding hands.

Finally, Lynn said, "When we get to Rome, how about if I write your parents and you write mine. That will make them happy."

I agreed to the idea.

In Rome, as promised, a private limousine picked us up and took us to the grand Excelsior Hotel. While we checked in, the receptionist treated us with utmost respect, like visiting dignitaries. Later that evening, when we went to dinner—Lynn in a stunning white fox jacket over a clinging silk gown, and me in my spanking new tux—I saw heads turn and heard people whisper, "Who are they? Are they famous?"

With our private car, we enjoyed incredible sightseeing in Rome, at our leisure, on our own time. Finally, we had left our parents in another hemisphere, and Lynn and I could indulge in just being in love. It seemed like all our problems would dissolve away.

That first week, we did write to each other's parents as promised, with the result that my mother sent Lynn a curt telegram reading, "I'm glad you two are having a good time, but I would also like to get a letter from my son."

My mother's meanness brought up the old conflict Lynn and I had, for nearly a week, managed to avoid. Pretty soon, Lynn began insisting I should simply stop acquiescing to all my parents' wishes—that I should "be a man" and transfer my loyalties to her family instead. I felt forced to defend my parents, even though, ever our wedding day talk, I resented them. Still, I never went on the attack, citing Abner's violent temper. Instinct told me that subject was taboo.

Since that day in Lewes, on various weekend outings, I'd seen Abner attack a man on the street, throw plates around the kitchen in a rage, and get so drunk I had to haul him upstairs, help him urinate, and put him to bed. Yet, Lynn avoided discussing the subject—as if she wanted me to simply accept and pardon her father's behavior, like the rest of the family did.

When Abner gave Lynn away at our wedding, I saw the dynamic between them in full play—his stern face next to her smiling one, looking up at him with love and a desire to please. Lynn still thought someday she would succeed in pleasing her father; that much was clear to me. Though no expert in psychology, I hoped that our honeymoon—a chance to physically separate Lynn from Abner—would sever their strange connection. Yet here we were in Europe, and I heard Abner's words coming out of my wife's mouth.

"My parents aren't perfect, Lynn, but they are my parents and they always will be," I said, during one of our recurring arguments. I felt almost silly stating such an obvious fact, but afterward, when we headed to the hotel restaurant for lunch, it seemed like my statement tortured Lynn. She remained quiet throughout our meal. I realized this was the first time that Lynn had ever been separated from her parents. Me, I had several years of campus life to put my parents in perspective, understand their irrationalities and form my own conclusions of the man I want to be and the life I want to live. Lynn was just days in to her new life and, maybe through anxiety or maybe simply being overwhelmed, retreated to the only life she understood—that of being 'daddy's little girl.' It's not that she wanted to marry a man just like her father; it was the only life she knew. She'd come around.

As the days of our honeymoon wore on, Lynn's aggravation with me grew worse and finally turned into overwhelming anxiety. I didn't realize how much inner turmoil she felt until, in Venice, a pimple sprouted up on her cheek. After washing her face a few dozen times, she started to pick at it with tweezers. She squeezed the thing until it popped, but overnight, it emerged again, redder and angrier than before. She panicked, insisting, "I can't go out like this!"

Lynn wouldn't leave the hotel room for a couple of days, so I stayed with her, and we sent in for room service. Meanwhile, she picked compulsively at the pimple until it became seriously infected, and I called for the hotel doctor. He kindly gave Lynn an antibiotic and somehow soothed her nerves in a way I could not. The tension between us healed along with the pimple, and Lynn and I moved on, according to schedule, until we arrived in Portofino, Italy, where we nuzzled one another like lovebirds again.

The quaint homes by the seashore, the colorful fishing boats, the romantic lanes winding between ancient walls—Portofino painted a picture of perfection. Our suite at the Splendido Hotel, high on a mountainside overlooking the entire village and harbor, even exceeded perfection. French doors opened onto our own gorgeous balcony, where bougainvillea dripped down from the terrace and the scent of night-blooming jasmine pervaded the air. After a full day of sightseeing, and the freshest seafood and finest wine on the planet, what could we do but make love all night long? That's exactly what we did, leaving the French doors open for the warm night air.

We had placed a suitcase upon a small bench at the end of the bed, and deep in the night, in the midst of our exuberant lovemaking, I accidentally kicked the suitcase, which fell into a floor lamp, which in turn fell over onto a glass coffee table, smashing it to smithereens. With the French doors open, the entire hotel heard the CRASH! SMASH! And before we knew it, a team of security personnel came banging our door down. Speaking fluent English, they demanded to know what in blue blazes we were up to.

Since neither Lynn nor I had actually seen the suitcase fall, we couldn't exactly explain the crash, but by looking at the evidence, Lynn, the security team, and I finally managed to piece together the chain of events. We had a good laugh over it.

"We're honeymooners," I told the security guys, with trademark Kraidin charm. "What can I say?"

15

The orchestra swelled and twenty dancers strutted on stage: the women adorned in feathered headdresses and diaphanous gowns, the men shirtless with bow ties and slacks. Slowly, they all stripped off their costumes, piece by piece, down to pasties and G-strings.

"Ah, Paris," I sighed to Lynn, settling back in my seat.

We had decided to make a night of seeing the most risqué strip and burlesque shows in town. Our first, the Follies Bergere, topped the must-see list of nude reviews down in the Latin Quarter. The stage had been extended around and in front of the orchestra pit so that a runway curved out into the audience. Our tickets for coveted "club chair seats" plopped us dead center, eye-level with the stage, in the first of two rows of upholstered easy chairs. What heaven!

The highly choreographed, Busby-Berkley-style show featured fleshy lines of kicking chorus girls and interweaving patterns writhing with lithe, oiled bodies. Perfect breasts jiggled from every corner of the stage. I saw the most beautiful women in the world that night—long legs, firm stomachs, beautiful faces—I couldn't take my eyes off them; meanwhile, Lynn ogled the men.

"We'll certainly never see anything like this in the U.S.!" I yelled into Lynn's ear, trying to be heard above the crashing orchestra. Lynn giggled adorably. She loved audacity.

In the next number, while dancers wiggled down the runway, balloons fell from the ceiling. I thought about catching one for Lynn, but the balloon I aimed for drifted back behind me. In trying to catch it, I upended my club chair, fell over backwards, and got stuck with my legs up in the air like an overturned turtle. Immediately, the lighting crew trained a spotlight on helpless me with my feet waving in the air. The people in the seats behind helped me up again, but by then, the entire audience was roaring with laughter. The dancers got a big kick out of my embarrassment. They even stopped their routine to clap for me, so...what could I do? I waved to the crowd and handed my wife the balloon!

After the Follies, we headed over to another place, which looked more like a high-class strip club than a theater, but still, it featured live musicians and a very ritzy ambiance. Lynn and I arrived in time to get a table right on the edge of the stage, so when the dancers came out, we noticed a lot of them were the same as those at the Follies. Their taxis must have been racing ours through the streets of Paris to get there on time.

Once again, the dancers strutted out to the music, but this time, one of them recognized me. She caught my eye and smiled, then did a little move—throwing her arms up, arching her back, and kicking one leg out—simulating my backwards tumble.

"Marty, that was a tribute to you!" Lynn exclaimed.

The dancing here far surpassed that of the Follies in terms of improvisation and being risqué. Still, I couldn't believe it when one of the ladies approached and actually pulled me up on the dance floor. I stood there on stage, in my suit and tie, feeling incredibly foolish, while tasseled and sequined beauties stroked their legs up and down my torso, writhed their midriffs against me, and, finally, removed my tie. Then, my shirt. At first, I felt shy. Horrified, even. But when I realized I couldn't get out of this any which way, I fell into "gregarious Marty," the persona I had developed to get through high school and college, the winning personality everyone loved. I threw my arms up in the air, gyrated my pelvis, and put on quite a show with the lithe, luscious beauty who had brought me up on stage. Lynn laughed so hard tears streamed out of her eyes. I showed off my pelvic thrusts for the audience members, many of who had just come from the Follies, like we did. They recognized me and applauded my antics with glee; meanwhile, the dancer crept around behind me, stroked my bare chest with both hands, and in the midst of this embrace, went straight for my belt.

I pleaded, "Je vous prie d'arreter, mademoiselle!" (No, please, I beg you!)

Thankfully the music ended before the dancer got my pants off.

When I took a bow with all the showgirls at the end, I realized that by then, every man and woman on stage had stripped down to nothing—all but me! The audience cheered like maniacs.

I rejoined Lynn at our table, threw my tie down next to our drinks like a prize I'd won, put my shirt on, roguishly buttoned it halfway, and kissed my laughing wife.

A moment later, the master of ceremonies strode on stage and, as a spot-light fell directly on Lynn and me, announced, "to the newest member of our cast!"

The audience went wild again while I waved and grinned like a superstar.

When she caught her breath from all the laughing, Lynn exclaimed, "I didn't know you had it in you!"

"Neither did I," I replied quite honestly.

"I'm going to have to learn to do that, too!" she said, provocatively, right before a waiter showed up with a bottle of champagne, on the house. I asked the waiter, "Could you please ask that dancer, you know the one, if she would have a drink with us?"

A moment later, the dancer came out, wearing a robe. She enjoyed a glass of our champagne and laughed with us, as if even she hadn't had such a good time in ages.

That night, Lynn and I fell into each other's arms, exhausted and amazed at the whole adventure.

"At first, you were so nervous on stage," Lynn said. "I could see the sweat rolling off your forehead!"

"What did you expect?"

"But then...I didn't know you knew how to dance like that!"

"I didn't. I just made it up."

"Oh God, Marty, I'll never forget it. When she went for your belt...oh God, I thought I'd die!"

"No kidding. How do you think I felt?"

Finally, Lynn and I took the train to Le Havre and set sail on the Liberté, the ship destined to take us home, but our adventures hadn't ended, yet.

On the cruise, dressed to the nines as we always were, Lynn and I not only attracted a lot of stares and whispers, but also made some interesting friends. The first night aboard, at dinner, someone sent us two glasses of champagne.

I asked the waitress who had sent them, and she motioned toward a well-dressed fellow and his gorgeous wife, a few tables away. The man raised his glass to us and, later, invited us to their table for dessert. He turned out to be Warner Leroy, a grandson of one of the founding members of Warner Brothers.

He and his new wife Jenn were the only other young couple on the ship. Like us, they were cruising home from their honeymoon. Lynn and I became fast friends with them both.

As luck would have it, for once, Lynn and I received less-than-perfect accommodations. We bunked in an inside cabin with no window. When we flicked the light off at night, the cabin turned as dark and claustrophobic as a coal mine. During a dinner conversation with Warner and Jenn, we happened to mention this misfortune.

Warner said, "Marty, that's unacceptable!" He leaned across the table and whispered, "It's no problem to fix this. Just tell the cabin steward some story, but make it a very romantic story. The French love that. He will find you a better cabin. Trust me."

I lay awake half the night, coming up with a story. The next day, I approached the cabin steward with a fifty-dollar bill and whispered to him that my new wife was secretly three months pregnant. Nobody knew about it, of course, and we didn't want anyone to know, but that airless inside cabin made her terribly sick. I worried someone aboard would notice her illness, and we might be found out. The resulting vicious gossip would ruin our perfect honeymoon!

"The thought of the scandal it could cause," I moaned. "It's horrifying!"

That very day, with utmost alacrity and many congratulations, the steward moved us into a lovely outside cabin, which turned out to be a luxury suite.

I told Warner about the success of my little story, and he said, "Marty, you really have an instinctive understanding of the French! Of course he moved you! How could he resist the passion? The secrecy! The drama!"

Later on, I learned that Warner and his wife received a basket of fruit, cheese, and champagne in their suite every morning.

"How do we get one of those?" I asked, impatient, at twenty-two, to live like I had already arrived.

"Just ask for it!" Warner advised, so I did. Before I knew it, Lynn and I returned to receiving the royal treatment to which we had become accustomed.

When the ship passed into New York Harbor, Lynn and I stood on the deck, wrapped in each other's arms, watching the Statue of Liberty come into view. By then, I felt the worst of our disagreements had fallen behind us. The sight of that statue, presiding over her island, so lonely and beautiful, made me glad to come home again and eager to experience the day-to-day existence of a normal, married couple—a future that seemed to hold so much promise.

We had arranged for both our sets of parents to meet us at the dock, after which we would all travel to the Konicks' cabin in Lewes Beach for a barbecue and weekend of celebrating Lynn's and my return.

Surprisingly, when Lynn and I stepped onto the gangplank, before we even walked out to the dock, my parents appeared. Mother and Father ran up and crushed us with uncharacteristically exuberant hugs, but I felt confused. Dock rules didn't allow the public onto the gangplank, only passengers.

After greeting them, I asked, "How did you get on the gangplank, anyway?"

"Oh, I have some connections," answered Father. "Cashed in a couple of favors, you know."

"Where are my parents?" asked Lynn.

"Down there," replied my mother fiendishly, pointing beyond the barricade to where Mary scanned the crowd, looking everywhere for us, and Abner held his hand above his forehead to cut the glare of the sun.

"You couldn't have asked your connections to let all four of you onto the gangplank?" I asked.

"Well, you know..." my father replied.

As we descended to the dock, Mother put her arm in mine like a bride. But when the Konicks saw the four of us walking along together, Abner's face turned red and Mary straightened up to a full five feet and two inches worth of wounded pride.

After Lynn and I greeted her parents, Abner turned to my father. "I see you got access to the gangplank."

"I had some connections," my father replied. "But, you know, they only let two people up there. That's all. Only two."

"Poppycock," replied Mary. "I don't believe that for a minute."

"So that's the kind of people you are," growled Abner. "You've always got to be first, huh? Well, I'll not have you in my house! Don't bother coming!"

"Let's get out of here," said Mary, assuming Lynn and I would take her side against my parents. In point of fact, I did take Mary's side. I thought my parents had behaved despicably.

"How dare you? We intend to spend time with our son and daughter in law!" squawked my mother.

"My husband says you are no longer invited to our home," shot back Mary.

A real catfight broke out between the two mothers. Name-calling and accusations flew. Then, Father and Abner commenced yelling at each other. Once again, security personnel arrived on the scene to escort all six of us off the dock and out into the parking lot, where they left the four parents to scratch each other's eyes out if they wanted.

In the end, Lynn and I rode to Lewes with Abner and Mary, and my own parents drove home alone. During the long, silent drive, I marveled at how our four parents had perfectly bracketed our honeymoon with infantile displays of ownership.

That night, as Lynn and I snuggled into our bed, I whispered, "Honey, when I finish school and we settle down, let's not settle anywhere near either of our parents, okay?"

"Definitely," she agreed. In a conspirator's extra-quiet whisper, she added, "You know where I'd like to live? Connecticut."

We had always loved our Sunday drives through that area, so her desire to settle in Connecticut didn't surprise me.

"Connecticut it is," I whispered back.

But first, I had to survive three more years of dental school, as did our marriage.

16

Mary set up our new apartment, near the University of Pennsylvania, with brand-new furnishings befitting the successful professional couple we hoped one day to be. These included a gorgeous, four-poster bed. One evening, Lynn eyed the bedposts and said, "Marty, look at those poles. I know what to do with those."

To my amazement, she grabbed a bedpost, swung a leg around, and performed a sexy pole dance, just like a professional stripper.

After one thing led to another, Lynn and I lay in bed together, completely spent.

"Where in the world did you learn that dancing?" I asked.

Lynn smiled. "You won't believe it if I tell you."

"Tell me!"

"Well, you know our maid, Gussie? One day—I was in high school—she took me aside and said, 'Child, you're so funny lookin', I don't know how you're ever going to find a man.' So she taught me how to dance with this pole in the basement."

"Gussie?"

"Yeah, she taught me how to twist, too. Come on, let's try it!"

Lynn leaped out of bed, completely naked, and tried to drag me with her.

"I don't know how to do that," I protested, but she wouldn't hear it.

Lynn demonstrated the twist, planting one foot saucily off to the side and shimmying her hips. Without the audience cheering me on, like in Paris, my real self—the shy, insecure Marty—came to the forefront. But Lynn helped me, encouraged me, and believed in me, and sure enough, I soon succeeded in doing the latest dance craze, just like Chubby Checker.

"I'm twisting!" I said. "You taught me how to twist!"

"Stick with me, Babe," she said. "I'm going to teach you a lot of things."

That year, we also discovered a mutual love of entertaining and began hosting wonderful parties. Always, people packed the dance floor. After a while, I noticed the show-off dancers stepping aside when my wife and I stepped up to do our thing. We were so in love; it made people want to watch us.

"You're such a good dancer," she said to me, while we stole the show at one of our own parties.

"Only with you, Lynn. Only with you."

Our two sets of parents agreed to share the burden of supporting us while I finished school. They didn't give us a lot of spending cash, but we could afford our roomy, one-bedroom apartment, where, in addition to teaching me to dance, Lynn organized recipe cards, collected cookbooks, and shared with me her first attempts at casseroles, roasts, and even fruit pies.

I continued making my obligatory weekly calls to my parents, but with this being my final year of dental school, didn't have time to drive up to Long Island and see them, not even once a month. Meanwhile, Lynn talked to Mary and Abner daily and we spent our holidays, and some weekends, with the Konicks. At their home, Lynn's childhood bedroom became our own little love nest, where we talked, loved, and also fought—always about my parents and hers.

Predictably, Lynn seemed very concerned about being a good and dutiful daughter. At first, I felt grateful for her efforts. After all, Abner had been on good behavior lately, and the Konicks gave us far more than their fair share of the expenses—what with the apartment furniture and our weekend outings—so I considered it prudent to keep our benefactors happy.

As for my own parents, I strove to fulfill their expectations of a good son, and, as always, respected them, but I didn't miss them or seek their advice. That element had never emerged in our relationship. Over time, however, I watched eager-to-please Lynn undergo constant frustration. When she called her parents, she usually wanted to share wonderful news—like when she baked her first cake, or when she threw a successful party—but she always came away from the calls upset.

"I don't know," she told me once. "Whenever I think I've done something good, after I talk to Mom, it seems like it wasn't such a big deal, after all. And Dad, he's never impressed by anything. But I keep calling. I keep thinking my next success will really amaze them, then when I get off the phone, I feel blah."

Usually ebullient and talkative, sometimes Lynn grew moody now, and snapped at me after these phone calls with her parents.

Then, one weekend, Lynn and I attended a party at Abner and Mary's club. No sooner had I begun sipping my cocktail than I felt Mary's hand clamp onto my bicep. She hauled me around the room, introducing me to all her friends as, "Martin Kraidin, my son-in-law, the future-dentist." My mother behaved similarly when introducing me to her own friends, so perhaps I should have been used to it, but this treatment made me feel like some prized pet spaniel, not even a human being. Between this event and the way Lynn seemed far too dependent upon her parents for approval she'd clearly never be able to earn. I resolved—again assuming physical distance would solve the problem—to get Lynn and myself away from the Konicks permanently.

In March of 1961, shortly before graduation, I found a very special letter in our post box. When I read it aloud, Lynn screamed with delight. This, my acceptance to the dental school at Columbia Presbyterian Medical Center, in New York City, enabled me to complete my post-graduate work in the most prestigious periodontal school in the country.

"This means it's time to take my board exams," I told Lynn. "Darling, do you still want to settle in Connecticut?"

Lynn knew the question implied more than tall trees and snowy winters. It meant making a permanent move away from Philadelphia and her parents.

"I don't know," she replied. "I don't see what's wrong with living near my parents."

"For one, they make you feel bad. Every time you get off the phone with them, you're upset. You always snap at me, and we fight about something, stupid things!"

"It's not their fault! They're trying to help us out! They give us everything!"

"I don't want their money, Lynn. I won't be bought." Of course with the handouts and supplemental stipends Lynn and I had been receiving along the way for everything from rent to tuition, one could say I was slowly but surely being bought. I just didn't see it that way.

"You are the most opinionated, pig headed, stubborn human being I have ever met!"

"Listen Gorgeous. We're a team. We'll do whatever you want."

"Good."

"Just remember I have two votes and you have one."

Lynn gasped and punched my arm.

"Just kidding, Darling! Please, please, I'm just kidding!" I pleaded as I dodged her swinging fist.

When Lynn finally calmed down, I spoke with her seriously. By this point, I felt determined not to live near the Konicks and fall under the spell they seemed to be casting over both Lynn and myself. I knew we would have to pay for their largesse with our loyalty, prioritize the Konicks over the Kraidins, and bend to Abner's every whim. The Konicks wanted my very soul, and I wouldn't give it. I didn't need to. Smart, successful, and moving into a very lucrative field, I could make it on my own, and on my own terms. But I had to make Lynn understand our need for independence. I wanted her to agree to my plan, not just go along with it.

Over the ensuing weeks, I kept working on Lynn, selling the Connecticut idea, her own idea, back to her. I painted a picture of a lovely, two-story home surrounded by tall trees, where children played in the yard. A tire swing hung from a sturdy oak. Friends gathered every weekend for spirited parties on our broad veranda. Our family. Our independence. No Mom telling Lynn her fruit pies weren't good enough, no Abner flying into rages, just us, enjoying our perfect lives.

"Yes," she finally answered. "I'm ready, Marty."

That spring, I took the New York exam, knowing I would need that certification to work at a clinic during my postgraduate work. Then, without telling any of our parents, I took the Connecticut exam, too. The sly move of not taking the Pennsylvania exam ensured Lynn and I couldn't settle near her parents, no matter what they offered us, no matter how hard they tried to convince us to relocate to Philadelphia. With Lynn's permission, I gladly burned that bridge. Abner and Mary had treated us well, but the time had come for Lynn and I to grow up, establish independence.

We knew we would catch hell for it later, but for now, that decision felt like our first independent step as a couple. The decision even seemed to bring us closer—two conspirators in the same crime. We dared to hope, though, that by the time I finished school at Columbia, our respective parents would have adjusted to the idea of Lynn and me being on our own.

A month or so later, we accepted an invitation to dinner at Abner and Mary's exclusive club. The clink of fine china, waiters' soft footfalls, and the low hum of conversation filled the room.

It should have been a casual evening, but Abner asked the million-dollar question: "Tell me, Marty, when do you take the state boards?"

"I already took them," I answered. "In May."

"You didn't tell me."

"You didn't ask."

"Pennsylvania, right?"

I crossed my knife and fork on my plate, placed my hands gently on either side of my place setting, and looked Abner in the eye. As calmly as I could, I answered, "Ahh, no. Connecticut."

"Connecticut?" Abner countered with a frown. "What'd you do that for?"

"Lynn and I have been talking about living in Connecticut more and more. Just talking, you understand."

Abner pulled the linen napkin from his lap and threw it down on the table. "That's awfully far! And anyway, Marty, isn't Connecticut practically a suburb of New York?"

"No, actually. Connecticut is…Connecticut."

"Why, you'd be closer to your own parents than to us! What are you, some kind of mama's boy? Be a man, Marty, and move back to Philadelphia!"

I sipped my drink quietly, allowing emotions to dissipate a little before I answered Abner. From opposite sides of the table, Lynn and Mary silently watched us. Then they looked at each other, got up, and left the table.

Once we were alone, I said, "I've had enough of this talk, Abner."

"Oh, calm down, calm down, Marty. You're so touchy," Abner said. "It's just that I have an idea. Listen to this," Abner bellowed. "I want you to take the Pennsylvania exam. I want you and Lynn to settle down right here in Philadelphia!"

"Thanks, Abner. I'm really touched that you'd like us to be nearby. I'll talk to Lynn…"

"No, Marty. Listen. I'm saying I'll help you get started. I will buy you a house. Build you an office. Right here in Philadelphia. Yes! What do you say?"

Suddenly the room seemed smaller; Abner's face, bigger. Nearby, the sound of a waiter stacking some plates crashed violently in my ears.

"That's so generous, Abner. I don't know what to say."

"Say yes!" he boomed.

"The thing is, the state board exams are over for the year. I guess I missed my chance to take you up on that."

"So, take them next year. So what? There's always a way. When I want what I want, I get it! Let that be a lesson to you. Just think—a house right on the Main Line, for you're very first home. Amazing! What a way to get started, huh? And I'll get you into the club, too. What do you think of that?"

"It's very generous, Abner." I cleared my throat. "It's just that Lynn and I haven't decided where we want to live, yet. We've got some time to think about it, so...I'll definitely keep your generous offer in mind."

"Just what are you saying? I said I'd buy you a house and an office, Marty. What more do you want?"

"Oh no, it not that. It's just that there are a lot of factors to consider. School districts and such. Lynn and I are still thinking..."

"I see," groused Abner.

Lynn and Mary returned to the table, and Mary tactfully turned the conversation to the weather.

That summer, Lynn and I relocated to New Jersey, as it was just over the George Washington Bridge from Columbia-Presbyterian Medical Center where I was going to be starting the next stage of my post graduate education. I got a part-time job in a dental clinic, and Lynn became a receptionist at the university. With all our family obligations, Lynn took it upon herself to become an expert event coordinator. Thanks to her, we attended synagogue regularly, kept four parents happy, and also found time to throw parties and build a base of wonderful new friends. For the time being, Lynn and I avoided discussing the Connecticut issue.

One morning that summer, Lynn snuggled up to me in bed and said, "Marty, I think it's time."

"Time for what?"

"Time for us to start a family."

"Are you serious?" I replied. "Don't you want to wait until we have some money?"

"No," she said. "I want to have our baby, now."

"Our baby. I like the sound of that."

"Let's do it, Marty."

"All right, Beautiful, if you think it's not too soon."

"I'm ready," she answered. "Oh Marty, I'm so ready!"

Before the end of the summer, Lynn got her wish.

The excitement of Lynn's pregnancy fueled even more visits to my parents' place. Mother actually stopped bitching about Sheila long enough to engage Lynn in some of that first-trimester girl-talk. Meanwhile, my father pulled me aside and complained about money incessantly. I felt guilty that I still required his support for two more years, but saw no other way to get through school, so I listened and tried not to sigh.

"Thanks for visiting my parents so much," I told Lynn one day, on the drive home. "I know they can be tedious, but I really need my mother and father to know we want them involved in their grandchild's life."

"Oh. I guess." She paused and added, "To be honest, Marty, I don't like making all these visits. I don't even think it's healthy."

"Healthy?"

"Yeah. For you to be so close to your parents."

"You're awfully close to your parents, too. Did you ever notice that?"

"Yes, but I'm a woman. That's normal. You're a grown man. You don't need to be pleasing them and worrying about what they think. After all, we have a baby on the way, and it feels like you're not focused on me and my needs."

I drove on in silence, incredulous Lynn had actually returned to this obnoxious subject, and incensed at her attempt to use the baby as leverage.

"I'm just being a good son, Lynn. They are supporting us, after all."

"So is my father," she spat with sudden venom.

I took my eyes off the road and looked at Lynn. Her face seemed puffy and pale, and her eyes had gone dull.

"Pull over," she snapped with sudden urgency.

I screeched the Impala to a stop on the side of the road, where Lynn opened the door and retched violently.

Thus began a very difficult pregnancy.

Lynn began to stain, and Dr. Johnstone, the Konick family's internist, prescribed bed rest, warning that her symptoms indicated a serious risk of miscarriage. The worse Lynn felt, the worse she made me feel. Our fights still revolved around the parents. If her parents called and I spoke to them, Lynn complained I hadn't spoken long enough. If my parents called, or God forbid I called them myself, Lynn complained about that, too.

"You're a mama's boy, that's what you are," she snapped at me, one day. "You're not even a real man! Do I have to go out and find myself a real man?"

The next day, she said I owned her heart and she could never live without me.

Dr. Johnstone told me that with any luck Lynn's sickness would fade away after a few months, so I hung in there and prayed her insanity would prove temporary, too. Nonetheless, Lynn's cruel accusations against my manhood hurt deeply. I looked forward to September, and the start of school, when I'd have to spend more time away from home.

17

Mere weeks before classes began, I received a surprise call from my father.

"Marty, things have really gone downhill, financially."

"I'm sorry to hear that. I'm sure they'll improve."

"No, I mean the business is...we had a bad year."

"Go on."

"We've had a few bad years, as you know."

"Is there anything I can do to help?"

"No. It's over now. I'm afraid I'm going to have to declare bankruptcy."

"I see. I'm so sorry."

"What I'm trying to say is, well, I can't pay your tuition or rent."

That moment, my world came screeching to a halt. Without my ambition to become a periodontist, life made no sense. Every decision I had made for the past five years laser-focused me on getting through dental, then postgraduate school, without delay. This felt like getting a phone call that someone in my family had died, only that someone turned out to be my dream for the future. I felt for my father but feared for myself.

"What should I do?" I asked.

"I don't know," my father answered.

Not exactly a font of wisdom, my father. When life got rough, he always froze up, as if he had never solved a problem before, never learned a damn thing to pass on to me.

Hoping for a miracle, I called the bursars office and told them my situation. They transferred me to a brand new department at the university: The Department of Financial Aid.

In 1961, government-backed financial aid to students had been only recently invented. It owed its existence to the space race and America's desire to train more scientists. Unfortunately, with a baby on the way, the loan I qualified for still wouldn't be enough. To finish school, I would have to break a vow I had made to myself. I saw no other choice.

I called Abner and told him everything. I said I could handle the tuition myself, and, between us, Lynn and I made enough to pay for groceries, but in order for me to stay in school, we needed him to cover the full rent on our apartment. Abner agreed to do it, and for the time being, didn't ask for anything in return. But a few days later, the phone rang.

"Marty!" boomed Abner. "I want to take you out to lunch at the club. You don't have to drive down to Philly, just take the train and I'll pick you up. How about Saturday at one? Sound good?"

I certainly couldn't say no.

Between courses at the restaurant, Abner made his proposal. "Marty, I'm prepared to offer you a position in my business."

"Doing what?"

"Helping me run it!"

"The garment factory?"

"It's a very hot business, Marty. Clothes just change style; they never go out of style. You can't go wrong in the garment business! Well, your father did, but you won't go wrong with me."

"Pop, I've dedicated my life to becoming a periodontist. I only have two more years to go."

"But you haven't got the money. What are you going to do?"

"I took out a student loan."

"A loan? I don't like that. I don't like the idea of you and Lynn going into debt."

Cocky as ever, I shrugged it off.

"I don't mind the debt," I told him. "I believe in myself. Besides, I'm at the top of my class."

"Sure, you're young, you're confident, but you have no idea what debt can do to a man."

"It's a very flattering offer. I'm honored you would consider taking me into your business."

"So you'll do it?"

"No, pop. I'm afraid I won't. I'm finishing my post-graduate work and becoming a periodontist."

Abner got red in the face, just like the time he threw the pasta. "What do you mean?" he asked.

"I've spent the last five years…"

"I know what you've done the last five years! You're a student. Who wants to be a student when he can be a businessman? I don't want my daughter's husband to be a student all his life!"

"Perhaps we should go now," I said, noticing stares from nearby diners, as the volume of Abner's voice steadily grew.

He drove me back to the train station in silence.

That night, I asked Lynn, "You still want to move to Connecticut?"

"Yes."

"Good," I replied. "Me too. We have to get away from your father, Lynn. You should have seen him today, practically ordering me to give up on my dreams so I could manage his factory."

"You know my father. He always wants it his way."

"Lynn, there is no way I'm giving up on my dream. I need you to know that. No matter what your father, my father, or anyone says."

Lynn sat in silence a moment, and then said, "I don't want you to, Marty."

In that moment, the first time I ever asked her to take my side over Abner's, I felt her waver.

I knew my father felt awful about having abandoned me financially, so, during that first month of school, even though Lynn insisted on staying home, I visited Long Island every other weekend. Walking to synagogue side-by-side with Father now felt like a way to demonstrate the strength of my respect for him, no matter what.

I explained the importance of this to Lynn again and again, noting that I'd expect my own son or daughter to show the same courtesy in a family crisis. She participated in these discussions erratically. Sometimes, she'd shrug and walk away. Other times, she'd applaud my loyalty. Occasionally, she'd tell me my clinging to this relationship with my father showed a weak will and an immature mind, then, she'd toss in that dreaded phrase: "You're not a man!"

To me, Lynn seemed to be trying very hard to establish her own opinions in the face of Abner's overwhelming influence, but so far she simply couldn't separate her father's viewpoints from her own. I understood. Abner steamrolled everyone around him, but Lynn was strong and I felt sure that, in the end, she would come around to seeing my side. In the meantime, we fought. I tried not to upset her at this crucial stage of her pregnancy, but sometimes the hurtful language she used proved too much. I'd snap back at her, we'd both raise our voices, and the argument would gain momentum.

The situation became so bad, my head told my dick to stop working, so I made an appointment with Dr. Johnstone, Lynn's family doctor, whom I had always liked. I told him about the tension between Lynn and me, and he counseled me for such a long time, his waiting room backed up with patients.

"I can't believe this," he said. "I've never known Lynn or Abner to act like that. I hope it passes, Marty."

Dr. Johnstone reassured me my problem only resulted from stress, gave me a shot, and said, "Go home to your wife now, kiddo. You're going to be fine."

Briefly, things improved between Lynn and me.

"Marty, I love you," she said, one day, while we relaxed on the couch. I hadn't heard that in a while.

"I love you, too, Sweetheart. Everything is going to be all right, you know?"

"I know. I know it is. I'm sorry I've been so nasty lately."

"That's okay. I'm tough. We're in this together, okay?" I replied.

"I know, but please, Marty. Please take me home this weekend. I want to see my mother so badly."

"Sure I will, Gorgeous." This wasn't just any ordinary weekend, but the start of the High Holy Days. Rosh Hashanah fell on Sunday; Yom Kippur, on Tuesday of the following week. "Let's spend Rosh Hashanah with your folks and Yom Kippur with mine," I added. "Fair enough?"

"Okay," she said.

"But won't you get carsick on the ride to Philly?"

"I don't even care if I do," she replied, leaning over and resting her head on my lap.

18

Lynn took blouses and skirts from her suitcase and placed them into her childhood dresser while I lay back on our bed at the Konicks, stretching my legs after the long drive. Then she shut the bedroom door and sat on the bed beside me.

"About Yom Kippur," she said in a soft voice—the kind of voice wives reserve for telling their husbands bad news.

"What about it?"

"I don't think I should walk to synagogue."

"Why not?"

"What do you mean why not? I'm concerned about a miscarriage. I can't be walking across town in my condition!"

"You're fine. You walk around the house. What's the difference?"

She looked at me long and hard. I looked right back, completely impassive. The thought of telling my father Lynn wouldn't participate in this important ritual terrified me, though I was unaware of that at the time. I only felt out of control and wanted that control back, right away.

"I've been spotting. You know that. We talked to the doctor."

"You're fine."

"Are you actually telling me you're willing to risk my life, and the life of our child, for the sake of some stupid ritual?"

"Stupid? Did you just call Yom Kippur stupid?"

Lynn and Abner, as much as I hate to admit it, were right when they said I wasn't a man. I didn't think for myself. A man would instinctively understand that no God would expect a woman to risk a miscarriage just to walk to synagogue. A man would find a middle ground between dogma and the demands of real life. And a man would be willing to look his father in the eye and tell him, without fear, that he'd made an independent decision, such a letting Lynn ride to synagogue in a car. I still thought like a boy—trying only to gain approval from my father—when I should have held my wife's health and safety above all else. By standing up for her needs, Lynn placed us on the deck of that sinking ship Abner once spoke of, and did I save Lynn? No, I saved myself and my family's orthodox beliefs. I left Lynn teetering there, all alone.

Our argument continued for some time, though we kept our voices soft. Neither of us wanted Abner involved. We both stubbornly held our ground until I became furious and Lynn burst out crying. In that state, we walked downstairs to the kitchen to get a couple of cups of tea and try to calm down. There, we found Mary and began to tell her about our conflict. Lynn expected her mother to take her side, of course, but because I knew Mary had been brought up orthodox, I actually thought she'd take mine.

Mary didn't have a chance to respond though, because as soon as we started talking, Abner burst into the kitchen and screamed, "I've heard enough!"

"Heard enough of what?" I asked.

"I know what's going on between you two!" he said. "And Lynn is not walking across town on Yom Kippur! Forget it!"

Abner couldn't have heard our quiet argument unless he'd been pressing his ear to the keyhole. Of that, I felt certain. "You've been listening at our door?" I asked. I felt my head and neck expanding. The tie at my throat became a tourniquet and I reached up to jerk the knot loose as I matched Abner bellow for bellow. "You listen outside our bedroom door? Eavesdropping? Spying? Oh boy, Abner, you're a real piece of work, you are!"

"I do as I goddamn please in my house," he spat back. "I want you out of here! For good!"

I knew this wasn't just about Yom Kippur. It was about my refusal to go into business with him, my refusal to settle in Philadelphia, and every other time I had resisted Abner's attempts to control me. Confronting him, I tried to modulate my voice and stay calm for Lynn's sake.

"Stay out of our lives, Abner," I replied. "It's none of your business." I took a deep breath then, and turned to my wife, coaxing. "Lynn, most of our stuff is still in the car. All we have to do is walk out that door. Come with me." I grasped her arm and tried to lift her to her feet, but she sobbed now, and the tears seemed to anchor her to the very foundation of the house.

Lynn's slender shoulders crumpled over the table and she wouldn't look me in the eye. "My father," was all she said. "But my father, my father...I don't know what to do." Her body collapsed around her little ball of a belly. "What do I do? What do I do?" she wailed.

"Lynn," said Abner. "Get rid of him. Marty's no damn good. He cares more about his parents than he does you. You're going to be miserable with this loser all your life. End it now, Lynn. Do you hear me? Call my lawyer, now!" Abner grabbed the phone receiver off the wall and held it out to his daughter, the line's ringlet stretched taught.

Lynn began to shake all over and shiver as if in a deep freeze. I had seen this reaction before, during our very worst arguments. She put her hands over her eyes and wailed and wailed, so many wordless sounds. I crouched by my wife's side, stroked her back, and murmured into her ear, "C'mon, beautiful. Let's go. Let's get out of here."

"But my father," she cried. "My father. What do I do?"

"Come on, Lynn. Let's just go, Sweetheart."

Abner dialed the phone and its once-familiar clickety clack rattled my skull like machine-gun fire. "I'm calling my attorney, Joe, right now," he said. "You better talk to him, Lynn. I want Marty out of here and I don't ever want to see him again."

"Stop interfering in our lives, Abner. Just stop!" I yelled, and then I lunged at the man, tore the phone from his hand, and slammed it onto the cradle.

"Get out of my house!" he screamed.

"With pleasure!" I screamed back, but still, Lynn wouldn't budge. Her gorgeous, lanky frame shrunk into nothing but a ball of hurt. She ceased to be my wife in that moment and became Skinny Lynnie again, the laughingstock of the family. I put my arms around her, rocked her, and held her.

"Lynn, please, Sweetheart, please. Come with me now. If you don't, I'm afraid you'll never come with me again."

Abner resumed shouting. I didn't hear the words anymore, just the overwhelming noise of it. He warned, threatened, and accused. When I finally realized I couldn't budge Lynn, I stood to face Abner. He cocked his elbow back and suddenly I knew he planned to hit me. I drew my hands up to protect my face, but everything moved in slow motion. I knew I wouldn't be able to get them up in time.

Then suddenly Mary stood between us. She had sat silently throughout the entire event but now put her tiny, bird-boned body between her husband's and mine. "Ab, stop," she said. "Leave him alone."

Abner drenched his wife in spittle and foam, yelling, "Stay out of this!"

"No," Mary said calmly, almost sorrowfully. "Not this time. I will not. Leave them both alone."

"At least there's one sane person in this crazy family," I said. I took a step back from Abner and laid my arm across Lynn's heaving shoulders, but she shrugged it off and looked away.

I saw no other option but to turn around and leave the house.

"You're not a man!" Abner shouted after me.

Driving home, each mile I put between myself and that house seemed to ease a hundred pound weight from my chest. A single glare from Abner could make me—hell, any man—fear for my life, but this argument had escalated too far. As I drove, I had to remember to breathe. Feeling the air move in and out of my chest like a miracle, I thought of Lynn, my beautiful wife, and the love of my life. How had things come to this? I didn't know what I'd done to spark the conflict. I still felt completely righteous about the walking-to-synagogue issue and drove along stewing in hubris and fury.

Surely, I thought, Lynn would call and ask me to come get her in a day or so. In fact, I thought she might even wise up within hours, and as soon as I walked through the door of our apartment, the phone would ring. I imagined her asking me to drive back to Philadelphia and get her. I pictured it so vividly; I convinced myself it would happen. But when I came through the door, the phone was silent.

I never dreamed twenty-two years would pass before I saw her again.

19

September 1961

"Lynn," I said into the phone's hard plastic. "Listen to reason. Let me drive down and pick you up. I want to bring you home. I miss you so much."

"I'm not ready," came her faint reply. She had been living at her parents' house two weeks by this time. I called every day, but Lynn only seemed to grow more and more distant.

"What do you mean, you're not ready?"

"When you change," she said.

"What are you talking about? Lynn, I'm Marty. I'm the man you love."

"When you change," she repeated.

"Change what, Lynn? What are you talking about?"

"When you..."

I felt panic rising through my core. I yelled at her, "Stop it, Lynn! Make some sense! Tell me what you want from me!"

After a long pause, she said, "I want to stay here. At least, I'd be taken care of. I want you to come here, too."

"Lynn, Sweetie, I'll never set foot in that house again. How can you expect me to?"

After another lengthy pause, her voice—not Lynn, but only her voice—said, "We can live here."

"What in the world are you suggesting?"

"There is plenty of room in this house, and there's help here. It's easier."

"Never! And anyway, what am I supposed to do about school?"

"You can take the train."

"Are you serious? An hour and a half to Penn Station and another half hour up to the dental center? Each way?"

"Yes," she said. "Don't you love me?"

"Don't you love me?" I replied, beginning for the first time to really doubt that she loved me, really letting that sink in.

Then another voice came on the line, Abner's. "Forget about her. I'm through with you, and so is Lynn. We're finished with you! Understand?" That deadest of all sounds, a dial tone, followed Abner's exclamation.

Looking around our apartment, now cluttered with school books and dirty clothes, it seemed the traces of Lynn—her neatness, her way of arranging knick-knacks just so, her flair for color—had already disappeared. In two weeks, the place had deteriorated from happy home to bachelor pad to the dingy cave of a ruined man. On top of that, October first loomed, just days away, and Abner had cut off my financial support.

I drove around town until I found some cardboard boxes abandoned behind a grocery store and piled them in the car. They reeked of garbage, which seemed only fitting.

I packed up our things in no particular order, just threw them in the boxes. Each item I packed heightened my confusion and depression; made me want to call Lynn again, made me want to pound the walls, beat the ground. Instead, I loaded the boxes into the Impala, drove to my parents' house, and asked my father, "What should I do?"

"I don't know," my father replied, but he helped me move back into my childhood bedroom.

Mother stood by; arms crossed over her bosom, watching us carry my things up the stairs, too busy shaking her head to offer any help.

Eventually, she said, "All we know is we didn't do anything. None of this is our fault."

I brought the last box into the bedroom, shut the door, and curled into a ball on the creaky little twin bed. I felt so small.

After a nap, I pocketed some dimes and walked to a corner phone booth to call Lynn again. I didn't want my folks listening in.

"Lynn, please talk to me," I pleaded. "I can't live without you. I can't live like this, Lynn. Why are you doing this to us?"

"You aren't the man I thought you were, Marty," she said in a voice newly angry. "You're not a real man. I don't think I want to be with a man like that."

"That's not who I am at all, Lynn, and you don't sound like yourself."

"Well, I am myself."

"How long are you going to stay there? Don't you want me to come get you and we can talk about this in person?"

By now, I genuinely feared Abner, whom I now understood to be almost psychotic, capable of anything. I was sure he would physically attack me if he saw me again.

"I will pick you up anywhere, Lynn. Just not at that house. I'll pick you up on the corner, at a friend's house, at the grocery store, or anywhere you want. But I can't walk in that house again."

"I don't know," she said, then added, in a thin, weak voice, "I don't think I want to go back."

"Remember our honeymoon, Lynn? Remember our love? It can be like that, again. Don't you remember?"

"But my father," she said. "My father, my father."

I could only assume her pregnancy had driven Lynn into a delicate mental state. Since I couldn't get through to her, I tried a different approach.

I shook Dr. Rebecca Liswood's firm hand and sat in one of the two leather chairs opposite hers, eyeing not only the diplomas on the walls but the framed newspaper articles lauding her as a pioneer and the world's leading authority on sex therapy and marriage counseling.

"You're here alone?" she asked. "Where is your wife?"

"My wife is absent. That's exactly why I'm here," I began, and proceeded to tell Dr. Liswood the story of our recent separation.

I wanted Dr. Liswood to go to Philadelphia and talk to Lynn in person, since I couldn't. My father, with surprising generosity, had agreed to pay for it all. After hearing our story, Dr. Liswood agreed she should not only talk with Lynn, but Abner and Mary as well, to really get to the bottom of our problem. That week, Dr. Liswood called the Konicks. They all agreed to meet her, so she spent three days in Philadelphia interviewing and counseling each of them.

I came to our next appointment with wings on my feet, eager to hear the results, but this time, Dr. Liswood—saver of marriages, opener of hearts—shook my hand weakly and slumped into her chair.

"Marty, my professional reason for being is to help, counsel, and save a marriage. That's why it pains me greatly to say this to you, but with those parents..." She shook her head ever so slightly, averted her eyes, sighed, and stared at some spot on the rug, "The two of you don't have a chance."

"Her parents?" I answered. "Wow. You're saying that already and you haven't even met my parents."

A frightened, confused young man of twenty-two, I needed an authority figure to tell me what to do. As far as I knew, no higher authority on marriage existed than Dr. Liswood. Looking back, however, I'm ashamed of having listened to the doctor. Of course, a higher authority existed: my own heart. But I didn't know that, then. I felt so powerless. Listening to Dr. Liswood pronounce the death of my marriage, I finally surrendered.

Lynn, through Abner, sued me for divorce. My father's lawyer dealt with the details while I continued to call Lynn daily, wanting only to hear the word "divorce" from her own mouth, but she refused any of my calls.

"What did you do to make your father-in-law hate you so?" asked my lawyer in one of our meetings.

"I stood up to him. That's all. I told him to butt out of our lives."

"Well, he's forcing you into a corner with this divorce. He not only wants you to divorce Lynn, but to swear you will never attempt to see her again. And Marty, I don't know how to tell you this, but he wants you to rescind all parental rights over your unborn child."

The lawyer placed a document on the table. "This is a blank adoption agreement he wants you to sign so Abner and Mary can raise the child as their own."

I pounded the table, "What right does he have?"

"No legal right. Abner can't make you sign it, but that will just leave your marriage in legal limbo. He's refusing to negotiate."

"I'm not divorcing Abner!" I shouted. "I want to talk to my wife, God damn it!"

I called Lynn from the attorney's office, but Gussie, who always answered the phone now, told me Lynn refused the call again. Mary wouldn't talk to me, either. I stormed out of the office and somehow made it home without crashing the Impala.

I can look back now and see how, to him, Abner's demand must have seemed perfectly logical. After all, he was so used to controlling every member of his family, he didn't see any point in stopping just because his daughter got married. He didn't think of it as control, though. He thought of it as building a kind of family dynasty—proof of his own manliness. Abner expected Lynn to recruit me into his circle of influence, so when I refused to go into the garment business, refused to move to Philadelphia, refused to compromise my family's religious convictions, I thwarted his goal. Abner viewed nothing as neutral. People were either friends or enemies, and he declared me the latter.

As for me, I was a lot more like Abner than I'd like to admit. Completely unyielding on the subject of walking on Yom Kippur (and in many other cases as well) I tried to control Lynn. My parents, in their orthodox tradition, expected to have a say in nearly every aspect of my life, and I didn't dare stand up to them. Abner, in his tradition of abuse, also expected to control Lynn and me. Abner and my father played tug-of-war with me, even as Abner and I played tug-of-war with Lynn. Abner fought dirty, something I didn't know how to confront.

In addition to requiring old-fashioned physical bravery, going back to the Konick's house would have required humility on my part—I would have had to acknowledge I'd been wrong in the argument about Yom Kippur and apologize to Lynn. I couldn't do it.

Not a man? Indeed, I wasn't a man. What twenty-two-year-old is? When it came down to doing what I had to do to get Lynn back, I couldn't.

Abner's adoption agreement was nothing less than a kick in the groin. He would build his family dynasty—if not with me, then with my baby. This was revenge, pure and simple. Oh, the contract made all kinds of claims as to why it would be better for the child never to know a father that was shunned from the family home, and how Lynn could start her life over without the baby, and how the Konicks would be much better parents than two divorced kids barely out of their teens. Nonetheless, I knew revenge when I saw it.

That evening, the phone in the breakfast nook rang. My mother answered and held the receiver silently to her ear. Standing at the kitchen sink, drying dishes, I turned to face her with a building sense of dread.

Mother put her hand over the phone's mouthpiece and stared at me warily, unblinking. "Abner," she mouthed. "For you."

"Now, you listen to me," began Abner. "I'm not wasting any more time on you. Understand? You have heard the terms of the contract and you are going to sign it, you little shit."

"Why can't I talk to Lynn?" I countered. "Why won't you let her come home to me?"

"She can do as she likes, and she doesn't want to see you."

"I want to hear it from her, Abner."

"Listen to me, young man. You are never going to see Lynn again or talk to her. Ever! We want you out of our lives, forever. We never want to hear your name again."

"When did you become so cruel? You're a heartless man, Abner. I think you're sick."

"Don't you dare talk to me like that."

"Are you threatening me?"

"Listen carefully. I can ensure you never finish your education, never become a periodontist, and that your license to practice medicine is revoked. I can publicly humiliate you, cause a scandal, and ruin your life. Do you hear me? I know people everywhere. Do as I say."

"So you are threatening me."

"I'm warning you. Stay away from my daughter. Forever. Do you understand?"

"I understand," I said. "But I won't agree to the terms of the contract."

"If you don't, you'll live to regret it," Abner said, and hung up.

I dropped the receiver, and it smashed into a plate on the cluttered table. As I steadied myself against the wall, pieces of porcelain fell to the floor, and then I felt it: a big ball of Abner's hate turning inside me.

I ran to the bathroom and vomited, over and over, but never felt relief.

When Abner said he would ruin my life, I believed him. In fact, I felt quite positive if he wanted to, he could ensure I never got so much as a dishwashing job for the rest of my life. He might hire a hit man to come after me, break my legs or something. I couldn't forget how the venom in his voice oozed right through the telephone.

That's when I realized why Mary put up with him. Standing up to Abner brought on unthinkable repercussions. The man did not own a conscience. He had embedded himself in Lynn's brain and held Mary by the throat—surely she couldn't leave him or he'd ruin her, and their children, too.

And now he had me by the balls.

Just thinking about Abner made me feel covered in fire ants. All I wanted was to get him off, get him off, get him off! Yes, I decided again, Dr. Liswood was right. As long as Lynn remained under Abner's spell, she would never give me her heart. I couldn't have Lynn without becoming Abner's lackey. Abner sent that message, loud and clear. But I didn't lose sight of the irony of the situation either. Abner wants me to be a man? I thought. What kind of man would I be under his thumb?

"A man" described the opposite of what Abner wanted me to be.

All night and the next day, wrenching stomachaches tore my guts apart and piercing headaches came and went in waves. I sat in my darkened room and cried, alone. Hope tortured me whenever the phone rang, but the callers always turned out to be my mother's friends, excavating the neighborhood for gossip. All day, I could hear Mother discussing my imminent divorce with one busybody or another.

"I have just stayed out of it," she insisted to her friends. "What have I done? Nothing, that's what. I never interfered, so don't blame me."

Finally, I pounded down the stairs, grabbed the phone from Mother's hand, dialed my lawyer, and told him I couldn't take it anymore.

The next day, I signed everything.

I may not have been the man I thought but I was not going to ruin the life of the woman I loved for some Pyrrhic victory. To be any sort of man, I had to let go. It was God damned Shakespearean in it's tragedy. How could a human be so cruel to another human being—family no less? I had fallen on my sword for the woman I loved and the son I was never to see. I couldn't be bought and yet paid the ultimate price. How could that be?

20

Every morning I woke up, felt for Lynn beside me on the bed, and then remembered: it's over. With practice, I developed the habit of powering through each day like a man running through waist-high water. Keeping myself busy helped—I had my work at the clinic, classes at the dental center, and parties on weekends. I didn't enjoy the parties, but they kept my mind pleasantly obliterated.

One day in late March 1962, I came home, threw my books on the kitchen table, and, as usual, ransacked the fridge for a snack. The phone rang. It startled me, and I knocked over a milk carton.

When I picked up, Dr. Johnstone said, "Marty? Lynn just gave birth to a boy. She is asking for you, and I really think you should be here."

I felt my heart pounding. I had become a father. And yet, I hadn't.

"I can't," I told him.

"What do you mean, you can't?"

"Abner made me sign that I'd have no contact with Lynn or the baby."

"What?" he asked. "I don't know anything about this!"

"The man threatened me, and frankly I believe Abner would follow through." I told Dr. Johnstone the details of the contract I had signed.

"Oh my God," he said. "Oh my God. Oh, dear God. This is so much worse than I thought."

"I'm going to be honest with you," I said. "I think Abner is probably waiting for the slightest provocation. I think it would give him great pleasure to see me destroyed—financially, professionally, emotionally, every way there is. I'm petrified of the man."

"I understand," said the doctor. "Listen, let me handle this, Marty. I'll get back to you as soon as possible."

I never heard from Dr. Johnstone again.

I worked hard at convincing myself I'd done the right thing. My rationalization began with: it's better if Lynn remarries, the child has another father, and he never knows me. The voice in my head insisted it would also be easier for me, too, if I never saw the child, never formed an attachment, especially if the boy was to be raised by Abner and Mary. There is no point, I told myself, in getting close to anyone in Abner's home.

These loops of logic repeated through my head while I studied, drove, took tests, ate, slept, worked on patients at the clinic. They never stopped because they never fully convinced me.

Somehow, along the way, I found out Lynn had named the boy Stephen, but knowing his name made everything worse. I began to retreat deep inside myself and never talked about my misery. When I stewed, I blamed everyone else in my life for my predicament. I felt I'd done exactly what my parents had raised me to do, tried in every respect to honor Jewish laws and traditions, and yet God had punished me for all my efforts. What's the point? I thought. My attendance at synagogue became sporadic. On the surface, I still acted like the good son and the smart, charismatic, president-of-student-council Marty, but I also began to live a secret life. I started sleeping with several of my patients at the clinic—fashion models looking for a good time and nothing more. I saw them at lunch, after work, between classes. I didn't feel anything for them, didn't want to. I just wanted something, anything, to look forward to each day. And mostly, I wanted to be bad.

I also tried to date, not because I thought I'd fall in love again, but simply in an effort to act normal. Oddly, whenever I called on friends to double date with me—something Lynn and I used to do—my friends always turned me down, now. Soon, all my married friends excluded me from gatherings, dinners, and nights out.

After months of this treatment, I finally asked Fred, who had come along to Columbia with me from U. Penn, to tell me what he knew.

He said, "Marty, it's not us guys, it's the wives who don't want you around. They know you divorced Lynn when she was pregnant, and they think you're...well, they think you're a bad influence. They don't want you around their husbands."

Shut out of the social circle at school, I became best buddies with my old friend Ken, also from U. Penn. He lived on Long Island now, near me, and practiced dentistry. He found us some girls to go out with now and then. For me, this merely passed the time, but Ken actually fell in love with one of them. He told his folks about his intentions, and they asked to meet her family. Then, one day, Ken called me, hysterical.

"Can I come over?" he asked. "I have to see you."

Ken pulled up drunk, parked his car on the curb, and proceeded to tell me that his parents didn't like hers. His own father had called his girlfriend trash. "He said, 'If you marry her, I'm washing my hands of you!'" Ken told me, adding, "Then he said, 'By the way, your mother and I are leaving tomorrow for three weeks in Europe. We can discuss this when we get back.' Boom! Just like that!"

"What are you going to do?" I asked.

"I want to die, Marty. I just want to die, that's all."

Now we both had sorrows to drown, so, one night, we borrowed Ken's father's Fleetwood Cadillac and drove two and a half hours up to the Catskills. The Catskills reigned as the ultimate place to see Frank Sinatra, Buddy Hackett, Tony Bennett, Martin and Lewis—all the big, big names. With nothing to lose, we drove up there and threw away all our money, drinking all night, picking up women, dancing like lunatics. We didn't drive home until 6:30 in the morning, at which point we swerved up to my house and basically poured ourselves out of the car.

My father came out just then, on his way to work, took one look at me and said, "You're ruining your life. You'll never amount to anything."

I pretended Father's disdain affected me not in the least: I strode inside, shaved, changed clothes, drove off to work at the clinic, hung over, made my lunchtime appointment for sex with some girl and my afternoon appointment for sex with another. Then, for dinner, I showed for a date with a quietly attractive virginal young lady named Barbara. Her conversation amused me, if mildly, but unlike the others, she seemed to genuinely like me.

The fact that Barbara might like me felt very impressive at that low point. I didn't have any feelings for her, though. Her personality was rather bland, but I thought having a steady girlfriend would provide yet another layer of distraction from Lynn and the baby and everything I wasn't allowed to think about. I started seeing Barbara every weekend.

Completely chaste, Barbara believed in "saving herself." Even with the sexual revolution well underway, that concept still hadn't gone out of vogue. I didn't mind. After all, I enjoyed all the sex I could handle every lunch hour and afternoon with fashion models, budding young actresses, and one certified nymphomaniac.

Eventually, after many months of my dating Barbara, my parents launched a harassment campaign about getting me married again.

"You are taking up an awful lot of Barbara's time," my mother hinted one day.

"What are your intentions toward her?" asked Father.

"She's got her future to think about, after all," added Mother.

"You think I should marry her?" I asked.

"I would like to see you settled," replied Mother.

"Sure," I said. "I'll ask Barbara to marry me. Why not?"

To me, the idea of marrying Barbara felt like buying a house cat—set it up with a ball of yarn and some food, keep the water bowl full, and how much trouble can it be? Besides, I had finished post-graduate school by this time and was very busy preparing to set up my first practice. I had envisioned doing this with Lynn, and now going it alone seemed unthinkable.

With my mind at an all-time creative nadir, I planned a reenactment of my engagement to Lynn: dinner with both sets of parents, napkins on the plates, surprise ring, etcetera, etcetera. I bought a cheap ring and set the date for the dinner: November 22, 1963.

The morning of the big event, I drove up to Stamford, Connecticut, to talk to a dentist about a potential business partnership. Driving through the countryside—Lynn's and my favorite countryside—I exerted a monumental effort to not think about Lynn, our imagined home in Connecticut, and how those plans had begun the unraveling of everything. The effort of trying not to think about it weighed so heavily I felt like I had a head cold.

In the middle of my discussion with the Stamford dentist, a nurse barged into the room.

"I'm sorry to interrupt, doctor, but I thought you would want to know!" she blurted out. "The president has been shot!"

By the time the hysterical nurse finished replaying the telecast for us, John F. Kennedy's death had become official.

Shaken to the core by the assassination, I drove home to be with my parents. I should have known, as usual, they would offer no comfort. I found Mother vacuuming the drapes, and Father hadn't found the occasion momentous enough to come home early from work.

I stomped around the house, shouting, "The world is coming to an end, and you're vacuuming drapes? We could be at war in an hour! Where the hell is Father? This is a time for families to band together, for God's sakes!" Finally, I collapsed in a chair and told Mother, "I can't go through with this engagement. I'm too upset."

"Oh, grow up," she snapped. "No matter who is president, you still have an obligation to that girl."

I tried to convince Mother to call off the dinner. I thought it would have been tacky to do otherwise, but she fought me on it. In the end, I acquiesced to changing the invitation to "coffee and cake," and politely sat through some sort of banal conversation with Barbara and the two sets of parents. I don't remember what we discussed, but I do remember that afterwards, I took Barbara out for a drive.

Still deeply shaken, I talked to Barbara about feeling devastated over the assassination and how JFK had been the first vote I ever cast. The image on the television of the spray of blood coming from the president's head after those three gunshots, then poor Jackie reaching for him. The way Jackie had, in her panic, crawled over the trunk of the car; meanwhile the motorcade kept rolling steadily down the street. I couldn't stop thinking about it. I felt like evil overran the world that day. The fact that my parents seemed relatively unconcerned about it all disturbed me even more.

Barbara listened attentively and kindly that evening. I remember well how sweet she acted, patting my hand and telling me she cared. I guess that's why I did it. I pulled the ring out of my pocket and put it on her finger. I didn't say I love you, nor did I look her in the eye, but she didn't seem to mind. In fact, she shrieked with delight.

Later on, my parents beamed at the news of the engagement, Barbara showed off her ring to everyone, and Barbara's parents congratulated us.

Pleasing all those people made me feel content, or perhaps satisfied. Whatever feeling dwelled in my heart that day, it impressed me as the closest thing to happiness I deserved.

21

Father brought the bridesmaids in his car, and Mother and I drove to synagogue in mine. Along the way, I pulled over into the parking lot of some fast food joint.

With uncharacteristic honesty and in a vain attempt to not ruin yet another life as well as my own, I spewed, "Mother, I can't go through with this. It's a huge mistake."

White-gloved hands in her lap, she turned her head, but not her shoulders, toward me. "You're just having bridegroom jitters. It'll be okay, you'll see."

"Mother," I said, through gritted teeth. "May I remind you I've done this before?"

Her pretense at kindness fell away instantly.

"Stop this behavior this instant, young man," she said. "And get back on the road. You are not leaving that girl at the altar. Oh my God, think what people would say!"

I gripped the wheel and stared straight ahead. Mother's right, I thought. My reputation is already at rock bottom, and if I leave Barbara now, that'll be it. I'll never get another date as long as I live. A handsome, smart, charming, twenty-four-year-old man, I thought my life had ended. My life, my troubles, and my future: that's as far as I thought. It didn't even occur to me to wonder what entering into marriage with a man who didn't love her would do to Barbara.

I swerved back onto the road and eventually trudged down the aisle. But I thought of Lynn the whole time and just wallowed in pain. What with Barbara being a virgin, our wedding night loomed as a momentous evening for her, but as soon as I kissed her, my nose began to bleed in a torrent. I spent the rest of the night trying to stanch the bleeding, glad for the distraction. I didn't want to touch her. Thoroughly regretting this impulsive and completely fake marriage, I wondered why Barbara didn't ask me what was wrong. In fact, I wondered why she herself had gone through with the wedding. I didn't sense that she loved me, exactly, only that she was intent upon completing some expected rite of passage. I began to think, Barbara is a smart girl and surely she wants to be happy with her life, so why is she playing out this charade? What I didn't realize is that she had never been in love and didn't have a basis for comparison like I did.

The next night, on our honeymoon in the Virgin Islands, we finally did the deed. I tried to make the sex nice for her, but Barbara kept her eyes closed the whole time. She didn't seem to realize I expected her to participate. I felt none of the sensuality, the depth, or the raw emotion I had felt with Lynn. Of course, proper society girls like Barbara were taught that appearing to enjoy sex would make them seem 'fast'. Lynn instinctively ignored that silly advice but Barbara was a "good girl" to the core, so I don't know why I expected anything different. After the sex, I got another nosebleed and kept on getting them throughout our vacation.

While we lay beside the pool, basking in the sun, Barbara thought about God-knows-what and I beat myself up for not shoving my mother out of the car and driving straight to the south pole instead of marrying Barbara. But now I had married again, and I'd be damned if I would fail at relationship number two. Failing again, I felt, would prove something deeply wrong dwelled within me, as my parents' frequent criticism always seemed to imply. Reaching between our deck chairs to hold Barbara's hand, I resolved to make this marriage work or die trying.

Barbara and I moved into a rented apartment on Long Island. As soon as we crossed the threshold, which I didn't even have the gentlemanliness to carry her over, Barbara ordered, "Take off your shoes!"

"What? My shoes? Why?"

"I don't want a mess on this rug!" Her tone implied the reason should be obvious.

I hadn't spent much time with Barbara in a private home. When we dated, we went out to restaurants, the movies, and for drives in my car, but she didn't come over to my folks' house much and I didn't spend time at hers. That must be how I managed to remain completely blind to the fact that Barbara was a fanatical neat freak. Worse yet, when guests came over, Barbara never thought to offer them a glass of water or a snack, unless she wanted something from them, like an invitation to a party. Then, she became the most charming hostess in the world.

I came home every night to "Take your shoes off! Don't make a mess!" The sweetness and love she had showered on me before our marriage gradually diminished after the honeymoon. I'm sure this change was partly due to her finally sensing how little I loved her and maybe even realizing she didn't love me either. How could any woman have loved the distracted, shallow man I became after Lynn? But I was bright and ambitious, had good prospects, and to Barbara, at first, admiring those traits must have seemed like love, or what she have been taught love was. Barbara, like me, followed her training and latched onto a "good breadwinner".

Of course, she could have actually been in love with me all along. I'll never know and don't want to because, if she did, then the immediate deterioration of our relationship is too sad to bear. Despite the face my marrying Barbara had been one gigantic farce, I still resolved to succeed at it. Despite what Abner thought, I knew what it meant to be a man; damn it, and I could make a marriage work. I needed to prove that to myself.

I finally started my practice, which became an immediate success, and Mother and Father seemed pleased. Here they could boast of the "happy" son they always dreamed of: successful dentist, own practice, and lovely wife. I played the part to the hilt, and gave them bragging rights to all of it. Having longed all my life to make them happy, I should have felt proud and delighted, but instead, I felt disgusted with all of us.

I bought Barbara clothes and furs and handbags and whatnot, which always seemed to make her happy, at least for a while. But she never ceased with the cleaning and the scolding. She began cleaning before I left the house in the morning and I'd find her cleaning when I got home at night. If I made myself a midnight snack I'd have hell to pay, simply because she couldn't supervise the cleanup. I hired housekeepers and maids and all kinds of people to try to give my wife some peace of mind, but Barbara micro-managed them so much they always quit.

Worst of all, Barbara considered throwing parties, like Lynn and I used to do, completely out of the question.

"Think of the mess!" Barbara shrieked, when I suggested it.

When Barbara's parents came to visit, they smoked. Barbara would empty the ashtray each and every time someone flicked an ash in it.

I liked both of Barbara's parents and they liked me. In fact, before we married, I told them and Barbara all about Lynn, though I neglected to mention the fact that I still longed for her, and our child, every moment of the day. Barbara figured my first marriage had completely ended, so she didn't mind my being divorced. Her parents both felt I had done the right thing in signing those adoption papers so my child's life wouldn't be too complicated. In fact, they thought I had handled the whole thing courageously. I appreciated their support, though, in my soul, I couldn't agree.

I also told the three of them about my estranged sister Sheila. For some reason, this disturbed the Lesser family far more than the circumstances of my first marriage and divorce. Like Lynn, Barbara asked Sheila to be our maid of honor. Of course, Sheila refused. Her parents found this fact astonishingly troublesome.

Despite how much they liked me, I didn't dare confide in Barbara's parents. Whenever they, or anyone, criticized Barbara, I defended her through gritted teeth. Above all, I didn't want anyone to know how miserable I felt with her. That would destroy the entire illusion I worked so hard, each day, to create.

During our first year of marriage, I found it easy enough to justify staying away from home; after all, I had to work very hard to get my practice up and running, and Barbara understood that completely. I also had to work very hard to keep my lunch and dinner sex dates, but somehow I managed that, too. And I never got a nosebleed with any of those girls.

Gradually, I moved on from the fashion model and actress set to the vast population of horny, dissatisfied, wealthy, married ladies living in situations much like mine. Unlike the single girls, they didn't expect a phone call, nor did they expect to fall in love, but just wanted a reason to get out of bed every day. Also, I think, like me, they wanted someone to confirm they weren't the only lost, miserable souls out there.

Not only did I learn to fake my way through my marriage, I even faked my way through my affairs. I didn't possess anywhere near the confidence necessary to pull off these kind of hi-jinx. Sexually, I felt shy and repressed, though for some reason, I had never felt that way with Lynn. During sex with my various partners, I always had to hide my shame and insecurity. I hid it well, though—after all, I had been practicing that trick my whole life.

These married women made it all possible with their incredibly aggressive attitudes—products of a society balanced somewhere between the freedom The Pill gave them and a desire for the respectability of a house wife. Most of them came back for more, again and again, yet I always wondered if I had performed adequately.

22

Despite out incompatibility, Barbara's and my union did bear fruit, and in 1965, Barbara gave birth to our son Jonathan. Two years later, I built a house in Flower Hill, on Long Island's affluent North Shore. At 27, I headed the youngest family on the block.

The day I signed the papers on that house, Barbara's father Seymour crowed like a cock, "Look at my son in law! He graduated dental school substantially in debt, and now look what he has done!"

My own father, the perpetual naysayer, only muttered, "You're not making enough money, yet. You can't afford this." I never discussed my finances with him; he just assumed. From the Konicks, I had picked up the habit of enjoying money, and naturally, Father disapproved. Deep down, he probably also intuited my growing apathy towards Judaism and our family's conservative traditions in general, but I never talked about it. I still walked to synagogue with him once in a while, even though my heart wasn't in it.

Every morning, I woke up in our beautiful mini-mansion, complete with entryway chandelier and cascading double staircase, and resolved anew to make this marriage work. Every afternoon, I met some new hottie eager to get my pants off. The way I viewed it, I cheated on Barbara in order to save my marriage. As long as my latest fling gave me something to look forward to at lunchtime, I could tolerate my wife in the evening—a strange rationalization perhaps, but it enabled me to get a little of what I thought was pleasure. I didn't realize that where compassion exists, love and even pleasure can grow. But I had not compassion, no fellow-feeling for the others. I felt sorry for myself and acted out like a child. I certainly never stopped to wonder whether Barbara was happy or sexually satisfied.

In 1968, our son Adam came into the world.

For both the boys, we hired a baby nurse named Bess—a grandmother so full of love, and so on top of things, in my eyes she could do no wrong. Big-hearted

Seymour, who remained very concerned about the animosity between my sister and me, befriended Bess, and the two of them insisted that she and I reconcile. For the sake of Seymour and Bess, I extended a tentative hand to Sheila, and she, Walter and their two kids did begin to attend family functions, but things between us remained guarded. The endeavor proved futile anyway, because Sheila didn't like Barbara. Barbara felt the same about Sheila, and, though I spoke of it to no one, I didn't like my sister or my wife. Every Thanksgiving, I longed to sit at the children's table.

I enjoyed being a father and spent my days off at home, with the boys. Instinctively, I parented differently from my own mother and father in every way. Though a strict parent, I still showered my boys with kindness and praise. When they got to school age, I sat down with them every evening, asking, "What are you studying now? Do you need help with your homework?" I helped my children through their conflicts in school, gave them advice, provided them with flash cards and research books, whatever they needed to excel. Barbara loved the kids just as much, but her parenting style was much more laissez-faire.

As soon as Jonathan grew big enough, I asked him to spend Saturday morning in synagogue with me—perhaps trying to recreate and then better the relationship I had growing up with my own father. We lived too far away to walk, but I insisted he dress up and ride with me in the car. He didn't want to do it, of course.

"It's not supposed to be fun," I explained. "It's a tradition. A special time between a father and eldest son." I acted stern, like my own father, and insisted he participate, but every Saturday Barbara would flutter by this little scene and say, "He doesn't have to go if he doesn't want. He's just a boy. Let him run and play." And run and play he would. Only beating him would have made the boy obey, so I accepted defeat.

Though I felt Barbara was thwarting my family tradition, I couldn't pretend to be pious. These days, I only partly valued the ritual from a religious standpoint; mostly, I just wanted to bond with my son. I didn't know exactly what drove me to synagogue anymore. In the early days, with Lynn, I'd known where I stood on issues of faith, even if she didn't agree. Now, I did the same things I'd been raised to do but only pretended to care.

As parents, Barbara and I stood at perpetual odds. At dinnertime, playtime, study time, and every other time, I tried to insist upon my agenda, usually a more conservative approach. Meanwhile, Barbara insisted upon hers, usually a very liberal approach, and since the boys always wanted to play or wrestle each other, Barbara generally won. Because we avoided being alone together, Barbara and I didn't discuss parenting strategies or try to present a united front. We just fought our battle of wills at every turn. It's no wonder our boys fought with each other all the time. Monkey see, monkey do. Despite this mess, I felt sure the children would be better off with both parents than with a divorce. That was the prevailing wisdom of the time. So, I tried to escalate my efforts to find happiness within this marriage.

Lynn and I found happiness but it was through magic, through chemistry, and when we lost the magic, we lost each other. I had learned nothing from our breakup, had no conflict resolution skills at all, so I only avoided Barbara more. She matched my avoidance and raised me one by feeding the children dinner before I returned home from work and the bitterness between us grew.

Happiness, for me, meant interacting as little as possible with my wife. I usually brought home a take-out dinner because Barbara's idea of a meal consisted of plopping down some disgusting concoction from a can. After dinner, I helped the boys with their homework, tucked them into bed, then retired to my den to do some paperwork, watch Johnny Carson, and sip brandy until Barbara fell fast asleep in bed. Only then, would I tiptoe into the bedroom and lie down to sleep beside my wife. Each day, thoughts of my next sexual liaison pushed me forward.

Early on, Barbara used to make the children wait until I came home for our family meals, but she grew tired of that, and soon, eating alone became part of my standard evening ritual.

After a few years of this, I tried to improve our lives by doing charity work in Israel every summer. The children got to experience life on a kibbutz, and I positively impacted the world. All of this should have made me feel good about myself, but still, every day, I woke up next to Barbara and felt like a shell of a man that nothing in this world could fill.

From the start of my practice, I had the receptionist bring the mail directly to me every morning—every bill, every envelope, every advertisement. I still secretly hoped Lynn would write to me one day, though I had no idea what I would do if she actually did.

Then, in 1969, something finally happened.

I received an envelope with no return address. Inside, I found only a picture of a five-year-old boy. He stood on the deck of a boat, wearing a stripped T-shirt and denim shorts. With his mother's oval-shaped face and my eyes, the boy looked like a perfect blend of Lynn and me.

I cancelled my appointments for the day and retreated to the movies, where I could cry all I wanted, in the dark. I didn't know if Lynn, Mary, my parents, or someone else had sent me that photo, but I felt both angry and grateful at once.

When the movie ended, I called my friends Steve and Jimmy. A businessman and a dentist, those two had become my closest friends and the only people I talked to about Lynn. In a dark bar, the three of us nursed vodka cocktails. I slapped the photo on the table and said, "Well guys, what do you think of that?"

Steve put on his glasses and picked up the photo, "Is this you?" he asked.

"It's my son Stephen, God damn it. I'm sure of it. Who else could it be?" I replied.

"Oh my God," said Jimmy.

"It came in an unmarked envelope! Is someone trying to torture me? I even wonder if Abner sent me that, just to rub my face in everything. 'Here's your son, who's my son now, you sack of shit.'"

"Are you going to contact Lynn?" Jimmy asked, "I think you should."

"You know I can't."

We drank quietly then, for quite some time.

"All that's in the past now, anyway," I said. "She stopped loving me, and I have to let it go."

Steve said, "Do you think they're lying to the boy? Telling him Abner and Mary are really his parents?"

"Hell if I know."

"One day, Marty, that kid is going to put two and two together," Steve added. "He's going to find an old picture of you and say, 'Who is this? My doppelganger?'"

"Or else," added Jimmy, "he'll figure out Mary can't possibly be his mother at age sixty something. He is going to learn Lynn is his mother, not his sister, and he'll want to meet his real father, too."

"I'm counting on that," I replied. "In fact, I'm living for that day. He'll do it when he turns twenty-one. And I'm going to be waiting."

"How do you know?" asked Jimmy.

I tucked the picture into my wallet and told my friend, "I just know."

23

Professionally, I made a name for myself at the top of my field—solving problems other doctors refused to touch, pioneering cutting-edge technology, traveling the country to give lectures on the latest methods, and running a well-respected charity clinic in Israel. But personally nearly a decade into my marriage to Barbara, I felt miserable as a dog.

I decided I needed something new to make me happy: a little girl. So, Barbara and I used the unscientific but very optimistic rhythm method to predict the gender of our next child. And despite not really enjoying the chore of lovemaking with Barbara, we got lucky. In May of 1972, we perfectly timed our intercourse to produce baby Elizabeth.

I loved having a little girl. Elizabeth used to lie on my chest at night while I watched the news, and I'd stroke her back while she fell asleep—my little darling. Yet, the emptiness I had felt since divorcing Lynn still lurked inside me, so before Elizabeth turned one, I started thinking about some new way to improve things.

"Barbara," I said one day. "Let's get a nicer house."

"What for? This one's huge."

"I've been thinking we should move to the Gold Coast of Long Island's North Shore. What do you think of that?"

"Oh, you mean a mansion?" she said, brushing back a strand of hair with sudden seductiveness.

"Better! A private estate surrounded by acres and acres of land. I'll be a country gentleman, and you'll be a lady of the manor. Picture it: a swimming pool, tennis court, and caretaker's cottage. Something so private you can't even see the house from the road. And when we do venture out, we'll be rubbing elbows with Vanderbilts and Roosevelts. Not a bad idea, eh?"

"Oh Marty, Honey, you're so good to me!" Barbara threw herself into my arms with uncharacteristic affection in her 'buy me something' mode.

The Gold Coast, setting of The Great Gatsby, shone as the ultimate place to buy an old-money mansion oozing with provenance, a way to tell the world I have arrived. I knew Barbara would like that, and hell; I'd like it, too. Foolishly, I concluded that doing something to make us both happy would make us happy to be together. The children existed as living proof of the fault in that logic.

We consulted with Barbara's father, who dealt in real estate, and throughout the time we looked at properties, Barbara acted sweet as sugar. I never met a more caring and attentive wife. Barbara and I could have bought anything at all; we had that kind of money, but the search for an estate turned out to be harder than expected. No matter what we liked, Barbara's father vetoed everything. He knew too much. This one concealed a crumbling foundation that one threatened to have electrical problems—he always found something amiss. Finally, we found an estate that seemed perfect. I nearly closed on it, but during a final walk-through I noticed a decrepit shed on the property, just an old root cellar, really. I could practically watch it crumble into bits before my eyes, and the door hung crookedly on a single hinge. I claimed the place endangered the children and withdrew my offer. But really, I backed out because that old shed reminded me of my crumbling marriage, and I realized moving to a new house wouldn't solve our problem at all.

That night, I poured myself a stiff scotch and confronted Barbara. "With this move, we'd be forcing the children to move to a new school district, and for what? A different view? We're not going to be any happier on the Gold Coast, and we both know it."

Barbara pursed her lips and looked at me long and hard. "Fine," she said. "Then I want a separation."

Shadows snaked around the room. The ice in my glass crashed together like cymbals. In the back of my head, I heard Abner's voice booming, "You're not a man!" and my mother whining, "Look what you've done to us!"

I couldn't let this marriage die. Sure, Barbara would be able to endure a divorce—it would be a mark on her personal history, but not such a big deal. She could be charming when she wanted to be, and could surely find second husband if she put her mind to it. But I felt a second divorce branded me permanently undesirable, a bad element. I remembered being shunned out of my circle of friends after divorcing Lynn and felt I couldn't survive that again. I had worked too hard to build my reputation, both socially and professionally, to see my whole life come crashing down.

The fact that I had become the opposite of the man I set out to be simply tortured me. Early on, I established a vision for myself: successful doctor, good son, faithful husband, and loving father. Except for the faithful part, I had accomplished all of that, but the vision also included a deep inner pride and sense of fulfillment, which I found desperately lacking. Happiness remained elusive. These days, I looked in the mirror at a drunk and a philanderer, a man I didn't recognize, whose eyes held no luster. All evidence indicated things would not improve from here, but I sure as hell didn't want to sink any lower.

If Barbara and I separated, I'd be alone, I thought, and unloved, forever. And what about the children? How could I condemn them to a life of switching back and forth between parents? I considered it my responsibility to save them from that fate.

"Barbara," I said. "Don't be hasty. We can work this out. I know we can. I want to make you happy, so listen, let's do something you've always wanted to do—move to Florida!"

"Really? Miami Beach?" she asked, eyebrows arched in skepticism.

"Miami Beach!" I declared, and surprised her by planting a kiss on her lips to seal the deal.

Personally, I envisioned a brand-new home, on beachfront property, filled with modern appliances to make life easy for us. But Barbara harbored a romantic notion of "Old Miami Beach." She wanted a movie star's home from the 1940s—something out of Casablanca. We travelled to Florida several times over the course of the year, and finally found something we both liked. A 1936, New Orleans-style Colonial, the house still sheltered its original owner and boasted a big, southern, two-story balcony; wrought iron embellishments; and gingerbread under the eaves. I plunked down the money, hired a contractor, and started renovations. Then, I began the process of selling my practice in New York. Barbara, who had spent many childhood summers in Miami Beach, declared herself happy, for once.

Selling my practice took seven years, during which time we remained on Long Island. Little Elizabeth grew into a delightful child and, with my encouragement, the boys excelled at school. I also received three more of those mysterious photos in the mail: Stephen at 7, again on a boat; Stephen at 10, grinning next to a captain's wheel; and Stephen at 13, holding a fishing pole. Unlike my other two boys, who took after Barbara, Stephen grew tall, like me, and developed my hair, my eyes, my smile. But how and why, I wondered, did he spend so much time on boats?

The photos tortured me. Just when I thought I had put Lynn out of my mind, here would come another envelope. I scanned the background of the photos, once even with a magnifying glass, hoping to catch a glimpse of Lynn, but she never appeared.

I didn't mention the pictures to Barbara, but showed them to my friends Steve and Jimmy, and we spent hours theorizing about Stephen and his life—taking clues from each of the photo's backgrounds, his clothes, the look in his eyes, whatever we could find.

Around the time I sold my practice, my parents had also moved to Florida, like old people do, so my father volunteered to supervise the renovations on our Miami Beach home while I prepared my family to move. He called me every day with doom and gloom predictions.

"Boy have you bought a piece of junk," he said once. "Wait until you see all the problems."

"What problems exactly?"

"It's a mess! What a big mistake you made! This is a disaster!"

I had long since grown used to my father finding the negative in any situation and took his comments with a grain of salt. In this and all similar conversations, Father never gave specifics, just did his best to work me into a lather of regret. While Barbara thought I parented like a conservative, ogre-like, taskmaster, my father found me disgustingly liberal with my showcase homes and free-spending ways. These endless doomsday predictions were his way of admonishing me for straying from the tribe. By this time, I had finally ceased to try to please anyone but myself, which left me open for criticism from all sides.

In much the same way that Barbara and I never sat down and worked out a mutually agreeable plan for child rearing, my father and I never discussed the waning of my religious devotion. He wouldn't have known where to begin such a discussion, and neither would I. Very much like Abner, my father and I still viewed the world in terms of extremes: people were either with us, or against us. Since neither of us could meet people halfway, neither of us could agree with anyone at all, for long.

The day we arrived in Florida, Barbara, Jonathan, Adam, Elizabeth, and I stood in the doorway of our new home, suitcases in hand, horrified. The owner, a widow and proud member of the D.A.R., turned out to be one of these "ladies who lunch." And by lunch, I mean drink until their eyes pop out. She left the place a complete dump. I had to hire a dumpster and crew to clean out the results of her hoarding.

My contractor, a barrel-chested man with an eternally knit brow, took me aside and said, "Dr. Kraidin, I want to make sure you know what we're up against, here."

He showed me how if he went to change a wall socket, the plaster crumbled. I tried opening a window, and it came off in my hands. Whenever he tried to fix an electrical socket, the brittle old wires snapped into pieces.

The wiring needed to be replaced, which meant the plaster walls had to be torn up. The plumbing would require a complete overhaul; too, so there went the floors.

Up in the attic, he said, "See those beams?"

They looked like they had been attacked with a buzz saw.

"Those are full of wood boring beetles," he said. "This roof is going to go any day now."

Then he took me down to the crawlspace under the house, where he proceeded to show me how salt-air had worn down the concrete slab to the point where the house practically sat on sand. Perhaps I should have listened to my father after all. For once he saw the obvious and was more pragmatic than pessimistic.

With no choice but to move forward, I hired two work crews—one for daytime, another for night. I could have built the identical house from the ground up for cheaper. I renovated the old place, doing whatever it took to ensure Barbara got what she wanted and didn't leave me. Finally, we finished all the renovations, built a swimming pool, and restored the manse to its true nature: a glamorous, world-class, luxury home of yesteryear.

My parents visited for our grand opening. After I toured them through the oaken doors, across the marble foyer, beneath the crystal chandelier, through the living room outfitted in period-appropriate antiques, and out onto the flower-strewn veranda, Father said, "What a money pit!" Mother frowned and sniffed.

I had hoped this move would straighten me out, as a husband, because I'd get away from my sex partners in New York. In my fantasies, Florida, with its sunny and pleasant weather, would warm up Barbara a little, too, and maybe we'd grow to like each other. I even dared to envision throwing parties in our gorgeous home, but things didn't work out that way. What with Florida's ever-present sand and our home's white marble floors, before long, Barbara's obsession with clean floors sent her into a tailspin worse than anything I had seen yet. She declared parties, and even houseguests, out of the question. The fact that I hired enough household help to clean up a third world country made no difference to her at all.

Fully understanding that Barbara's severe cleanliness obsession had to be a sign of something more than a simple propensity toward neatness, I knew I ought to feel sorry for her, but I just couldn't. Today, I'm sad and a little ashamed to say that, In Miami Beach, my dislike, distrust, and aversion to Barbara turned into full-blown hate.

While the renovation continued, I founded a new periodontal practice. True to my nature, I quickly became even more successful in Florida than I had been in New York. Shmoozing and networking, something I had always been good at, made up an integral part of this endeavor. And what with all that shmoozing, my extra-curricular sex life got off to a running start, too. A parade of hot, eager women threw themselves into my lap. I couldn't resist. Didn't even want to try, anymore.

One evening, Barbara and I attended a party at another mansion in our neighborhood. The hostess, a lovely young blonde, pulled me out on the dance floor. Mid-dance I suddenly felt a hand down the back of my pants and another cupping my balls.

"Why don't you come over for lunch tomorrow?" she purred. The blonde brought me to a bedroom with mirrors on the ceiling over the bed. Seeing that made me feel innocent all over again. Oh, I didn't know debauchery like Miami Beach knew debauchery. No, I did not. But don't blame me…EVERYONE, it seemed was doing it. Or at least, that was part of my justification.

The incredibly hot women in Miami Beach impressed me as absolute sex goddesses, who left me feeling pleasantly destroyed every time. I don't know if it's something in the water down there, or what.

After a while, I felt like I needed an appointment secretary just to keep track of all my sex dates. It got to where I had to stop and ask myself what the hell I was doing. I was driving myself crazy with all these women. They crawled all over me, and still happiness eluded me. I considered quitting, but life without them seemed too bleak.

On Miami Beach—a small island with a tight-knit, old money, predominantly Jewish culture—all the society people married one another, of course, but promiscuity defined their way of life. So many people carried on affairs, many of them neighbors, and many of them married men with other men, that one could hardly keep track of who had come out, who remained in the closet, who had a marriage of convenience, and who kept a second family on the side. Despite the great sex I enjoyed, I didn't like this gossipy and incestuous little world one bit.

I thought the new atmosphere would change my sexual ways. I had long since come to understand that sex was just a validation because I felt so beaten down by the life I felt forced to endure. This change to Miami was supposed to change all that. Instead, it just fueled the fire and I took to the empty sex with as much, if not more, vigor as ever. And, as always, it was just as empty and unfulfilling.

Florida lies so near to the Bahamas, I learned I could hop over to the islands on a one-hour plane ride. Enjoying an excellent excuse to get away from Barbara, I extended my charity work to the Bahamas. One thing led to another, and I established a second full practice there as well, making money like an oil baron.

Moving to Florida had done nothing for my marriage, but now at least I could retreat to my condo in Nassau and live like a bachelor any time I wanted. Barbara and I stayed out of each other's hair enough to remain married, and I viewed that as a small victory over the alternative, a second divorce. In Miami Beach, people considered divorce relatively commonplace, so that outcome would no longer doom me socially, but failing at a second marriage would definitely have destroyed my few remaining shreds of self-esteem.

24

The last remnants of afternoon sun slanted through the lilac bushes, through the sliding glass door, and onto the kitchen table where I sat. I held my right hand in my left and manipulated it gently. Sure enough, the wrist hurt no matter which way I turned it.

Barbara entered from the patio. "What are you doing in here? I thought you were going to change that patio light so the kids can play outside before bed?"

"The screws on the damn thing were stuck, so I used a pair of pliers..."

"Oh God, am I going to have to do this myself? Seriously, Marty? You can't change a light bulb?"

"God damn it, Barbara! I was trying to tell you I hurt myself! Listen to me, for once. I strained too hard to turn that damn screw and now I think I've torn something in my wrist."

"Well, go see a doctor." Barbara breezed back out the door and ordered the children inside.

A chorus of whines accompanied Barbara through the house while I sat there, slowly opening and closing my hand, feeling for the source of pain.

I saw a hand specialist, who took some ex-rays and told me, "Nothing's broken, but your wrist is very inflamed." He put me on a brand-new, anti-inflammatory drug called Feldene.

By the third day of taking the drug I felt terrible, so I returned to the doctor, only to discover the Feldene had given me a duodenal ulcer. The doctor stopped me as I put my shirt back on.

He said, "Wait a minute, Marty. I don't like the color of your skin."

"I just have a sunburn," I growled.

"No," he said. "That's not it. There is also a yellowness to the sclera of your eyes. I want you to go to the hospital for some tests."

"Oh, for crying out loud!" I complained, "Okay, I'll go in tomorrow if I have time."

"No, Marty, I'm not kidding. I'm admitting you right away."

Pretty soon, a feeding tube snaked up my nose and a pump emptied the contents of my stomach. After a while, a doctor entered the room.

"The tests just came back," he said. "You have hepatitis B."

HIV was just a headline and not a hysteria yet and we were still practicing "wet finger" dentistry—no gloves. I must have treated a patient while I had a tiny cut on my hand. He or she turned out to be a hepatitis B carrier, and that's how I got it.

By the next day, my skin and eyes had turned completely yellow. Barbara brought me a pair of pajamas from home—also yellow. I looked like a big stick of butter.

I didn't feel sick or weak—not yet—and I didn't want to be there, so I sat up in my hospital bed all day, annoyed as hell, puffing away on cigarettes until the doctor made me stop.

The ulcer disappeared, and gradually my wrist felt better, too, but day by day, the doctors became more worried about my hepatitis. They observed my test results over the course of a week, and then called in a world-renowned Hepatologist to consult. My case turned out to be very severe, even though I still didn't feel much in the way of symptoms. I certainly didn't feel like I knocked at death's door each day, but apparently, I did.

Barbara told me later that the Hepatologist warned her if my test results didn't improve by the eleventh day, my liver would shut down and I'd be dead within 48 hours. On the tenth day, they started drawing my blood every hour on the hour to recheck.

Miraculously, on that eleventh day, my numbers did improve.

On the twelfth day, I received a mysterious phone call.

"Hi," a woman said.

"Hello," I replied. "Who is this?"

"Don't you know?"

"No, I don't. If I did, I wouldn't ask. Please tell me."

"I thought you would recognize my voice," she said.

"I don't. Please, this isn't fair. I'm really sick and I don't have the energy for this. I'm going to hang up."

I hung up, went to sleep, and forgot about the whole thing.

Two weeks later, they sent me home.

If I ended up a lifelong carrier for Hepatitis B, that would spell the end of my dentistry career; however, a chance remained that my status as a carrier would revert back to zero, so I recovered at home, meanwhile going in for weekly blood tests.

As the weeks of my recovery rolled by, I felt weaker and weaker, to the point where I couldn't lift a fork to my mouth. I hadn't much appetite, but when I did eat, I had to actually lay my head on the table and scooped the food in. My doctors had warned me the recovery would feel worse than the disease, but the fatigue I endured turned me limp as an old sock.

Then came the depression—also a typical side effect of hepatitis B. If I thought I had experienced depression throughout my marriage to Barbara, I now entered a whole new realm of wishing I had never been born. For six months, I shuffled around the house like a butter-colored ghost, immersed in utmost despair, unable to pick up a pen, dial a phone, or feed myself without herculean effort. I remember, at one point, huddling on the bathroom floor, between the toilet and sink, hopelessly sobbing and considering suicide.

Worst of all, I had to keep my condition a secret. If the general population found out I might be carrying hepatitis B, a public panic would end my practice in no time, and for good.

My depression brought my years-long crisis of faith to a head. Not for the first time, I mused upon how I grew up doing everything "right" and expecting to be rewarded with the good things in life as a result, but Lynn divorced me, Abner threatened me, and I entered into this unhappy marriage as a result. What good had really come out of being raised with stern adherence to Judaic law? My own son wouldn't go to synagogue with me, everyone in my family fought constantly, and my wife didn't respect a single one of my family's traditions. In fact, whenever I tried to enforce them, she mocked me in front of the children. The stern conservatism I'd been brought up with simply wasn't accepted anymore, not in the world I occupied. What's more, I didn't even believe in it myself. Why, I asked myself, was I still beating my head against a wall? Because I was so used to it I didn't know how to stop? In this, my time of greatest need, Judaism ceased to give me any comfort at all, and I finally abandoned it.

I began to explore Christianity, Buddhism, eastern religions, western philosophies, the principles of psychology, and every other new mode of framing the world that I could find a book on. These studies helped me realize that ever since divorcing Lynn, I had struggled desperately to give life meaning. Money didn't do it. Status didn't either. Sex offered nothing but a way to forget my sorrow for a few minutes at a time. I loved my children, but even they didn't fill that emptiness in my soul. My efforts to help the less fortunate gave me no real sense of inner satisfaction, either.

Finally, I understood there was something about me that set me apart from Barbara, my parents, and most of the people I had ever met: the fact that I had once known true happiness. Ever since Lynn, I couldn't stop trying to recapture the feeling of having her by my side. Where others saw a satisfying life, I felt a giant emptiness. I looked at each of life's events as either bringing me closer to, or further from, the sense of inner peace I'd felt in Lynn's arms. Propped up in bed like a rag doll, it occurred to me, finally, to let my yearning go and just accept, like everyone around me, that I lived a good enough life. I truly wanted to believe that, but I couldn't, largely because I still didn't know why Lynn had abandoned me. In my heart, I didn't believe she really meant it.

I had grown used to filling my days with activity, sex, worry, plans, work, and everything but introspection, but now I could do nothing. Nothing but think. And try as I might, I couldn't stop doing that. I thought about how I had tried all my life to please my parents. I had amassed a fortune, given them three grandchildren, held together a socially acceptable marriage, and even grudgingly allowed Mother to introduce me to her friends as, "my son, the dentist." Yet still, both my parents complained incessantly. Now, at forty-five, I finally realized that their complaining would never stop, and though their gripes often focused on me, the cause of their deep unhappiness never really had anything to do with me. That small, much-overdue realization freed me profoundly.

During these long hours of contemplation, I realized Abner differed not a whit from my own father. Each man withheld love to make his children work for it—a goal they both pretended was actually attainable. Both our fathers came from the school of thought that expressing love was like admitting defeat. Once the child felt loved, then—according to this philosophy—the father couldn't control him anymore. That's why Lynn's behavior, during our marriage, actually didn't differ much from mine. We both checked every decision, consciously or subconsciously, with, "What about my father? What will he think?" Still a girl and boy, not a man and woman, we felt tortured by the need to please our fathers.

In the old days, I dreamed Lynn and I would help each other out of the emotional holes our parents had dug for us, but I never could help Lynn, and, not even realizing I had a problem, I wouldn't let her help me. Surely, I thought, our divorce hadn't won that sought-after fatherly love for her any more than it had for me. The circumstances of our separation simply set up new obstacles toward attaining that elusive prize.

Reclining in my luxurious bed in my gorgeous mansion in one of the most prestigious, affluent neighborhoods in the country, I felt as miserable as a bum and knew I wouldn't be happy until I again experienced the deep-soul satisfaction I felt with Lynn. I knew that feeling hadn't just been due to youth. True happiness, true love, electrifies the soul and manifests two destinies as one. To this day, many call me a hopeless romantic, but I have felt this phenomenon, and it is real.

I turned to astrology.

I would assume I found Ginger on a lark but given her profession perhaps it was more fate than fluke. I was walking down Lincoln Road by the beach one afternoon and came across a professional building. My eye caught her nameplate and the word astrologer. I don't know if it was simple curiosity or a burning need for answers but I went inside.

"I see you married," said Ginger, whose long, blonde tresses swept the clipboard that held my natal chart. I couldn't see her face through her curtain of hair.

"I am married," I replied impatiently. The ring on my finger could have told her that.

"No," the astrologer said, sweeping her hair back and looking out the window at the lush garden surrounding her house. She tapped my chart with a calloused fingertip. "This is different. I'm trying to understand it."

Ginger put the clipboard on her desk and ran her hands through a head of thick, silky hair, gently clutching hanks of it as if to pull the thoughts out of her head. In the last few weeks, I had become accustomed to this quirk and knew it usually led to an interesting revelation.

"It's not the same person," Ginger finally said.

I liked Ginger's face, ruddy and sunburned from working in her garden, and her hands, clearly, enjoyed communion with the soil. The woman saw visions, but she didn't paint castles in the sky for me. She talked about my life in down-to-earth terms. I told her nothing, but just from looking at my chart, Ginger figured me out—my outward success, my inner emptiness, and my despair.

"Are you talking about the past or future?" I finally asked.

Ginger sighed. I loved that she never asked me to make it easy for her. Using a combination of my astrological chart and her psychic abilities, she saw what she saw and never asked for confirmation.

"You were married once, before," she said.

"Yes."

"I see you married again, and not to the wife you have now. I'm sorry, but I see you married to the same person as before. I know that doesn't make any sense."

"I haven't spoken to my first wife in almost twenty-one years. Ginger, please don't stop there. Please keep talking. What else do you see?"

"That's all."

My face contorted with pain. Finally, I couldn't hold it in any longer and bawled like a baby. "I feel worse now than I did before!" I said. "What am I doing here? What am I doing to myself?"

Calmly, she answered, "You know why you're here, Marty."

"Why?"

"To learn about yourself."

"But tell me the future!"

"All right. I want to look up some information. Tell me, when was your first wife born?"

I told her Lynn's birthday and time and place of birth.

She opened a book, took out a pencil, picked up the clipboard, and made a few mysterious scratches on my chart; meanwhile, I blew my nose and pulled myself together.

"The two of you are very old souls and have shared quite a few experiences together," she said.

"Our marriage only lasted a year and a half, and we fought most of the time," I admitted.

"No, not those experiences. I'm talking now about past lives. I'm sorry, but that's all I can do, today. I'm drained," she said.

"You're drained?" I replied, "I'm completely unhinged!"

I looked at Ginger and indeed the light ebbed in her ice blue eyes. Her hair fell over one side of her face, and she didn't bother to push it away. While I watched, lines formed on the tender, nearly translucent skin around her mouth and eyes. Ginger, usually vibrant, became suddenly tired after whatever she had seen and appeared to age right before me. Still, I pushed her.

"Ginger," I pleaded. "Can you tell me more?"

She took my hand in hers. "Yes," she said. "But not now."

After I left her office, I drove around town aimlessly, wondering how the psychic knew about Lynn. Ginger's revelation had shocked me to the core. That night, instead of slipping into bed after Barbara had fallen asleep, as I usually did, I stayed in my easy chair in the den all night. I couldn't sleep.

Throughout the week, I called Ginger's office trying to move my next appointment up, but she remained booked solid. While I waited to see her again, I felt the life returning to my limbs. I pulsed with a new reason to get up in the morning: Ginger. A reason to hope for the future: Ginger.

That week, I drove to the lab for yet another blood antigen test. Miracle of miracles, I was clean! I had ceased to be a carrier for hepatitis B! I called my office staff and told them I planned to return to work the following week.

In the middle of that first week back, I drove to my appointment with Ginger.

"I've been studying your chart side-by-side with that of your first wife," she said. "It seems there is a third person. A child."

"Yes," I replied, "Our son. What can you tell me about him?"

"I'm going to go into a trance this time," Ginger said. "Let's see what I can see."

She sat silently in her battered, pink armchair. I gazed outside at the blooming jacaranda and noticed beauty for the first time in a long time. A passionflower vine hung heavily over the garden fence, swooping and curling the same way Ginger's hair flowed over her shoulders. I wondered if that happened by design, but how could it? This natural miracle touched me, and I realized I believed again—believed, like a child, that wonder lay everywhere.

Finally, Ginger spoke. "You are always leaving her alone."

"What?" I snapped, "Are you trying to hurt me?"

"Not in this life. In your past lives, the two of you always found each other, but ultimately got separated again. Once, for instance, you died in battle. It was World War One, and you died in an airplane crash. Another time, it was the battle of Gettysburg. You fought for the north. The two of you were in Atlantis together, too. But again, you died very young. You two are caught in a karmic cycle, always unable to finish the life you must live out together. And now...again. In this life, you have left her. But this time it is different. You will be given a second chance. A chance to make things right."

"What can I do?"

"Oh," she said. "You will see her again. But it is going to make a lot of people very angry, when it happens."

"What do you mean?"

"I see a dark cloud over this meeting. Nonetheless, it's destiny. But you must remember. Time is precious. Do not squander the time you have together. You will never get another chance."

When Ginger's garden gate swung shut behind me, I nearly skipped home. The very notion that I would see Lynn again brought life back into my wasted body. Even though my skin was still yellow and one hour in the office tired me like ten, I held onto hope.

I had sleepwalked through most of the previous year, and now a new year dawned, so I bought a calendar and looked at it in amazement. My God, I thought, I've been waiting all my life for this year. 1984. This is the year! This is the year! I silently rejoiced.

Five months later, I received Stephen's letter.

Dear Marty,

For 21 years now, I have been wondering who my father is...

25

May 2, 1984

Stephen wrote the return address on his letter, "care of Je Vonna Moxley," whom he described, in the letter, as "a close friend."

When I called, a woman picked up.

"This is Je Vonna."

Everything about this moment felt magical to me. Je Vonna's voice rung with music. I loved her instantly, whoever she was.

"Hello. My name is Martin Kraidin. I'm calling for your friend, Stephen Levenson...I'm his father."

"Oh my!" she exclaimed. "Stephen is going to be so happy!"

"How is he?"

"He is very nervous."

"So am I."

"He is right here, and he knows who I'm talking with. Let me put him on the phone," she said. I knew my son had to be smart to have chosen such a sweet, friendly woman.

"Je Vonna," I said, "I hope to meet you some day."

"Oh," she replied. "I think we will, Dr. Kraidin."

A male voice came on the line. "This is Stephen," it said.

I had no idea what to say. "This is Stephen," he said again, after a silence.

"Stephen, this is Marty."

"I can't believe you called."

"Of course, I called," I said. "I want to meet you as soon as possible. I'll fly to Philadelphia right away."

"You will?" he asked.

"Oh Stephen, of course I will. I want very much to meet you."

"You do?"

The fact that my enthusiasm surprised Stephen really tore me up inside. God knows what Abner, and even Lynn, must have told him about me for him to be so skeptical.

He told me the following week would work for him. "Does that work for you?" asked Stephen.

"I'll make it work for me," I answered.

"You will?" he replied.

That night, I told Barbara about Stephen's letter and our conversation.

"Oh, that's wonderful," she said. "I'm so happy for you." I flew so high I didn't notice the flatness in her tone.

I called my parents and told them, too. I had to share this joy with everyone.

"Oh?" replied Mother, as if sensing trouble.

"I have to meet him," I said. "Don't you see? For his sake, but also for mine."

"I see," she replied.

Since Thursday was my day off, I didn't delay, and flew to Philadelphia that evening. When the plane landed, too nervous to deplane, I sat in my seat until everyone else left. My legs and hands shook, and I felt nauseous. Getting off that plane felt akin to launching myself into outer space. Finally, a flight attendant came over and asked if I was okay.

"No." I said. "I'm not. It's a family thing. I'm emotionally overwrought."

"Do you want me to call for help?" she asked.

"No, no. I can do it," I answered, imagining myself being led off the plane in a wheelchair and straightjacket. Hell of a way to make a first impression.

I walked down the jet way and through the gate. There he stood. I would have known my son anywhere. Stephen wore blue slacks and a pink, button-down shirt—very preppy and straight-laced, just like my style at that age. And what a good-looking young man. His handsome, tall, broad-shouldered frame supported a kind face.

We stood before each other, just looking, and then we shook hands.

Walking down the airport corridor, by his side, I said, "I didn't know what to expect you to look like. The last pictures I saw were when you were a little boy."

He stopped in the middle of the concourse. "You saw pictures of me? I didn't know."

"I promise I'll tell you about it," I said. "You're a handsome young man. You sure look like your mother." We continued walking.

"That's interesting," he said, "because she says I look just like you. And when I saw you, I felt like I was looking at myself. I guess I'm a good mix," he said.

We passed the shops, picked up my bag at the luggage carrousel, and then walked out to the parking lot. While we drove away from the airport and down the freeway, I looked out the window, watching Philadelphia's factories, neighborhoods, and parks flash past. Finally, I asked Stephen, "How's your mother?"

He drove a moment in silence, and then looked at me. "She's fine," he said. "You probably wouldn't recognize her. Her hair has turned gray. They call her The Silver Fox."

I laughed and said, "That's cute."

Stephen drove me to a diner, where we sat in a booth and ordered burgers. He folded his paper napkin into small squares; meanwhile, I pressed my feet to the floor, hard, to stop my legs from shaking.

"I want to say something, now," Stephen said.

"Yes?"

"Bob Levenson will always be Dad to me."

"Bob Levenson?"

"My mother's husband. He adopted me when I was five."

"So, Lynn is your mom? You call Lynn mom?"

"Of course. Who else?"

"Your grandparents didn't adopt you?"

"What? No. Why would they?"

I couldn't answer his question. A lump filled my throat. At least they hadn't taken Stephen away from Lynn, I thought.

"Mom married my dad when I was five, and he adopted me."

"I see. And has Bob been a good father?"

"He was. I mean, he is. We've had to go to some family therapy, though. I always knew I wasn't really his son. I remember living alone with Mom, when I was little. And I remember the wedding, of course, so Bob not being my real father wasn't a secret. No one lied to me about it, but no one explained it, either. I guess the situation has been upsetting me for a long time."

"I'm sure it has!" I replied. "What do you know about me? Anything?"

"Nothing. But when I was in high school, Mom told me if I wanted to contact you, she'd help me."

"You didn't want to?"

Stephen sighed. "Honestly, up until recently, I was afraid."

"I understand. What made you write the letter, now?"

"I just decided to, one day. My girlfriend Je Vonna helped me make the decision, actually. She suggested I look you up in the Miami phone book, and there you were."

"How did you know I lived in Miami?"

"Somehow Mom kept track of you all these years. She knew when you moved to Miami Beach, and she knows you're married and have three children," he said, and took another bite of his burger.

I contemplated this information before replying. "Stephen, we've all had an emotionally disruptive twenty-one years, and I want you to know from this time forward, I will never be out of your life, again. I will always be there for you. I want to be a positive influence on your life. Okay?"

"Thank you," Stephen replied. "Now, can you tell me what happened? Nobody has ever told me anything."

"What do you mean?"

"Nobody talks to me. Your name is taboo in the family, and I'm sick of it. I want to know about you and my mother. I want to know who I am and where I came from. And I want to hear it from you, Marty." His tone felt light and eager, not angry.

"Of course," I said.

"Let me fill you in on the news, first," he added. "Gram, I mean Mary—she died a year ago."

"Of what?"

"Cancer."

"I'm sorry to hear that." My heart dropped. Even after everything that happened, I had always loved Mary. I remember how much I loved calling her Mom."

"Pop...I mean Abner, lives in Palm Beach," Stephen said.

Apparently Abner, who had been 45 at the time of Stephen's birth, sold his business a few years later. He and Mary left Lynn and Stephen behind and retired to Palm Beach, Florida, to live on a yacht.

"Yeah, I've spent a lot of time in Palm Beach," said Stephen. "Just sixty miles away from you."

"My God."

"Gram used to say to Mom, 'One of these days we're going to run into Marty or his parents,' and Mom would always reply, 'No, they're not the Palm Beach types.'"

"Palm Beach types..." I repeated like a robot. The fact that I had lived so close to Stephen, let alone Lynn, for so long struck me dumb. I cleared my throat. "The whole family lived on a boat?" I asked.

"Oh, no. Just Gram and Pop. Uncle Howard went off to live in Europe, and Uncle David was still in high school. He stayed behind in Philly with Gussie."

"Sixteen years old? Left alone with no parents?"

"Yeah. He set fire to the house."

"Whoa."

"I was just a baby, but I've heard the story. Anyway, Mom and I lived in an apartment in Philly until I was five, when she married my dad. She worked as a paralegal back then, but now she's an art consultant. But I don't know the story about you and Mom at all." Stephen said, gesturing broadly with a French fry. "No one will tell me. I was surprised you were willing to see me. I thought you had, you know, abandoned us."

Tears sprang to my eyes. "No, Stephen. It wasn't like that at all. Oh God, where should I begin?"

"When you and Mom met."

I told Stephen about that moment on the university lawn and didn't mind that he saw me lingering over every juicy remembrance. I could picture every second in my mind's eye so clearly. Lynn's legs. Her hair. Stephen smiled.

"God, she was gorgeous," I said.

"She still is," my son replied.

"I don't doubt it," I added, with all sincerity.

I proceeded to tell Stephen about our first date, even our first kiss. Every detail. "She was hot," I said. "A real piece of ass."

"That's my mother you're talking about!"

"Yes. And I'm your father. And this is how you came into the world. If it's upsetting you, I can stop now."

I look back on this moment in profound embarrassment. To my friends and I, growing up, "piece of ass" was used as a compliment, not a derogatory term. Now, I realize how demeaning the comment sounded to my son. To his credit, he ignored the offensive expression and pushed forward.

"No," he said. "Go on."

I told him about our date at the opera, the first time I slept over at Lynn's house, and how I proposed. I didn't leave out anything—how desperately I loved her, how much I wanted to please all four parents and how jealous my parents became of the Konicks.

Stephen shook his head. "I didn't know any of this."

"Did your mother lie to you?" I asked.

"No," he said. "Mostly, she just refused to talk. Whenever I asked, Mom just told me you two didn't get along. She said you fought a lot. She told me the divorce had nothing to do with me. No specifics, though. But still, I always thought I must have had something to do with it. Maybe you never wanted a child..."

The waitress took our plates, and I ordered dessert for us both.

"All my life," Stephen said softly, "I've secretly wondered what I did to chase my father away."

"Oh Stephen, when you hear the rest of the story you'll know what happened never had anything to do with you." Stephen tilted his head, just as I am wont to do. He scooted his plate away. "Okay. Let's get back to the story: so you proposed, you got married...then what happened."

I told Stephen about the difficult pregnancy, the arguments, and the conflicts between Abner and me, silent tears streaming down my cheeks all the while. I couldn't hold the sadness in any longer. I hadn't spoken in detail like this with anyone since it happened, and the memory brought up excruciating pain.

"I don't know if I want to hear this," said Stephen, when I got to the part about that fateful weekend at Lynn's house: the last time I saw her. Stephen put his head down on the table.

"I'll stop," I said, through my tears.

Then, just like I would have, Stephen pushed himself up straight, looked me in the eye, and said, "No, go on. I want to hear the truth, once and for all."

With shame, I told him how I had insisted Lynn walk to synagogue despite her pregnancy, how she'd cried, and then how Abner kicked me out of the house, said he was through with me, said I wasn't a man, and how Lynn refused to leave the house with me. I told Stephen about my loneliness, fear, and pain afterwards, about Abner's threats, and how the resulting depression drove me to sign the divorce and adoption agreements. I explained my fear of what Abner would do to me, but I tried not to vilify the man. By the fond way Stephen called Abner "Pop," I could tell the two of them had grown close.

Stephen stared at me. His jaw hung open until he spoke. "You didn't have to sign it," he said.

"Stephen, I wasn't much older than you are now. I didn't know what to do."

"You didn't have to do it!"

"I was scared, Stephen, and alone, and frightened of your grandfather..."

"You didn't have to do it!" Stephen raised his voice. He was angry now, blaming me, just as I had always blamed myself.

I took a deep breath. "This isn't going to get us anywhere. Let's just stop."

"No," said Stephen. "I want to hear it all."

I proceeded to tell Stephen what happened after the divorce: my marrying Barbara, opening my practice, and how someone had anonymously sent me pictures of him growing up. When I finished the story, Stephen drove me to my hotel room. By then, he had calmed down and returned to his normal, friendly demeanor.

"I'm staying just around the corner, at Je Vonna's," he said. "What time do you want me to pick you up, tomorrow? I want to show you around town."

"I did live here for four years, you know."

"I know," he said, "but a lot has changed."

"Okay. And what about the young lady? Why don't we arrange to meet her for lunch?"

"Oh, terrific!" he said.

The moment felt strange for many reasons, including the fact that Stephen and I stood eye-level to eye-level. Being 6'4", that doesn't happen to me much. Then Stephen hugged me. I felt like every moment of the last twenty-one years had led to that blissful instant in time, with my arms around my eldest son.

After he left, I broke down crying hysterically. This day seemed completely unreal. First, my mind reeled at the fact of finally meeting my son, but the way he took after me, in both looks and mannerisms, really amazed me.

The next day, Stephen and I walked around Rittenhouse Square and talked. I had to make believe interest in seeing everything I already knew about. But I did find it interesting how women on the street eyeballed Stephen when we passed by, just like they used to do to me.

Je Vonna joined us for lunch. During our walk, Stephen warned me his girlfriend had a few years on him. He also told me that before she became a dental hygienist, Je Vonna used to wait tables as a Playboy bunny. When I met her, my eyes nearly fell out of my head. Je Vonna, who wore her mid-thirties very well, arrested me with her beauty. Along with the presence of my long-lost son, it was all too much. My stomach twisted me into a nervous wreck throughout lunch.

After we ate, Stephen said, "I want to show you where I live."

We drove to Lynn and Bob's home in Haverford—a gorgeous old manor on heavily treed land.

"That's my house!" he proudly proclaimed.

"It's quite beautiful," I replied.

"No one's home," he said. "Come on in. I want to show you my room."

"I don't want to take a chance like that," I said firmly.

"Okay," he replied. "But let me drive you around the other side, too." He drove me all around the property, but I felt very anxious. Here I had come secretly to Lynn's house, so close I could practically smell her, but we had both remarried, life had moved on, and I held no place in her world anymore. I knew I shouldn't be there. Though I had been dying for two decades to get this close, suddenly I felt eager to get away.

Stephen wanted to show me the whole neighborhood, but I objected.

"Please, Stephen," I said. "Let's just go back to Center City. Someone around here is going to recognize you and talk to your family about seeing me. I don't know how Lynn and Bob will react."

"But I want to walk around with you."

"Let's do it in Center City," I said. I felt myself perspiring, thinking of Lynn finding out, imagining her anger at my showing up unexpectedly, worried she might accuse me of trying to break up her happy home.

We ate dinner, again with Je Vonna, but Stephen and I had finally run out of things to say. We wanted to talk about so much, but didn't know where to begin.

"I'd like to see you, again," Stephen finally said.

"I'd like that, too," I replied.

I could tell my son still thought this might be a one-time meeting. He didn't seem sure I would stay in touch with him, or if he even wanted to stay in touch with me.

On the flight home, I cried and cried like a little boy with a broken heart. The stewardesses kindly brought me tissues. Barbara had said she would pick me up from the airport, but when she didn't show, I hailed a cab to get home. During the ride, I transitioned from sorrow to anger. I had been hoping Barbara would show at least the barest amount of concern for me on the momentous occasion of my meeting my long-lost son. Instead, I returned to an empty house.

When Barbara arrived, hours later, I asked, "I thought you were going to pick me up?"

"Oh," she said, hoisting a bouquet of designer shopping bags. "I had things to do."

"What did you buy?" I asked.

"A lot!" she replied.

"You're not going to ask me how it went, meeting Stephen?"

"Oh yeah," she said. "How was it?" Then she ran the water in the kitchen sink so loudly she couldn't possibly have heard my answer.

Now, so many years later, I finally realize how threatened Barbara must have felt by Stephen's presence in my life, and rightfully so. A good husband would have said something to reassure her, but I didn't. I was too wrapped up in my own drama.

26

I took the children, one by one, into my study and told them about my first marriage and the fact of Stephen's existence. Adam and Elizabeth acted excited to meet Stephen, but Jonathan, 17 at the time, felt rather put out.

"So I'm not your oldest son anymore?" he asked, indignant.

"From the minute you were born, you were never my oldest son," I replied. I tried to be as honest as I could, but what I said hurt him. All the time I had spent thinking about meeting Stephen, I never gave any thought to how his presence in my life would affect my other children.

Later that summer, when Stephen came to Florida to see "Pop," he told Abner he wanted to go out and visit a friend for a weekend. Of course, that friend turned out to be me. Stephen and I spent some time together, walking along the beach, just talking, and becoming comfortable with each other. And later that night, I took Stephen, Barbara, and Jonathan out to dinner so that my two eldest sons could get to know each other.

I wanted all the men in a jacket and tie, so I loaned Stephen some clothes. I have always sent out my shirts and jackets for special tailoring, because of my extra-long arms. Well, lo and behold, my clothes fit Stephen perfectly. The resemblance amazed us both.

A couple of weeks later, Stephen visited again, this time with Je Vonna. I threw them a pool party and barbecue at the house. All my children liked friendly, outgoing Stephen, and Elizabeth fell instantly in love with sweet Je Vonna Moxley. Barbara acted polite, but not warm. Regardless, I put on a bit of a show, kissing Barbara on the cheek and putting my arms around her. I wanted us to look happy.

During the party, while Stephen and I ate our burgers on the patio, Stephen told me his mother hadn't actually met Je Vonna yet. Apparently, Lynn knew about her and didn't approve of the age difference. The situation seemed awkward for all three of them. On top of that, Lynn still didn't know Stephen had met me. I sensed tension between Stephen and Lynn, and it saddened me.

"Between seeing Je Vonna and meeting me, you're leading quite a double life," I said.

"I know," he replied.

"This can't go on, Stephen."

"I know," he said. "Tomorrow Je Vonna's flying home and I'm going to Palm Beach to stay with Pop. I'm going to tell him."

"And when are you going to tell your mother?"

"When I get home, I'll tell Mom everything. I promise."

Stephen slept on the extra bed in Jonathan's room that night.

Afterward, Jonathan told me, "What a weird kid he is! He kept asking me, 'What is Marty like? What was it like growing up as a kid?' He wanted to know if you took us on vacations, if you played with us. He wanted to know day by day, hour by hour, how we spent our time."

The very next day, Stephen called me.

"I told Pop about you," he said.

"And?" I wanted to know if I should expect to open the door to someone swinging a pipe at my kneecaps.

"He was very angry. He said, 'Why didn't you talk to me first? I would have told you not to do it. Now, you've opened up a can of worms. No good will come of this!'"

I didn't say it out loud to Stephen but I thought that fucking bastard was back to his old ways. My stomach was in knots just thinking he could be back in my life once again.

"I'm sorry to hear that, for your sake," I replied.

"Later on, he said, 'You've done it. Okay. Now you can be finished with him.' I told him I wasn't going to be finished with you. No way." Stephen became silent and I could tell his emotions overwhelmed him. Then, Stephen added, "Pop said, 'If you love me, you will never have anything to do with him again.'"

"How do you feel about all this?" I asked.

"I told him I wasn't going to cut you out of my life. I don't want to, Marty."

"Good. Neither do I."

"Then he asked me if I'd told Mom. I told him I hadn't and he said he was going to call her himself, but I talked him out of it. I told him, like I told you, that I would tell her as soon as I got home."

"Okay," I said. "I know you will."

Being in touch with Stephen brought me absolute relief, but without Lynn, as ever, I still felt like a puzzle missing pieces. Perhaps she would never reach out to me. I tried not to be greedy. I had Stephen now, and I might not get Lynn, too. I had no right to step into the life of a happily married woman. So I waited for Stephen's next call.

I only had to wait a day, but it felt like eternity.

"I told her," Stephen said, when he called.

My heart stopped beating. "What did she say?" I asked.

"She broke down crying. I told her in the car on the way back from the airport. She had to pull over to the side. She was completely overcome."

"Why was she crying?"

"Happiness. Gladness that you hadn't rejected me."

"Good God! Of course I didn't reject you. Your mother should know me better than that."

"She was very happy for us. I told her a little about what you told me, about the divorce, but she got really upset. She couldn't listen to it."

"That's not surprising. You saw how hard it was for me to talk about."

"Yes, I did. Thanks for telling me the story, Marty. I know it wasn't easy, but I've needed to know my entire life."

"Your mother should have told you a long time ago. That wasn't fair."

Stephen sighed. "I don't know what to say about that," he replied.

A week later, I received another letter from Stephen. He wrote:

You didn't have to do it. You abandoned me and Mom and you didn't have to. It was your choice. I'm glad I met you, because at least now I know what you did. But I don't want to have anything to do with you anymore.

I went into shock. The thought that Stephen would reject me now, just when my dreams began to come true, felt too awful to bear. I descended into darkness, blaming myself at an even deeper level than Stephen did. Yes, I had been a scared little boy my whole life, running from Abner, afraid to face the fact that I still loved Lynn, afraid of her rejection, afraid to get involved in my son's life. I thought, My God, there is no way I'll ever make up for this terrible crime I have committed against Stephen, an innocent child. My memory of the fear and confusion I felt when Abner served me those divorce papers, and when Dr. Johnstone told me of Stephen's birth, disappeared. I could only remember my cowardice.

The more I thought about it, the more I realized I owed Lynn's husband a debt of gratitude. Here Bob Levenson had adopted Stephen and raised him as his own, and Stephen had grown up to be a fine young man. Bob Levenson had righted my wrong. I hoped if I humbly acknowledged that debt, Stephen would understand how contrite I felt about it all.

I called directory assistance and received Bob Levenson's number. Somewhere deep down, I knew my real motivation was just to hear Lynn's voice, even if only in the background.

"Hello?" a man answered.

"Hello, Bob Levenson? This is Martin Kraidin."

"Oh, hello."

"I called to speak with you. As I'm sure you know, I met Stephen recently, for the first time, and I just wanted to say thanks to you, for bringing him up to be such a fine young man."

Bob remained completely silent, which I found strange, but little did I know that Lynn was standing there the whole time, and when she recognized my voice, she furiously gestured for the phone. But Bob didn't know what to do. He was made utterly speechless by my statement and then Lynn's gesticulating confused him even further.

Finally, Bob asked, "Would you like to talk to Lynn?"

"Yes," I replied, "If she would like to speak with me."

I heard Lynn's voice say hello, and just like that, after almost twenty-two years, I found myself talking to the love of my life. Then, she petulantly snapped, "Where have you been?"

Taken aback, I took a defensive tone. "Don't start with me again after all these years!" I replied. "You've known exactly where I've been and why!" Then I added, "You sound like Golda Meir!"

"I'm sorry," she said. "That was uncalled-for."

This was no distant reunion of two childhood crushes. No, we regressed right back to being the very same Marty and Lynn we used to be. Inside the anger expressed was contained by a deep familiarity, which contained our love for each other. Decades had gone by—long enough for a baby to grow into a man—yet, in talking to Lynn, I felt like no time had passed at all.

The sound of her voice drew me in, made me feel home again, and no matter what Lynn felt, or didn't feel, for me, I knew we couldn't speak freely with Bob standing by.

"I can tell this is awkward," I said.

"Yes," she replied.

"I'll call you tomorrow morning," I added, guessing Bob would leave for work.

"That would be nice," she said.

The next morning, from the office, I called Lynn again. This time, we didn't argue. We talked about Stephen, his letter, and my visits with him. She told me a little about Bob, a sales manager for an electrical supply company. They had produced a daughter together, Julie. Lynn spoke to me like in the old days—so familiar. We felt like best friends again.

After our call, the rest of the day dragged on. I wanted to call Lynn back every hour, talk to her again about anything at all. Somehow, I managed to wait until the next morning, but this time, she lit into me.

"I had to give birth to Stephen alone, in that hospital, with only my parents, and you weren't there. You abandoned us! You ruined Stephen's life! He never knew his father!" she screamed at me. As ever, Lynn hadn't buried her anger at all. It perched right on the surface, like a buzzard on the corpse of our marriage. One thing about Lynn, she knew how to hurt a man. She could cut me down to size in a single breath.

During our conversation, I quickly realized Lynn had been telling herself a version of our story that differed vastly from mine. Here we had both been thinking about each other for all these years (that much was clear immediately), but neither actually knew the full story of our break up. We had spent more than two decades stewing over assumptions.

144

It took until our next phone call, but I finally knew what to say to her. "Lynn," I said. "You signed those papers. You wanted a divorce. You said you didn't love me."

"I was confused," she said. "I didn't know what I wanted."

"Then why did you sign the papers?"

"What papers?"

I froze. I spoke of the papers that had ruined my life, and she asked, "what papers?" I couldn't believe it. "The divorce and adoption agreements," I said. "Your father threatened to destroy me, my reputation, my career, and my future if I didn't sign them."

"He did?"

"Are you actually telling me you didn't know that?"

"I was so sick at the time. I didn't know what my father was up to. All I remember is I was in bed when he came to me with the papers. He said, 'Sign them. It's for the best.' So I signed them."

"You didn't read them?"

"No, I couldn't bear it. I didn't read them."

I wanted to throw the phone across the room. "Don't you know what you signed?" I yelled into the phone.

"A divorce?"

"An agreement that I would never ever endeavor to contact you or Stephen again as long as I lived. And that I would give him up for adoption, for his own good. That is what your father made me sign."

The silence following that statement broke my heart. A silence as wide and deep as the years that separated us. Finally in a very small voice, Lynn repeated, "I didn't read them. I couldn't bear it."

"I died that day!" I shouted.

I sobbed, and so did she. We sat there—she in her home and me in my office, separated by most of the length of the eastern seaboard—sobbing both at and with each other through the miracle of fiber-optic cables. I wanted to throttle her, and then hold her in my arms...again.

27

Our next phone call proceeded more sedately. I had to hear Lynn's voice again, and to do that, I risked the conversation turning into a fight once more. But this time, neither of us brought up the divorce.

"My hair is going gray," she said.

"I'll bet it's beautiful," I replied.

"You wouldn't recognize me. I'm so old, now."

"Oh Lynn, I'm sure I would. Tell me, do you still have that dimple on your right cheek?"

She laughed and said coyly, "Of course I do."

"And those well-defined calf muscles? I'll bet your legs are still sexy as hell."

"No, they're not."

"Do you still have those legs?"

"Marty!"

"Okay, just checking. And how about that little birthmark on your abdomen? I can see it now. Oh, man."

"Yeah? Well, how about you? Do you still have hands?"

"Last I checked."

"Because I wish I could feel them on me, right now…"

With that, we launched a session of phone sex that could have curled the paint right off the walls. Immediately, it felt as if nothing had ever come between us.

In our next conversation, that very evening, Lynn accused me again of abandoning her. I alternately apologized and defended myself. I could tell she still hadn't faced the truth of what happened and how her father manipulated her. I also got the feeling she still hadn't stopped trying to please him.

I asked if Abner and Mary had really moved to Florida a few years after

Stephen's birth. She said yes. I couldn't fathom it. First, his obsession with Lynn and me moving to Philadelphia to be near him, then his sudden decision to leave town when his 20-year-old daughter became a single parent.

"My parents told me it wasn't their fault I couldn't hold onto a man."

"Lynn, no."

"Yes, Marty, that's what they said. I believed it, too, for a while at least. I blamed myself, but I blamed you, too. Oh boy, did I blame you."

In another conversation, Lynn said, "I understand you met Je Vonna. What do you think of her?"

"She's lovely," I said, sincerely.

"What about her age?"

"What about it?"

"She's a lot older."

"Lynn, come on. They're not getting married. They're just having fun."

"I can see what kind of influence you would have been!"

"This has nothing to do with influence. It's happening whether you like it or not, so just let the thing run its course."

"I think Stephen should break it off," she said. Like Mary, Lynn had always been concerned with propriety.

"Tell him, then," I replied.

"Why don't you tell him? You're his father!" Lynn exclaimed.

She seemed to be living in some fantasy world where we had stayed married. Shocked into silence for a few long seconds, I finally answered, "That would be overstepping the bounds."

On another call, Lynn cited the cost of repairs to Stephen's car. She worried about money, what with Bob's income dropping and Stephen's college tuition coming due. She progressed from crying about it to being angry with me, in the space of five minutes.

"Why don't you pay for it!" she yelled.

I said, "Sure. I'm happy to do anything I can for Stephen."

I hadn't heard from Stephen since that last devastating letter and knew he wouldn't accept money from me, so I mailed Lynn a money order to use as she wished. Not long after that, Lynn said she wanted to buy Stephen a new suit of clothes at the most expensive men's store in Philadelphia. I told her to send me the bill. It came to thousands of dollars. She's testing me, I thought. Let her! I'll pass every test. I'll do anything for her and Stephen, anything at all.

A few weeks after his last letter, Stephen wrote me again.

I think I overreacted in my last letter. I really do want to have a relationship with you. I'm not sure I approve of what you did, leaving us when I was born, but I understand you did the best you knew how. I really enjoyed meeting you and think of you often. Feel free to write or call me at my school address.

Relief swept over me and I realized that after all Stephen had been through, our meeting had turned his life into an emotional roller coaster. Meanwhile, Lynn and I rode that coaster as well. I resolved to be patient with Stephen, should he continue to run hot and cold like this.

I called Lynn and told her about Stephen's letter.

"Did you write him back?" she asked.

I told her I did.

"Will you read me the letter?"

I read it to her. It simply said that I understood Stephen's pain and agreed to accept any role in his life he felt comfortable assigning me.

"It's the most beautiful thing I've ever heard," she said. "You write such beautiful letters," she said. "You always did. Marty, will you write me a letter?"

I said I would, and when I sat down with paper and pen, my hand flew across the page. My handwriting became large and messy, and I experienced a great moment of truth. Here are some excerpts from that fateful letter:

One thing is certain; we were two very young people in 1960. After we were married, we not only ceased to grow and grow-up, but we actually regressed. What happened? First, you and your parents in different ways and for different reasons were unrelenting in chopping me to shreds, both as a husband and as a man. Your father was determined to convince you that I didn't love you, and so he did...they wanted to control us. I fought that control and therefore was guilty by implication. Didn't anyone wonder why I didn't take the Pennsylvania board exams? I would have gone to China! Anyplace except New York or Pennsylvania. I wanted us to be away from everyone. It was wrong, but I can only say that after the fact.

Mostly, I wrote down the plain facts of what happened so long ago, but it had taken two decades for me to separate these facts from my opinions, her opinions, my parents' opinions, and all my self-blame. In the letter, I simply reviewed, step-by-step, the actual events of our marriage and divorce. I hoped this recounting would help to us both.

As I wrote, I fought with a voice inside my head: my mother's, and probably Abner's as well. I knew Mother would reduce what happened between Lynn and me to "puppy love" or some such platitude. I preempted the offensive notion with these words:

How can I possibly remember these things? It is because I never stopped remembering...I will not be implicated in the concept of being in love with a memory or that either you or myself were in "heat." The outrageous audacity of it. Human beings don't fall into such neat categories...

Finally, I pressed my case to a dangerous degree. Lynn had remarried, as had I, but I dared to hope for a future for us.

And now, what about you and me? If we want, we will learn to trust again, to believe again. We are going to meet; we will speak, we will talk, we will touch, and we will share. More than that, we cannot plan.

When Lynn received the letter, she called me, in tears.
"This spells it all out, doesn't it?" She said. "Marty, we have to end this pain. We have to talk about all of this."
"We have to meet," I said.
And so, we did.

When Stephen first wrote me it was in secret, then I visited him secretly, and now my visit to Lynn became a secret from Stephen himself. He didn't even know she and I had begun speaking on the phone. Lynn and I approached the meeting very respectably—both of us telling our spouses we needed to meet one another in order to put to rest some old misunderstandings. It all sounded very responsible and adult. We decided to meet in New York City, because Lynn traveled there anyway for meetings with her art consulting business.

Lynn drove. I flew. We planned for her to pick me up curbside, at arrivals. Just as with Stephen, I delayed deplaning as long as possible, then walked down the jet way last. Inside the airport, I paced frenetically before finally working up the nerve to step outside.

What Lynn had described on the phone as "a small black car" turned out to be a classic Mercedes sport coupe. Of course, I thought—elegant as always. I let myself into the car and looked at her. No longer brunette, her gray hair ran through blonde like silver.

"Lynn," I said. "You're more beautiful than you ever were."

She looked me over, head to toe. "You look pretty good, yourself," she said, adding, "How about a hello?"

"Picky, picky, picky!"

"Smart-aleck, I see you're still the same!" Lynn drove off towards the Park Lane Hotel, where I had made our reservations, and for a few minutes, we tried some awkward small talk.

"Marty," she finally said. "You look nervous, why?"

"Why? I can't believe this is actually happening! I'm sitting in a car beside you, and it seems just like yesterday. So normal, so natural. I'm in disbelief."

She put her hand on my thigh the way she always used to.

"How come you have an erection?" she said.

"That's a hell of a question! I always did around you. Don't you remember?"

"Oh, I remember all right," she said, removing her hand. Her face took on a look I hadn't seen before—the saucy spark of a sexually experienced adult.

"I think I should go back to the airport," I said.

"I'll let you out here. You can walk back," she replied.

"Damn it, that's not nice! What in the world is wrong with you?" I shot back.

"I'm very nervous," she admitted.

150

"You look cool as a cucumber."

"Oh God, Marty, I'm soaked with perspiration."

"Can we start again from the beginning? And this time, leave my erection out of it?"

"I don't feel so grown up, right now," she admitted, replacing her hand on my thigh.

At the hotel, I checked us in and retrieved our room keys.

"Why two rooms?" she asked.

"To keep up appearances," I replied, with a smile.

Inside one of the rooms, we faced each other. I must have been sweating bullets.

"Marty?" she asked. "What's wrong?"

"I'm worried that you hate me and this is a revenge meeting. Maybe you're going to kill me, I don't know."

"I am angry," she admitted. "Not just with you, but with myself. But I don't hate you. I never have. I never fully understood what happened to us, not until I read your letter, and then it all started coming back. I've been enduring wave after wave of memories—things I didn't want to face. I know you have been, too. But right now, I just want to be in your arms...and I would like you to kiss me."

Standing in that hotel room, I felt so awkward, I could have been a teenager again. I put my arms around Lynn, but apprehensively. I kissed her lips, but stiffly. It felt like I was kissing an illusion, a dream, a vision. Who in the world ever gets a second chance at the most perfect love of his life? Nobody! What's gone is gone. I had been telling myself that for decades, and yet I held my queen, my heart, in my arms. I felt sure one wrong move would wake me from the dream.

We looked into each other's eyes. In those deep blue pools I saw my girl, my Lynn, my love. She is real, I said to myself. She is really here in my arms. I wanted her so much I felt it as pain. My organs tied themselves in knots. I tried another kiss, and this time made it deep, passionate, wet. The real thing.

I slid one hand along her back, to the deep curve of her waist that I remembered so well. Then I easily slipped my fingers beneath her white silk blouse and ventured up. Her slender, lithe body responded as always. She breathed deeply and pressed herself into my chest. I cupped a breast through her thin, lace bra and felt her nipple pop up to greet me.

"You haven't changed a bit," I whispered into her ear.

"Let's go to bed," she whispered back.

I froze a moment, and then wrapped both my arms around her again, tightly this time, as if she would flee my embrace. "I'm so frightened," I said. "I don't think I can make love. I'm afraid of disappointing you."

"I know," she said. "I know you so well. And do you think I'm any different? I just want to sleep in your arms. I want to feel you wrapped around me tonight. And tomorrow...we'll deal with tomorrow when it comes."

That evening, my life began again.

28

Lynn and I awoke to a bright, sunny, perfect, summer day. I grabbed the telephone and ordered breakfast in bed. We ate and talked, sipped coffee and talked, and teased each other and talked all morning. We talked about everything from the glorious blossoms on the trees in Central Park, which we could see through the window, to the pain we had each felt, missing each other over the last two decades. Finally, through tears, Lynn told me about Mary's death.

"She was only sixty-two," Lynn said. "Mom had ovarian cancer. We know that now, but she wouldn't go to a doctor. She had a lump in her groin the size of a grapefruit. When she finally did go to the doctor, it was too late."

"I'm so sorry, Lynn."

"She did it on purpose, to get away from my father."

"She died on purpose?"

"Mom knew she was dying, and she wanted to die. Things were so bad between her and Dad. They fought constantly, screaming matches, and right in front of Stephen. Even his presence didn't stop them. Dad selling the business started it all because then Mom and Dad actually had to spend time together, which they had avoided all those years. He would threaten her, too: 'You better not leave me or I'll do this and this.' You know how Dad is."

"Yes, I certainly do."

"Mom just let herself die. It was the only way out. That's what I think."

I held her, and after a while, we told each other about our spouses, too. Contrary to what I had heard from Stephen, Lynn didn't enjoy a happy marriage with Bob. She had married him for practical reasons—he'd been willing and eager to adopt Stephen. Like me, Lynn figured she would never find love again, so she settled. We also talked about the surreal quality of our reunion, even as we lived it. Neither of us quite believed we actually held one another again, after all these years.

We still lay in bed when the telephone rang. Barbara's voice surprised me.

"Hello, Barbara," I said. "Why are you calling?"

"Where is Lynn?" she demanded.

"I don't know. She's out on appointments. She has her own business, and a lot to do while she's here."

"You're lying," Barbara hissed. "She's with you. I know it."

"You don't know anything of the kind." Of course I lied. What was I to do? "She's not with me, and she has her own room. I'm going to see her later for lunch. We have a lot of talking to do and old, unfinished business to settle."

These days, Barbara and I sometimes put our dislike for each other right on the table but I never revealed my affairs to her. And I didn't see any reason to change that tactic now..

Two minutes later, the phone rang again.

"What do you want, now?" I asked my wife.

"I don't believe a word you're telling me," she said.

"That's your problem. This trip is difficult enough for me, and I don't need any extra aggravation from you. Don't call again. When I have something to tell you, I'll call you."

I hung up.

Two minutes later, the phone rang again. I didn't know what effect Barbara sought to achieve with her harassment. In hindsight, I think she probably didn't know either. Since the day I'd met Stephen, I think Barbara felt me moving, emotionally, into a more independent place. I'm sure this gave her incredible anxiety. Predictably, she lashed out at me every which way she could.

Without answering, I hung up the call, dialed the hotel operator, and told him to block all incoming calls.

Lynn rolled her eyes. "So that's what you have to live with?" she asked. "I really feel sorry for you."

"I feel sorry for me, too," I replied.

I wasn't a good enough liar to make things up out of whole cloth, so my lie to Barbara had been loosely based on the truth. Lynn did have a business appointment that morning and had asked me to meet her for lunch at the Four Seasons afterwards.

"I've never been!" I replied.

"You're going to love it," she said, with a big smile.

"But don't we need a reservation?" I asked.

"Let's see what happens," Lynn whispered mysteriously, before clicking the door shut behind her.

We walked into The Four Seasons at the height of lunch hour. Many people waited to be seated, but, just like on our honeymoon, all eyes turned to us. After all those years, we still made a strikingly good-looking couple. The maître d' gave us a look both quizzical and deferential, like he knew we must be important people but couldn't place our faces. He seated us immediately.

At our table, Lynn and I held hands and gazed into each other's eyes, reliving the feeling of our honeymoon all over again. With no effort at all, we fell back into that psychic cocoon, that little world of our own.

"I don't want to go back to Philadelphia," she said with a sigh.

"I don't want to go back to Miami," I replied. "I wish we could just run away together, right here, right now, but we can't. You know we can't."

"We're not ending this, are we?" she asked.

"Lynn, I'll never leave you alone again as long as I live. That, I can promise you with all my heart."

After lunch, we returned to the hotel room, and to bed, where we fondled and held each other some more. After about an hour, a knock sounded on the door. I answered it to find a uniformed security guard.

"A Mr. Lesser called security on your behalf," the man said. "He was worried about the phone block and wanted to make sure you were okay."

Barbara had turned on the waterworks and manipulated her father into doing her bidding. I wanted to punch someone. Instead, I smiled and said, "Wait here, please." I retrieved my wallet and handed the security guard a $100 bill. "I'm fine," I said, "and I'd appreciate no more interruptions, please. Thank you very much for your concern."

After I shut the door, Lynn exclaimed, "I don't know how you live with this!"

I paced the room and took a few deep breaths to calm down. "It's funny," I said. "Barbara never before gave a damn where I was or what I was doing—as long as she had her precious credit cards. Now she's suddenly being possessive?

Pulling her father into it? God knows what story she told him. I've traveled all over the country, and the world for that matter, and she never once called me before."

"Somehow," said Lynn. "She knows."

"What about Bob?" I asked.

"He'll never suspect," said Lynn. "I'm sure he's been watching sports on television all weekend without a thought in his head."

We spent the afternoon strolling among the blossoms of Central Park. There, I remembered something.

"The strangest thing happened when I was in the hospital," I said. "A woman called and said, 'Don't you know who I am?' But she wouldn't identify herself."

"Oh," said Lynn, "That was me."

I stopped walking. "You? That was very unkind! I was really sick!"

Tears sprang up in Lynn's eyes. "You're right," she said. "It was selfish. I'm sorry."

"Why didn't you just say it was you? I would have been so happy!"

"When you didn't recognize my voice, I got scared. I thought you had forgotten me."

"Never! I never forgot you, even for one day."

"I know that, now. I know."

I asked Lynn how in the world she knew about my hepatitis in the first place.

"Fred," she replied. "I've been in touch with Fred all along."

"Fred? He never told me he still talked to you. That's so strange, I wonder why."

"Marty," Lynn replied, looking down at her perfect manicure and long, tapered fingers. "Fred is no friend of yours."

"What do you mean?"

"He only speaks of you in the harshest, most demeaning terms. Ever since you left me, he never liked you."

"Because..."

"Because of how you left Stephen and me."

"Did you tell him the position Abner put me in? Did you tell him you signed those papers, too?"

She looked away, through a stand of trees.

"No! You didn't, did you? You let him believe the divorce was all my doing!"

"You're right," she answered quietly. "I didn't tell him."

"Oh, you got some satisfaction from that, didn't you? Letting me take the rap for that my entire life? God knows how many other people think it was all my fault. And you never corrected them, did you?"

"That's true," she said, turning to face me. "I admit it."

"At least you're being honest, now! And what about Fred? You're saying he hasn't liked me all these years?"

"No, he hasn't," she answered, "I let him believe..."

"You are actually telling me Fred has only stayed in touch with me over the years in order to be your spy?"

"I think that's true," she whispered.

"I can't believe this!"

I wanted to rip off my clothes, tear out my hair and take a sledgehammer to the park bench before us. Lynn enraged me with her self-centered attitude— just like during our marriage. But somehow, within the hour, I held her in my arms again.

While we walked, she told me about her life as a wealthy suburban housewife. It sounded very glamorous. She had gone to school at the famous Barnes Foundation and become an expert on contemporary art. With one of her classmates, Lynn started a business doing corporate art consultations.

"What got you started down that road?" I asked.

She looked at me funny. "Seriously?"

"Of course."

"You. You never stopped talking about art and literature the whole time we were together. You really planted that seed in me."

I squeezed her hand, amazed that our brief marriage, so long ago, had affected Lynn as deeply as it had me. We returned to the hotel room after a while, but there, we lapsed into reviewing the old resentments.

"Where have you been?" she asked, pounding my chest with her fists. "Why didn't you come back?"

"I wrote you all about this, Lynn."

"I want to hear it from you!"

So I talked her through the events again and tried to remove myself, emotionally, from the turmoil of that period. I simply recounted the reasons, as far as I remembered, for everything I did. All the while, I held Lynn in my arms, in our bed.

"I was genuinely frightened of your father, Lynn," I told her. "I had to get away from him. He directly threatened me. At the house, and over the phone, I asked you to come with me, begged you to, but you wouldn't. Over the phone, you said you didn't love me, and that you didn't think I was a man. And then you refused my calls, so I accepted what you said at face value. I decided the best way to be a man about the whole thing would be to move on."

"I wanted you to come back. I missed you every day. I cried and cried! And no one ever told me you kept calling! I stayed sick in bed for practically my whole pregnancy."

I held her tighter. By now I knew she had never stopped loving me. Back in 1961, in her physically weakened state, her father had essentially kidnapped and brainwashed her. I had given up too quickly. I now envisioned myself barging into Abner's house, grabbing my wife, throwing her over my shoulder like a cave man, and stealing her back from Abner. But I didn't barge in, so many years ago, and I couldn't go back. Slowly, painfully, I accepted that giving up had not been the right thing, the manly thing, to do. Now, I needed to find a way, in my heart, to live with my actions and all that had transpired as a result.

"Maybe it was a rationalization on my part," I said. "But I had been working towards my career for so long, and I wasn't going to let your father destroy my life. You forget, Lynn, I had seen Abner in action. I knew he was violent, and I knew what he was capable of."

"Yes," Lynn replied, resting her head on my chest. "He was violent. Even more than you know."

"Don't you see, my choice was a matter of survival, pure and simple? And then somehow, over time, I think my fear of him increased. My imagination got the better of me, I guess. It became harder and harder for me, psychologically, to keep resisting him. I feared what Abner would do to me if I persisted."

"He kept telling me you weren't a man," she said. "I didn't know what a man was. I didn't know what I was supposed to want in a man."

"Your father presented me—actually he threatened me—with an or-else divorce and blank adoption agreement. I was sure you knew about this. Abner said, 'We're going to adopt our unborn grandchild and give him or her our name so this child never has anything to do with you.' That's what he told me. Do you understand that?"

Lynn sobbed in my arms. "I never looked at it," she said.

"Then how in the world did you agree to it? I kept calling you and pleading with you! Don't you remember? I said, 'I'll pick you up anyplace, but not at your parents' house!' Remember? Oh God, Lynn. I'm sick to my stomach, now. I have been unhappy ever since that day."

I held her closer and we lay in our pain together, feeling the effects of the lack of trust that had developed between us over the years. We felt the hurt ebb and flow through our bodies. It physically linked us. The pain made us cry and made us yell and made us hold each other tighter. It felt so bad, and yet so good, to know, finally, that we endured this together, no longer separately.

Lynn sat up in the bed and took my hand. "Sweetheart, this is it. Our second chance and our only chance to get on with the next part of our lives. I want the next part of my life to be with you."

Over the last two decades I had hated her, loved her, mistrusted her, and cursed her, but now I finally saw that I couldn't live without surrendering myself to Lynn again. I let go all the old hurts and put my soul in her hands.

"I've hated you," she said, looking down in shame.

"I've hated you, too, Lynn. But hate is easy."

"I know," she said. "Love is hard."

"Yes," I said, "but loving you is what I was born to do, and from now on, I'm going to do a better job of it."

The next morning, we made love perfectly, better than ever before. The old rhythm and flow between us came back, just like in our youth, but now our souls connected on a much deeper level. Best of all, she still wrapped her long legs around me with the same abandon. I had actually forgotten the feeling of being touched with love. Afterward, just like the first time, we cried.

"Marty," she said. "How did this happen to us? I don't understand it. I do understand it, but I don't. I'm so angry, still."

"That's no way to start a new life together."

"Why weren't you like this in nineteen sixty-one?"

"Like what?"

"So patient and understanding."

"Because I was twenty-two. I didn't know losing you would mean losing half my life."

I studied every inch of her face and finally said, "You know there is no turning back for us now, don't you? We can only go forward, together."

Afternoon snuck up on us. I heard a rustling and saw a note emerging from beneath the hotel room door. At this point, Lynn and I could only laugh at the additional interruption to our tryst. Barbara's subterfuges finally amused us.

To my horror, the note said, "I know that you are in bed with her, and I have told the children I am throwing you out of the house because you are a disgusting, no-good father, and you are in New York City, sleeping with another woman."

"She actually dictated that to the desk clerk?" I wondered out loud.

What I should have done at that point was worry about my wife's already fragile mental state. In fact, years before, I should have gotten Barbara into psychiatric care. Surely, if anyone was to blame for her decline to this level of disturbance, I was. But, although, I was 45, it would still take me years and years to develop a sense of compassion for others. Even that, I can't take credit for. It was Lynn. She gave that to me. She inoculated me with kindness. But that day in New York, I admit that I cared nothing for Barbara's pain.

"I've never heard of anything like this!" exclaimed Lynn.

"What does that mean?" I asked angrily. "Hasn't this happened to you before with any other men?" By now, we knew we had both been unfaithful to our second spouses.

"That was a low blow," Lynn muttered. "And uncalled-for."

"I'm sorry," I said, knowing she would forgive me, knowing we could survive any storm together, even a storm of our own making.

We had planned to spend another day together, but Lynn said, "I think we should pack up and go today."

"Yes, you're right. I'm sorry about this, Lynn," I said. "I'll work this out with Barbara and I am going to see you again, soon. That is a promise."

29

June 1984

"Barbara, honey!" I exclaimed, grinning and embracing my even more distanced wife as soon as I arrived home. "What has got into you? I came back a day early because of all these crazy phone calls of yours. Listen, I had to work out a few things with Lynn. That's all. We had some unfinished business. It wasn't an affair. Don't be ridiculous! Oh my goodness, you have such an imagination! Now what do you say we take the children and all go out for a nice dinner? I'm worried about your stress level, Barbara. I really am."

She might have believed me. It's hard to say.

I didn't like myself for this overt deception, but if Barbara had really done what she said—told the children I was having sex with another woman—she had finally gone over the edge. A divorce, I thought, would make Barbara even more vengeful, and I predicted she'd take it out on the children. In a couple of years, the boys would both be in college. Perhaps, I thought, I could postpone our inevitable divorce that long, and, in the meantime, somehow prepare Elizabeth.

With this reasoning, I was thinking of the kids and myself but not of Barbara. If I had stopped for even a moment to consider her mental health, I would have probably suggested a divorce right away. We both knew we were living a lie. The difference was, I had the fortitude to keep on living it. But for Barbara, this life aggravated all her obsessions and compulsions to a dizzying degree.

In my office the next day, I spoke quietly to my assistant Sharon. "I'd like you to find another conference for me to attend in another two or three weeks," I said. "Anywhere but Miami. I feel like traveling."

"Consider it done," she said.

"And if my friend...I paused, trying to come up with a code name for Lynn...'Jane' calls, as long as I'm not in surgery, put the call through."

Sharon smiled, perfectly aware I had been talking to "Jane" several times a day for the past few weeks. Sharon also knew the depth of my misery most days, so I think her sidelong glances and goofy smirks meant she wished me well.

I returned to my usual routine—ten hours of work daily, interspersed with various sex dates. The women called me; I didn't go out looking for it. After a few weeks of that, I felt disgraced by my behavior. I had to stop thinking like the old, hopeless Martin Kraidin. I needed to trust that, even though we both wallowed in loveless marriages, Lynn and I would find a way to be together again. The world had finally given me the opportunity to be the man I always meant to be: Lynn's man. I wouldn't squander my chance. One by one, I broke it off with my sex partners.

Lynn and I continued to talk three or four times a day, always on my office phone. Sometimes we voiced our love, but other times Lynn regressed to the anger she had held in for so long.

"How could you have left me?" she asked, one time. "I gave birth to Stephen all alone. I cried all day, every day, for a week! The doctors wouldn't let me go home from the hospital, I was so hysterical. How could you do that to me?"

"Lynn," I replied. "I just don't have anything to add to what I've already told you. I have always loved you. That's all I can say. Please stop this."

No matter how much anger she expressed, Lynn's eagerness to meet me never abated. The following month, she and I returned to New York, this time staying at the luxurious Plaza Athene. I set up a professional conference, as cover, and Lynn set up a meeting with a client. But within twenty-four hours of our arrival, the hotel's general manager, a Frenchman, asked to see me in his office.

"Dr. Kraidin, I'm sorry to have to tell you this, but a Mr. Lesser has been calling, making inquiries about you and the young lady. I realize the two of you are not married, but that is not my business. I want you to know that at the Plaza Athene, we are perfectly discrete."

"I appreciate that very much," I said. Thank God for the French. They came through for us a second time.

Her parents still lived in New York, so I'm sure Barbara asked her father to actually travel to the hotel, sit in the lobby, and spy on us, but luckily, when the manager held him off, her father gave up the inquest. He must have been happy for the excuse.

I had travelled for conferences many times before, so Barbara really surprised me by guessing correctly of the affair, yet again. Somehow, my wife possessed keen instincts I had never perceived before. Unfortunately so did someone else.

One afternoon, while Lynn and I relaxed together in the tub, the phone in the bathroom rang.

Lynn said, "Go ahead and get it."

"Hello, Marty," answered a sultry voice. "It's Helen."

I had already ended things with this particularly aggressive housewife.

"Why are you calling me?" I asked.

"I want to know how you're enjoying your stay at the Plaza Athene," she crooned.

To this day, I don't know how Helen tracked me down, but I panicked, stepped out of the bath, and grabbed a towel as if I could wipe my old lover off the face of the earth.

"I don't want to talk right now," I said, feeling my face flush.

"Why not?" she asked, clearly angling for an invitation to my room.

"I have to go!" I exclaimed, and hung up, but by now Lynn had figured out what was happening, and she jumped out of the tub, too.

"Hand me a towel!" she demanded. I did, and Lynn went on. "This is the third time! First it was Barbara at the Park Lane, then her father, and now this woman! Who is she? Never mind! I don't want any part of this!"

Though ashamed, I burst out laughing. I couldn't help myself. After all, Lynn and I were engaged in an affair. Even though we felt we had every right to be together, technically, we didn't. And here Lynn stood high and mighty, giving vent to the righteous indignation of...well, of a wife. She fumed at me for laughing.

I assured Lynn no call like that would ever happen again, but at that point, she wanted to know, in detail, about my past and all my lovers. I didn't want to come clean. I had never told anyone, not even my friends Steve and Jimmy, about the affairs, but Lynn insisted, so I sighed and explained how the fashion models had led to the aspiring actresses, then the housewives, and finally I told her about Miami Beach's veritable playground of adultery. Then, against my will, she told me everything about her own past.

Lynn wanted to "clear the slate," but I had no desire to learn about her sex life with other men. By her description, her affairs were passionate, involved, and a lot juicier than mine. Hearing about them made me angry, and we fought. Finally, I begged her not to bring the subject up again. It hurt me too much.

"None of that matters," Lynn said. "Now, we belong to each other again."

We really did belong to each other. Even though we navigated a bumpy road those first few months of our affair, Lynn and I continued talking to each other several times a day, every day. And we never stopped finding ways to justify traveling to the same cities.

One time, we met at the Miami airport and flew to the Bahamas together. In the waiting area, before the plane arrived, we fell into each other's arms as if enchanted.

"Is there something wrong with us?" I asked, and she laughed. It felt so right being with her.

On that flight, Lynn and I pushed up the armrest between our seats. She lay her head on my shoulder. I curled my palm around her thigh. She cradled my face, finger combed my hair. We couldn't stop touching each other. Finally, the woman sitting next to us said, "I'm so sorry to interrupt, but I have to ask you a question. I have never felt such energy between two people. I don't want to intrude, but...are you married?"

"We got married in nineteen sixty-one," I answered obliquely, smirking at Lynn with satisfaction.

Over the course of the next few months, Lynn and I extended our romance to cities around the country—New York, San Francisco, Chicago, Salt Lake City, Washington DC—wherever I could find a conference to justify a weekend away. I even attended a conference in Paris, where Lynn and I recaptured some of the magic of our honeymoon, so long ago. Every time we met, in addition to making love at every opportunity, we continued the discussion about what really happened back in 1961, repeating the same conversations over and over. We needed to.

We found it difficult to understand that we had been separated for so many years because, in our youth, we hadn't known how to talk, only argue. Neither of us had been raised to reason, but to obey. In 1961, we tried to question the demands of our parents—we really did—but neither one of us had the strength to follow through. We couldn't stand up for ourselves, because we simply didn't know ourselves. Didn't know our own priorities. Didn't know what we wanted and needed to be happy in this life.

Of course, we weren't the first pair of young lovers ever to lose one another because of naïveté, but I think some people have this experience and move on. They find other loves, marry happily, and the past fades away—not so for Lynn and me. In 1984, we both still felt the same sense of destiny, of belonging together, that we felt on our wedding day, in 1961. No, not the same: the feeling had multiplied ten-fold.

I knew without a doubt that my one last chance for real love and happiness stood before me. There had never been anyone for me but Lynn, and I did everything in my power to make her see it. I wanted all doubt gone from both our minds.

"Lynnie," I told her once, while we strolled the streets of Chicago, "You're a beautiful person with a heart that's bigger than you are. I'm so proud of the woman you've become, and I'm so upset that I've missed all of you. Never again. We are never going to be apart. I adore you. You are the love of my life, the heart of my heart, and the soul of my soul."

She looked at me shyly, the collar of her overcoat turned up against the wind. "Where did you learn to talk like that?" she asked.

"I didn't learn it, damn it! I feel it! It's the inside of me talking out loud. I love you and I want to trust you once more. Please, please let me."

She kissed me deeply then, right in the middle of the sidewalk. It reminded me of the old days, how we used to kiss and kiss all day long. Suddenly, I remembered something and broke away, exclaiming "Lynnie Luscious Lips!"

I had called her this nickname once before, back in our youth, during a passionate moment. I just couldn't get enough of her full, sensuous lips. Nothing had changed.

She remembered and laughed. "To think," Lynn said. "I'm forty-two years old, and you're still calling me that."

In a dark bar in San Francisco, where we enjoyed cocktails before a jazz show, Lynn and I sipped our drinks, holding hands. Suddenly her eyes turned dark.

"When is this going to end? When are you going to leave me again?" she demanded.

"Shape up, woman," I said, slapping the tabletop as if to snap her out of a trance. "What do you think this is? You think I'm here for some great sex every few weeks? That's not why I'm here, so stop it. I'm going to marry you, Lynn! Mark my words."

"Are you crazy, or have you just lost your mind? Kraidin, you are married already."

"Should have told that to your father when he forced you to divorce me."

"Enough," she said. "Enough!"

"You should have told him, 'I'm married. I took vows. Nothing can come between us, not even you. Marriage is for life!'"

She looked down into her cocktail, as if an apology swam around in there, waiting for her to drink it down.

"Our marriage is the only real marriage either of us has ever had," I said. "We both know it. Eventually, all the pretending has to end, and that means both our current marriages. Or do you want to keep pretending your whole life? What kind of life is that?"

"Marty," she said. "I don't like telling you this, but I have to. I wasn't a good mother to Stephen. He looked so much like you that whenever I saw him, I thought of you, and how angry I was at you. I took it out on Stephen. I did. I yelled at him, neglected him. I'm not proud of it."

"That's in the past, Lynn. We can't look back to yesterday."

"No Marty, let me finish. When Julie was born, I told myself I'm not doing that again. I'm going to be a good mother to her, and I have been. I've been much better, much more attentive with Julie, and I don't want to leave her now. What I'm trying to say is that I have to wait until she graduates high school before divorcing Bob. I have to think of Julie before myself."

"Okay, Lynn. I don't want to tell you what to do. All I can say for sure is I'm never going to stop loving you, and I'm never not going to be part of your life again."

"I love hearing you say it," she said.

30

Toward the end of the year, gift-giving season, Lynn and I trysted once more in Manhattan. After she drove home, I wandered around on the Upper East Side, awash in the glory of our love. In my wanderings, I found a record store and bought Lynn some jazz tapes in the style of the trio we had seen the night before. I asked the store to box them up and send them to Lynn's home address.

Back home in Miami, about a week after I returned from Manhattan, I came home from work one day and Barbara caught me completely off-guard. There she stood, in the foyer, holding a small cardboard box. She cocked one hip, sucked in her cheeks, and looked at me with utmost contempt.

Jonathan, Adam, and Elizabeth stood next to her, lined up in a row, eyes downcast, as if being punished.

With a flourish, Barbara pulled a note out of the box and read it. "Ahem. 'Please don't ever do this, again. Please don't ever send me anything again.'"

Barbara raised her over-plucked eyebrows, then turned the box over. Four tape cases fell out and broke into pieces on the floor.

"Do you see this note, children? It's from your father's first wife. He is sleeping in the same bed with her!"

Elizabeth started to cry.

My mouth hung open with shock and horror. I realized that, on top of Barbara now having evidence of my and Lynn's affair, the gift had also caused havoc at Lynn's home which left me feeling doubly mortified.

The children looked up at me, then, and I could see the struggle between allegiances in their eyes. I opened my mouth and, like everyone else, wondered what would come out of it.

"I'm sorry," I said. "This is never going to happen, again. I'm going to put an end to it."

Barbara crossed her arms and raised an eyebrow. "When?" she asked.

"Today," I said, unsure what in the world I planned to do.

"What are you going to do?" she asked.

If the children hadn't been there, I probably would have simply admitted I loved another woman and demanded a divorce. I wouldn't do that in front of the children, and well she knew it.

"I'm going to call her," I stated firmly, as if I had already planned this.

"I'm going to be in the room. I want to hear this!" Barbara crowed.

"You can do whatever you want," I said, and strode into the den. Barbara followed. I grabbed the phone and called Lynn, who answered very coolly. Clearly, she still seethed with anger at me for sending the tapes to begin with.

"I got your package," I said. "This is no good. We've really screwed up our lives, haven't we? We both have to work on our current marriages and just know that anything between us...it just can't happen."

I meant what I said. I hated what Barbara had done, confronting me in front of the children, and I didn't want it to happen again. Also, in the back of my head lurked those voices: my father's voice, telling me I hadn't tried hard enough; my mother's voice, telling me the scandal of a second divorce would ruin our family; even Abner's voice crept in, telling me a real man could keep a marriage together. I suspected Barbara enjoyed having a whole new way to make me feel like a complete failure as a man, but in fact, I now realize, this episode may have been her way of trying to fight for me. Maybe, deep down, she actually did love me, after all.

"I know," said Lynn. "I understand."

After I hung up the phone, Barbara spat, "Fine, that ought to make things a little easier around here."

Meanwhile, the arrival of the tapes made Bob extremely suspicious, resulting in a screaming fight between him and Lynn.

January and February dragged by, each day leaden with the absence of Lynn. Finally, in mid-March, I dared to call her.

"Oh God, Marty, I've missed you," she said. "I want to see you on my birthday. I can't bear spending another birthday without you."

Overjoyed, I made reservations for her birthday, March twenty-sixth, at a lovely Victorian bed and breakfast in East Hampton. Then I called Stephen and said I wanted to take him out for his birthday, too, which fell only a few days after Lynn's.

I told Barbara I planned to escape, alone, to the Hamptons, for some peace and quiet, visit my sister on Long Island, and, most importantly, take Stephen out for his birthday.

"Is that really necessary?" Barbara asked.

"It certainly is!" I insisted. "He's one of my sons!" Then, I made the mistake of telling her where I planned to stay, in case of emergency.

Lynn and I agreed to meet in the La Guardia airport car rental parking lot. Walking from the terminal to the lot, I spotted Lynn striding toward me. A mischievous look crossed her face, and she began to run. When I saw her running full-out, straight for me, I became confused and shouted, "Lynn, no!" but she leapt into my arms anyway, just like that time on the beach. Somehow I managed to stay upright and catch her. She wrapped her arms and legs around me like a little girl, while we laughed and laughed.

Lynn and I enjoyed a wonderful time in the Hamptons, and the hotel staff couldn't have treated us better. We had come off-season, so we practically enjoyed the whole town to ourselves. I remember one day, we took a walk among the beach's undulating dunes. Lynn always liked to walk along the beach, take her shoes off, and kick at the water's edge. The sun felt so warm, that day, and the water so cold, the contrast surprised and delighted her. We found a spot between two dunes where we could lay back, watch the lapping waves, listen to the whirling gulls, and hold each other. Alone with Lynn, in nature, I felt an incredible oneness and connection to everything.

After our stay in the Hamptons, we returned to Manhattan to spend one last night together before I met up with Stephen. That night, we talked about how melancholy Stephen's birthday made us feel. We both regretted my absence at the hospital that day, and while we discussed it, we replayed our usual routine—she blamed me, I told her she had pushed me away, she reluctantly admitted the truth of that, and then she regressed and blamed me again.

When I met Stephen the next day, I took care not to mention anything about Lynn or my weekend in the Hamptons. If I thought Stephen had been living a double life when he first got to know me, that deception paled in comparison to this. I lived my married life with Barbara, had my secret affair with Lynn, and a third life with Stephen. My love for Lynn had to stay secret from both Barbara and Stephen..

That day, Stephen and I talked at length, but stiffly. He still held a lot of resentment towards me; that much became immediately clear. I could see him working to move past it, so I tried to be patient with the process.

"I'm really angry with you," he told me, over his mustard-glazed shrimp.

"I know."

"I don't think you do know," he added.

"Tell me, then."

"Where the hell have you been, all these years?" Stephen nearly shouted.

All these years I had been thinking of him, dreaming of him, wanting to see Stephen more than anything, but I didn't speak of it in that moment. He knew. I just gave my son a soul-searching look.

We sat at that table for hours, sometimes not talking at all. He vented anger, love, confusion, and deep, deep sadness. Our lunch went on so long, I knew I would miss my flight back to Miami, but I simply sat with Stephen—talking a little, but mostly listening—until he felt ready to go.

When I dropped my son back at his hotel, I called the East River Teleport service, reserved a seat on an immediate flight to Kennedy Airport, and met their helicopter at a nearby landing pad. Yes, indeed, I thought smugly to myself as I boarded the plane just in time, Martin Kraidin can have his cake and eat it, too. But I spoke too soon.

In Miami, I walked in the door of the house to find Barbara, once again, standing there waiting for me. Beside her stood Jonathan, Adam, and Elizabeth, just as before, lined up like soldiers, all of them crying.

"You son of a bitch!" Barbara screeched at me. "You weren't alone. You were with Lynn!"

"You don't know what the hell you're talking about," I lied.

"Oh, don't I?" she replied. "Children, your father is no good! He was with his ex-wife! He goes to bed with her and has sex with her! He doesn't care about us!"

Not again, I thought. Not in front of the children. I couldn't believe I had been sloppy again, after all these years of successfully hiding my affairs.

Immensely proud of herself, Barbara told me exactly what she had done. She called the bed and breakfast the very day we left, calling herself Lynn Kraidin. Barbara had rightly guessed Lynn would check in as my wife.

"Hi, this is Lynn," Barbara said, demonstrating the cloying, sugar-sweet "Lynn" voice she had invented.

"Oh, hi Lynn," replied the friendly receptionist. Barbara acted out that part, too. "It was such a pleasure having you this weekend. What can I do for you?"

"I think I left my makeup kit behind," said Barbara, as Lynn. "Could you check for me?"

Barbara told me the desk attendant checked, and then informed Barbara she couldn't find it. "But say hello to Marty for us!" Barbara chirped, mocking the friendly receptionist. "Either you end this, or I want you out of this house, now!" she screamed.

Again, I called Lynn, with Barbara standing at my shoulder, and told her, a second time, that we had to end things once and for all. I hoped Lynn intuited Barbara's role in all of this, but I didn't dare let on.

Just like Ginger, the astrologer, had predicted—I always promised Lynn the world, but time after time, I left her. This phone call made it the third time in this lifetime I had abandoned my beloved.

31

December 1985

One Thursday afternoon, not long after that phone call where I, again, cut off communications with Lynn, I bustled around the bedroom, packing my case for a trip to my practice in the Bahamas, when Barbara walked into the room.

Unpremeditated, the words just came out of me: "Our marriage sucks."

"No, it doesn't," she replied.

"It's no good, and you know it!"

"What are you proposing?" she asked.

"A trial separation, just to see how things go."

"Okay. That's a good idea," she said. "But for how long?"

"I don't know," I said.

I did know: forever and a day. But my vagueness on the matter served to keep her calm.

I also knew that, for reasons having nothing to do with the love between a man and woman, Lynn may have needed her marriage to Bob more than she needed me. But I also knew I would see her again, somehow. I would hold her again. With that in mind, I could do what had to be done. In fact, I felt glad to have Lynn out of the picture, for the time being. I wanted my resolution to divorce Barbara to be independent of anything or anyone. The decision tested my faith in myself.

Barbara's hesitation to separate probably resembled what I, too, had felt for so long—she simply didn't know what the big wide world would be like without the hell she had become accustomed to living. Also, she probably wondered if another man would ever love her. Even a lousy marriage has an element of comfort to it.

When I returned from the islands a few days later, I gathered the children together and delivered the news. "Sometimes people have the best intentions, but it just doesn't work out." The children took it well, especially when I assured them I would still be spending plenty of time with them. Perhaps more, in fact, than before.

I found a brand-new, high-rise apartment overlooking Biscayne Bay. Happily removed from the incestuous little island of Miami Beach, I'd live just a half an hour from the children. I took out the very first lease in the entire building, which still clattered with the last touches of the construction process, so I regularly brought the children over to show them the building's progress. I wanted them to feel involved. Now that I could get the children alone, without Barbara undermining my authority, I enjoyed them even more. I think the children liked our times together, too. They certainly relished the opportunity to get away from "Take off your shoes! Don't make a mess!"

A month after we separated, Barbara called me. "The kids say your place is gorgeous," she said bitterly.

"It is."

"It doesn't sound temporary."

I didn't say a thing. I wanted this divorce to go by stages—stages that I controlled—to keep Barbara's spite from spiking into the red zone.

"I want to see it," she said.

"No," I said. "There's no reason for that."

I should have known Barbara would figure out a way to get what she wanted. She called the following Saturday and said, "I'm coming over."

"No, you're not."

"Oh yes, I am."

What the hell, I figured. I'd get it over with.

Barbara walked in and toured my apartment like an anthropological museum of the modern male.

"It's beautiful," she said. "And it doesn't look temporary. I think it's time for you to come back to the house."

"I'm not going to do that, Barbara." There, I said it.

I leaned against the kitchen counter, crossed my arms, and prepared for an avalanche of vitriol, so her reaction threw me off completely. She smiled, sighed and dropped her eyes. Then she reached out for me. I actually tried to respond to her seduction, perhaps out of some misplaced pride, but I just couldn't.

"What's the matter?" she asked, trying to arouse me every way she knew how.

"I just don't want to make love to you," I said, with a sigh. "I haven't wanted to for a very long time, and I'm never going to do it again."

The look on her face said, "but...but...but..." My message still hadn't sunk in, and I knew I needed to make her understand, once and for all. No more avoiding. My ongoing attempt to sidestep her wrath by refusing to talk about divorce was pure selfishness. It only confused her, and I finally understood, that wasn't fair.

"Barbara," I said. "I never want you to come here again, and I'm never coming back to the house. Never. It's too late for us. Let's separate so we can both live better lives."

Barbara stormed out of the apartment, making sure to slam the door extra loudly. I fell back into an armchair in a state of mental and spiritual exhaustion.

One Saturday morning, months after the incident with Barbara, I sat up in bed. I didn't have to work, so I leaned back against a pile of pillows and watched, through open terrace doors, as the sun rose over Biscayne Bay. No motorboats yet interrupted the pure sound of gulls calling and wheeling over the waves. I inwardly rejoiced at the imminence of my divorce and looked forward to getting dressed later and walking around my home actually wearing shoes. Oh yes, and on Saturday my cleaning lady came in order to keep the place exactly as clean as a normal person required. No cleaner than that, thank you.

I wanted a cup of coffee, but still felt too lazy to get up and make one, so I watched a sailboat cross the bay, far below, morning sun glinting off its deck. The telephone's ring disturbed my reverie. When I picked it up, I found myself talking to Lynn's business partner, whom I had only met once, briefly, on one of Lynn's business trips.

"Have you heard from Lynn?" she asked.

"What are you talking about? I haven't talked to Lynn in quite some time."

"I was just wondering if she was with you."

"Why would she be?"

"Well, we're in Miami, at the Grand Bay Hotel. We're here on business, and we have a really busy day ahead, but I woke up this morning and Lynn is gone. Her car isn't in the garage. I'm worried."

"Now, I'm worried, too."

I promised to call her back if I heard from Lynn. Replacing the telephone receiver, I resumed watching boats cross the harbor, but now instead of empowered, I felt helpless, thinking about Lynn wandering around out there, somewhere, and I couldn't take care of her. I had pushed such thoughts out of my head for so long, the dam finally burst that morning and all my anxiety over our separation rushed back. I wanted to hold Lynn more than ever. Frustrated now, I contemplated making that cup of coffee after all, as a distraction, but the phone rang again.

"Hello, Marty."

I let out a sigh of relief at hearing Lynn's voice. Immediately, I told Lynn about her partner's call and asked where she was.

"Oh," she said. "I'm back at the hotel, now. I was having one of those bad mornings. You know how I get."

"Yes, I do."

"I felt down in the dumps. I wanted to walk along the beach, clear my head."

"Yes, of course."

"I drove out to Key Biscayne, that's all."

"Lynn?" I asked. "Can I take you to lunch, today?"

"I'd like that," she replied.

The morning zipped by, and before I knew it, I greeted Lynn up at the Grand Bay, prepared for a civilized conversation with a respectable, married lady.

"Nice car," she said of my Mercedes.

"Thanks."

"I couldn't help but notice you have a new telephone number, too."

"Yes, Barbara and I have separated."

"I'll bet you picked out the best apartment in Miami," she said, with a twinkle in her eye.

"I did," I replied, uncomfortable with her flirting. I thought Lynn wanted to remain true to Bob, and I didn't know how to respond.

"I want to see it," she said, blunt as ever.

"Would that be proper? I don't know if you should go to a bachelor's apartment. What would Bob say?"

"Oh, I get it," she replied. "You're concerned. That's nice. Go ahead and be concerned. But seriously, I want to see your apartment."

As always, her wish became my command. Before long, I held Lynn again, and all felt right with the world. I knew she had no plans to leave Bob for me, but I also knew she loved me—the most important thing.

32

When Lynn returned to Philadelphia, I called Barbara for a lunch meeting. Over chicken salad, I suggested we sell the house and furniture and split all the money, so we could each start over anew. I agreed to give Barbara all of her jewelry and furs outright, suggested we each keep our respective cars, and split every bank account and pension plan right down the middle. We had one child in college, another on the way to college next year, and another in private school. I intended to pay for it all myself. I wanted to get the divorce over and done with. No more stalling.

"No lawyers," I insisted. "All they'll do is eat up our money, and we'll both end up broke."

While I spoke, Barbara sat in unheard-of silence, scribbling copious notes on a legal pad. She contributed nothing to the conversation until the end, when she asked me, "Is that it?" I told her yes, and she replied, "Okay, are you going to get the check?" before slipping out the door without so much as a goodbye.

Within days, I received a call from Barbara's new attorney, who said my wife wanted more, so I hired a divorce lawyer that came recommended by a friend. I didn't know the guy at all, and I'll never forget what a huge mistake I made in not looking into him further. This lawyer turned out to be a mean, aggressive son of a bitch. I had wanted to be fair and equitable, but now Barbara, who had actually hired a nice attorney, thought I wanted to cheat her. This set a terrible tone for the ensuing negotiations. As soon as I realized what I'd done, I fired the awful man, but by then, the gloves had come off. The easy, peaceful divorce I envisioned became a lost cause.

Lynn asked around among her connections, and gave me a recommendation for a world-class divorce lawyer, Marcia Elser, who turned out to be a brilliant attorney as well as a sweet, sincere person. Unfortunately, by the time Marcia came into the picture, Barbara had already decided to squeeze me dry.

Our lawyers negotiated a new settlement, but as soon as the agreement nearly finalized, Barbara fired her entire legal team and hired a new one, causing negotiations to begin anew. Month after month, Barbara pulled this same stunt, and each legal team she found excelled at maneuvering me into increasingly untenable positions for which, of course, I had to pay for everything. Every cent Barbara spent came from our mutual bank accounts, and I couldn't separate our funds. Her attorney held the job of negotiating that, of course, so as long as Barbara kept firing her attorneys, she maintained control over my money. At the bottom of Barbara's apparent fury lurked the fact that she refused to accept the inevitability of a divorce. I'm sure this stubbornness was based in equal parts on her not wanting to lose access to my ever-increasing income and her pain at being replaced by another woman. The fact that I had clearly lied for decades about my first marriage being a forgotten piece of history had to cut Barbara, too. I hadn't set out to hurt her, though. I may have entered into that marriage without love but certainly with the intention of putting Lynn behind me. I simply could not do it. I couldn't ever be happy without Lynn, and being with her was pure bliss. No happy medium existed.

Whenever I felt low, whenever I felt angry, I called Lynn, and she talked me down from the emotional ledge. Despite the fact that we conducted our affair with more gusto than ever, Lynn didn't play the role of "the other woman" when she helped me, but merely acted as a selfless, dedicated friend. She appointed herself my partner, my consoler.

"Keep your dignity," she used to say. "Don't even address Barbara in the meetings. Above all, don't insult her."

Elegant as always, Lynn knew how to maintain one's integrity. She taught me to stand up for myself without flying into a rage, to delegate the work I felt too emotionally worked up to handle. She taught me to shame Barbara's attorneys with my gentlemanliness and self-control, and Lynn reminded me, again and again, that my divorce from Barbara had nothing to do with her, or our affair. I had to do this for my own sanity.

Many times over the course of those months, I felt a dangerous tightening in my chest. One day in my office, during one of these incidents, I didn't want to call Lynn and upset any more than I already had, so I called my attorney, Marcia. By this time, Marcia had become a true friend of both Lynn and me. Thinking back, I wonder what made me call Marcia that day. I should have called a doctor, but I didn't want expert advice, I wanted a hug—a heartfelt, platonic hug from a woman.

"Marcia," I said. "I think I'm dying."

"What's the matter?"

"I'm getting pressure in my chest. I'm worried, and I don't know what to do!"

"Okay, cancel your patients for the day," she said, taking charge as I knew she would. "Call your doctor, and go to the emergency room. If it's not a heart attack, you should still make an appointment at Mount Sinai to have a stress test on a treadmill. You want to know what's going on."

I did as she suggested, and turned out to be okay. I only suffered from anxiety.

Barbara never tired of fighting me. She never reached the point where she just wanted this hell to be over with, like most people would. What's more, she harassed me with frequent calls, where she repeatedly accused me of having an affair with Lynn. Even after everything that had happened, I still stupidly denied it. In fact, Lynn and I took great pains to be discrete. We acted as if a private detective might be around every corner with a zoom lens and a tape recorder. I thought keeping the affair secret would help me prevail in the divorce. In the end, I needn't have bothered.

Once, Barbara even suggested, "If you tell me what you've done, I'll tell you what I've done."

I didn't give a damn what affairs she'd had, and didn't want to know. "All you do is clean the kitchen," I said. "That's all I know."

When Lynn came to Miami for business, which happened frequently, we found new restaurants to go to—places where no one knew me. One Italian restaurant down in Coconut Grove became our favorite. Word on the street had it the mob frequented this place, which suited me fine. Likely as not, those folks knew how to keep their mouths shut. We liked to sit at the banquette there, side by side, so we could touch, and touch, and touch some more all through dinner.

"Lynn," I said once, after finishing a delicious plate of ravioli. "I want to make a pact. This has nothing to do with divorce or marriage. It's about our souls, our true selves."

"A pact?" she asked. "Oh my God, Marty, you're so dramatic."

"Cut your finger," I said. I picked up a knife and pressed it into the pad of my index finger until a drop of blood appeared. Lynn saw I was serious, so she took the knife and did it, too, but couldn't help giggling. We pressed our fingers together.

"I am yours forever," I said. "My soul is yours and I want to grow old with you. And one day, far in the future, we will die together."

"And Sweetheart, I am yours forever," she replied, looking straight into my eyes.

I pulled the paper menu out of its leather case, turned it over, and wrote:

I am yours in this lifetime, as I have been in the past, and I will be yours throughout all eternity. I love you with my heart and soul.

We both signed our names to it.

"What do you mean by 'in this lifetime'?" she asked, so I told her about Ginger, and how she had told me about Lynn's and my previous lives together. "This is fascinating," Lynn said. "I feel like it's true. It explains something I've always felt, but didn't know how to say. Marty, can we go to an astrologer together? I'd like to do that with you."

Ginger had moved away, but we found another astrologer/psychic, a man named Jeffrey Brock, who met us as his door in a sport coat and tie. In his study, lined with rare books on Sanskrit, psychic phenomena, and occult topics, Jeffrey sat us down and asked a few questions to complete our natal charts. I had warned Lynn not to give anything about us away. I wanted to see how accurately the man would read us. Jeffrey didn't seem to mind our recalcitrance about providing information; he just launched into his reading.

Adjusting a pair of thick glasses, Jeffrey said Lynn and I had known each other in previous lives, but always ended up separated. He mentioned our past lives in Egypt and France, the battle of Gettysburg, and me getting killed in World War One, just as Ginger had done. From her face, I could tell Lynn marveled at the similarity of this reading and Ginger's, but I didn't. By now, I knew something stronger than mutual admiration held us together: Lynn and I held each other with a karmic bond.

At the end of our meeting, Jeffrey held our hands and shut his eyes. He said, "You two will marry, but many people will be made unhappy by this. I see everyone around you beating the ground. Beating the ground with their fists. There is anger. There is sadness. But you two are bonded, no matter what. I don't know why everyone is so upset, but there is no denying it. And this time your destiny will be fulfilled."

Come November, Barbara hired a firm that must have pledged to stop at nothing but my complete financial annihilation. One day, Barbara and her black-suited legal thugs met Marcia and me in Marcia's conference room, for negotiations. With true worry and concern for my state of mind, Lynn gave me a pep talk on the telephone beforehand, urging me to remain calm and dignified, no matter what. But the conversation grew so hostile, and it took so much energy for me to maintain self-control that I became a bit lightheaded. I actually stopped hearing what the lawyers shouted across the table. My soul felt like it left my body. Marcia finally called for a break and took me into her office.

"Marty, I want to talk to you not as your lawyer, but as a friend, somebody who cares about you a lot," she said. "Now, as you just heard, Barbara is asking for a lot more money."

"How much more?" I asked. "I kind of lost focus."

"Two hundred thousand dollars."

"What?" I yelled. I didn't mean to yell at her, I just couldn't believe Barbara's audacity. By now, I had already offered my wife a good two-thirds of everything I owned. I had lined up a buyer for the house, too, yet Barbara refused to sign off on the deal. I would have to give Barbara my half of the house money to meet her demands, so I don't know how she thought I planned to come up with this cash. She almost seemed to delight in creating an impossible situation.

Marcia sat down in front of me and took my hands in hers. "Marty, listen. Barbara says she is going to kill you. She said that out loud, just now. And you have been feeling sick, haven't you?"

"Yes, you know I have."

"No matter how much it is," Marcia said, "Pay it. Be done with it. I will work everything else out. Don't keep fighting. If you do, Barbara really is going to kill you."

I felt as I had when Abner forced me to divorce Lynn. I hesitated to sign another agreement under duress. Abner had manipulated me then and now. Barbara handed me her own deal with the devil. Just like Abner, Barbara really did want to kill me. At my age, 47, it wouldn't take a gun or a fist or a knife; only enough stress to give me a heart attack.

In 1962, facing Abner's evil contract, I stood alone. But this time, I enjoyed two advantages: first, Marcia's counsel. She prioritized not like a lawyer, but like a friend. At the end of the day, her concern about me as a person superseded her concern over my superficial trappings, including money. Second, this time, I knew myself. Sure, I enjoyed my money, I had worked hard for it, but it didn't define me. Barbara couldn't take away my children's love, Lynn's love, or my knowledge of myself as a man. Abner had done that, but Barbara could not. Not this time.

"Hell," I said to Marcia. "You're right. Give me something to sign."

I nearly ripped the paper as I signed the divorce agreement with a mean-spirited flourish. I gave Barbara all she asked for.

A week later, Barbara changed her mind. Again, she wanted more.

Lynn and I took a vacation in Bucks County, Pennsylvania, a place we used to frequent back in the sixties, driving through the beautiful countryside in the old Impala, with the top down. Those were the days. Now we cruised more sedately in a rented Cadillac, trying to forget our troubles.

When we checked into our country cabin at Burpee Farm, Lynn insisted I not call Marcia. "Leave it alone," she begged. "For one weekend, don't think about Barbara!"

"I can't," I said. "I have to know."

I looked out the window of our quaint guesthouse at the beautiful blanket of snow adorning each fence post, each barn roof, and called Marcia.

"So?" I asked. "Has Barbara accepted the terms yet, or are we going to take this endless bullshit into the new year?"

"I have called for an emergency session with the judge," Marcia replied. "He is tough, and I think he is going to settle this once and for all."

By the time I hung up the phone, I felt satisfied with Marcia's progress and content to resume our vacation, but Lynn's face looked distant and worried.

"I might as well call home, too," she said. "I want to check on Julie."

Lynn dialed and Bob answered the phone. After a moment, she yelled, "No, I'm not! That's ridiculous! You better get a handle on yourself, Bob! You're out of line!" Their argument continued for so long I had to leave the room and get some fresh air. When I returned, I found Lynn sweet-talking her husband with the grace and charm of Aphrodite.

She hung up and said, "Bob accused me of having an affair. He has caught on, but I denied it completely. I don't want Julie to know. I don't want her to feel betrayed by me. I couldn't take it. Not with Julie."

Lynn collapsed on the bed, crying softly, and I held her.

"I don't want to be that woman," she said. "I want to be a good mother. But I love you so."

Marcia called me right after Christmas. "Our emergency hearing is scheduled in the judge's chambers. All parties will be in attendance including us, Barbara, her lawyers, your real estate broker, the potential buyer of the house, your CPA—it's going to look like the U.N. General Assembly, and its going to happen on the first business day of the new year."

When I met Marcia at the courthouse, she said, "You just sit there quietly and don't say a word. Stay as calm as you can."

Yes Ma'am, I did whatever she said. All parties gathered around a conference table while Marcia and one of Barbara's attorneys retreated into the judge's chambers, shutting a thick, oaken door behind them. After half an hour, the pair returned to the room, along with the black-robed judge.

The judge cleared his throat and said, "I have gone over the separation agreement."

Then, he cleared his throat again, as if to ensure his words came out exactly right. Addressing Barbara, looking her straight in the eye, he told her that in his professional opinion, her husband had been more than generous. He even said I had been generous beyond anything that the court would require. "Yet," he added, "you refuse to sign any papers!" He reminded Barbara that she and I had three children together and her actions against me were harming the children. "So therefore," he finally declared. "This separation agreement is binding as of today. When you leave this courtroom, you will be divorced."

The judge signed the papers, then, holding her gaze, slid them across the table to Barbara. Under his glowering eye, she picked up the pen and finally signed them.

The whole time, Marcia squeezed my hand under the table and whispered, "Sh, don't say a word. Sit still."

I didn't want to say anything. I only squirmed in my seat because I wanted to run over there and hug the judge so badly.

33

"I can't believe Bob agreed to this," I told Lynn while I pulled some blankets and pillows out of my closet to create space for her things. "Is he an idiot, or what?" .

"He knows about us, sweetheart, and he isn't in denial," she replied," "We're using the same lawyer and splitting everything down the middle amicably. Would you rather he act like Barbara?"

"Oh God, no. Let him be an idiot, with my blessing."

Even though Julie was still in high school for another year, Lynn finally came clean with Bob about our affair. They worked out an agreement whereby Lynn spent two weeks out of every month with me, in Miami, and two in Philadelphia, where she and Bob now slept in separate bedrooms. This strange arrangement supposedly maintained a semblance of normal family life until Julie's graduation. As uncomfortable as the agreement made me—both for Bob's sake and for Julie's—Lynn wanted it that way, so I went along.

While Lynn found a place for her things in the bathroom, she told me about an argument they'd had. "Bob asked me if I had loved you all along, since before I married him," Lynn said. "I told him yes, I always loved you, even when I thought I'd never see you again. I didn't lie. I loved Bob too, though, in my way, but he didn't understand that. He shouted that our entire marriage was a sham from the beginning, and then threw my favorite fruit bowl on the floor. I've swept the kitchen ten times and still pick up shards of it."

"Both our marriages were shams," I said.

"I know, but I tried," she said. "I tried to move on from you and love him. I really did. I didn't set out to live a lie. It just happened."

"And what about your father?" I finally dared to ask. Did you tell him about us?

"Yes, I did," Lynn replied. "He came up to Philadelphia a couple of weeks ago, and I took him out for a walk and told him. He wasn't happy, of course."

"What did he say?"

"I said, 'I've started seeing Marty again,' and he said, 'Why did you do that?' And I said, 'Because I love him. I always have, and this time, things are going to work out.' I didn't cry or anything. You would have been proud."

"And he said..."

"Oh, Marty, you know what he said. 'Don't count on me for any support!' to which I replied, 'I wouldn't have expected less from you.' I meant less hostility."

"So that's that, then." I said, a little disappointed that after all these years Abner hadn't changed one iota.

The phone rang, and I picked it up to hear Barbara screeching, "Adam just brought some friends over from school and they ate a half a box of chocolate cookies! You owe me three dollars!"

"I'll take up a collection," I replied, clicking the receiver down.

Lynn wandered into the dining room and stood there eyeing my furniture with her art-collector's eye. "What was that about?" she asked.

"Barbara calls me every couple of days with 'alarming news,' like 'Jonathan got a B in chemistry,' or 'Elizabeth is dating a boy' or some such thing. She seems to think I need to know every time the children go to the bathroom."

"I'd change my phone number," Lynn said, pensively touching a mirror on the dining room wall. She straightened it ever so slightly.

"I refuse! I won't run from her. Barbara has to learn to respect my boundaries...somehow."

"I'd like to redo this dining room," Lynn said.

I looked the place over. I had carefully selected the chrome and leather furniture, and I loved it, but when I saw that glint in Lynn's eye, the glint I had missed for years, I said, "Go ahead. The place needs a woman's touch," and kissed her neck. "Afterwards, we can start having parties again, like in the old days."

"Oh Marty, lets!" she exclaimed, throwing her arms around my neck. Just then, the phone rang again.

Barbara screamed over the line, "You son of a bitch, do you know Jonathan hasn't called me from college in eleven days? This is your doing!"

"I have nothing to do with that."

"You know what else?" Barbara added. "Elizabeth's room is a mess. It's disgusting. This is what happens without a father!"

I took a moment to collect my thoughts while Barbara prattled on about various other slights and injustices. Finally, I interrupted her with something I had been trying to put into words for months: "Listen carefully, you bitch. Once and for all, we are divorced. I paid a lot of money for the privilege of not having to talk to you ever again. I bought my peace and quiet with that money. I don't ever want to hear your voice. Got it? Never! Never again in my life!"

I hung up the phone and silently congratulated myself on the well-turned phrase: "I paid a lot of money for the privilege of never speaking to you again." Indeed I had, and now if I could only get my money's worth, it would be well spent.

She didn't call again.

Julie appeared to adjust to some degree to her parents' separation, and luckily, when she met me, she tolerated "the other man". She even flew down to Miami to spend some of her school vacations with Lynn and me. Stephen, on the other hand, raged against Lynn and Bob's impending divorce. He had used his business degree to open a travel agency in West Palm Beach, near his grandfather, but despite his proximity to Miami, Stephen rarely spoke to Lynn these days, and never to me.

Over the course of that year, while I worked like the devil trying to put my financial life back together, Lynn redecorated my apartment. I should say we did it together, since going shopping for furniture, art, and antiques became one of our favorite things to do. While we browsed everywhere from top-of-the-line galleries to musty old warehouses, she taught me all about art—the era of this couch, the style of that water pitcher. I loved that she had become my teacher. My apartment became a reflection of us, and instead of what I would call "luxurious efficiency," the style I came up with on my own, the house now exuded a warmth and beauty born of mismatched pieces selected from different eras and cultures but somehow united by Lynn's decorating magic.

One day, she found a bench for ten dollars at a thrift store. It looked like a horrible old thing to me, but she said, "I like the lines." Sure enough, after a rub-down with linseed oil and a new upholstery job, the piece looked like something out of an old French castle.

"Where should we put this bench?" she asked glancing around the apartment, hands on hips.

I came up behind Lynn, wrapped my arms around her waist, and put my chin on her shoulder. "How about at the foot of the bed?" I suggested in a sexy whisper. I knew she'd remember our honeymoon debacle at Portofino, back in 1961.

"Never!" she exclaimed, before melting into my arms. "No furniture will ever stand at the foot of a bed in this house!"

Julie happened to be visiting us the day movers brought in our new dining table. Lynn had had the table specially antiqued, and the matching chairs painted, too—each one slightly different.

"What are you going to do with the old furniture?" Julie asked.

"I was thinking about giving it to Stephen," I said. Now that he had his own bachelor pad, the furnishings would suit him perfectly. "If he wants it, he can have everything—furniture, TV, sound system, the whole lot. We're upgrading it all."

"That's a great idea!" Julie said.

"Yeah, except for one thing," Lynn interjected. "Stephen won't talk to Marty. And with me, his conversations are barely hello and goodbye. I doubt he'll accept the gift."

"That's crazy," Julie said. "I'm going to call him."

She shut herself in the guest bedroom with the telephone and emerged twenty minutes later, frowning. She said, "His words, verbatim: 'I won't take a thing from them, especially if Marty has anything to do with it.' What an idiot. I told him to get over it, but..." Julie shrugged.

"Why does he have to be so stubborn?" Lynn asked of no one in particular.

Julie said, "You've heard how Pop talks to him. Stephen told me about the pipe bomb comment. Remember that?"

Lynn sighed heavily.

"Pipe bomb?" I asked.

Julie looked reproachfully at her mother until Lynn broke down and told me.

"It was the day Stephen and I met Pop for lunch in Palm Beach, a couple

188

of weeks ago, the day I drove your car. When the valet brought the car, Pop said, 'When did you get this car?' I told him it was yours, and he turned to Stephen, like the two of them were in cahoots, and said, 'I'm going to put a pipe bomb in this car!' He started laughing like a maniac. I reminded him I was the one driving the car, but that didn't seem to disturb him a bit."

"Pop expects Stephen to take his side," added Julie. "And then there's Dad. He's not exactly Marty's biggest fan. Stephen chose to take Pop and Dad's side," Julie said with a shrug. "I'm trying not to take sides."

If I longed to bring anyone into Lynn's and my ecstatic little world, Stephen topped the list, but I could only wait for him to come around. In the meantime, I introduced Lynn to my other children. Elizabeth came over first. She and Lynn got along so well; I could tell Elizabeth craved the presence of a calm, reasonable mother figure. Lynn and I fixed up one of the guest bedrooms with all kinds of pretty girl things for Elizabeth but my daughter would never stay with us. Sometimes she planned to, but at the last minute always asked to go home for one reason or another. Eventually, I realized she knew that it would hurt her mother too much.

Finally, one day, the inevitable happened: Elizabeth and Barbara fought so severely, my daughter called me, crying.

"Can you please pick me up?" Elizabeth asked, and I arrived in minutes flat.

At my apartment, Elizabeth fell into Lynn's arms, saying, "I want to leave the house. I want to move in here and live with you two. Oh God, I can't stand being there!"

I wanted to move my daughter in that very second, but Lynn wisely put the brakes on. "Listen, Sweetheart," she said. "We'd be very happy if you lived with us, but first you have to do your best to work out the differences with your mother. You don't want to make any big decisions in anger or haste. She's still your mother and always will be."

Lynn really impressed me with her level-headedness, especially since I reacted emotionally to everything having to do with Barbara and the children. Just as during my divorce, I still turned to Lynn for grounded, logical answers when I felt overwhelmed.

On Elizabeth's next visit, she and Lynn talked and cooked together in the kitchen, completely absorbed in each other. No one even noticed me. I sat and read a book while they did their thing—secretly spying on the two most amazing women in my life.

"You haven't met my brothers yet, have you?" asked Elizabeth, while the two of them whipped up a batch of marinara sauce. "I'll tell you ahead of time. The toughest one is going to be Jonathan."

When the boys returned from college, they finally met Lynn, and as it turned out, Adam approached her with just as much skepticism as Jonathan. The boys scrutinized Lynn no end, but she held up fantastically. Once, I walked into the den to find Lynn sitting on the floor with Jonathan, the two of them deep in a whispered conversation. She looked up and said, "Excuse me, Marty, but this is private."

Lynn amazed me like that—the degree of respect she gave each of the children, treating them like adults and listening to their ideas. Whatever they had to say, she listened intently. She also held them to high standards.

Adam, who used to lock horns with Barbara the most out of all the children, couldn't stand spending the summer of 1989 home with his mother, so he moved in with us for a few months. Lynn set strict boundaries. "You're going to keep your room clean, get up when we get up, not sleep all day, and wash your dishes," she told him. "You won't be staying out until all hours, either. If you want to live here, there are rules."

"I wasn't such a good mother to Stephen, Marty," she told me. "But I learned along the way. I did everything wrong with him. I was strict at the wrong times and lax at the wrong times. I did it all backwards. But with Julie, as much as possible, I did everything right."

Despite Lynn's stern lecture, Adam complained constantly and frequently broke our rule about late nights. He partied after work and came slamming through the front door in the wee hours of the morning.

Once, I complained to Lynn, asking, "What are we going to do about Adam?"

She only replied, "He's going through a stage. Be patient. It'll blow over."

I don't think Lynn even realized what she did as she threw the advice I'd given her about Stephen and Je Vonna right back in my face.

34

Even though Lynn hadn't yet divorced Bob, we couldn't wait to buy our first home together—something permanent, where we could throw parties. We found our haven on a tiny island off Biscayne Bay, studded with perhaps 100 other homes. A classic, Bermuda-style manor, with a peaked roof, quaint shutters framing small-paned windows, archways leading to a walled garden, and window boxes overflowing with fuchsia, it stood on the bay side of the island. To me, the house looked and felt like love. Lynn sensed it, too.

"Who lived here before?" I asked the real estate agent.

"A couple used it for a vacation home for many years. They both finally died, so their kids are selling it," he replied.

"They must have been very much in love," I said. The man shrugged. I don't know if the soothing colors on the walls; the open, breezy, architecture; or the abundant garden convinced me of this, but I just felt love there. Best of all, the house had been built in 1961, the year Lynn and I first married.

"I'm not going to lie to you, this is an old house and it has been neglected," the agent told us. "See those piles of sawdust? They're from termites. You can probably get a good deal, if you're interested. It's quite a fixer-upper."

"Are you sure you want this house?" Lynn asked me.

"Oh, yeah," I said. "This'll be fun to renovate. Besides, I've dealt with worse." I recalled the mini-mansion I raised from the dead to try to save my marriage with Barbara.

"But, how are you going to do it?" Lynn asked. "You work all day, every day!"

"I'm not. You are. I'm going to keep on working all day, every day, and you are going to supervise the renovation."

"I have no idea how to..."

I put two fingers on her lips. "You can do it, Darling. I trust you. And if you need me, I'm a phone call away."

That's how the project began. More than anything, I loved giving Lynn all my trust and watching her confidence grow. She still acted like the Lynn I knew, but nothing like that insecure, quarrelsome little girl I once married.

Stephen frequently travelled for work, so he began staying with Lynn and me on his way in and out of Miami International Airport; however, his visits never went well. Stephen and I argued, and Stephen and Lynn argued, and as a result, Lynn and I argued, too. Despite our love for each other, Lynn and I still lit into each other now and again, as hotheaded as ever. The old issues still came up, Lynn still blamed me for our divorce, and I blew up at her time and again for her unshakeable conviction that she alone was the innocent party in every conflict.

One day, after Stephen stormed out of our house for the umpteenth time, I told Lynn I could no longer endure the excruciating effort to be patient with him, nor would I continue to tolerate Stephen's zeal for provoking Lynn and me at every opportunity.

"I want to talk to Stephen about whatever is bothering him," I said.

"No, you are not," she replied sternly.

"Why not?"

"Because I said so!"

"That's no reason! I'm calling him and the three of us are going to sit down and talk, once and for all, and stop dancing around the issues."

Soon, the three of us sat in a triangle—couch, chair, chair—in the living room.

"Okay, Stephen," I said. "What's troubling you? Let's talk about it."

"Nothing."

"Stephen, don't talk like that," said Lynn. "We're not stupid, we're your parents."

"That's a laugh," he said. "You've treated me terribly all my life. Some parent!"

"What are you talking about?" asked Lynn.

"Oh, I remember you yelling at me to take my dirty boots off before coming in the house. Just yelling and yelling. And one time, as a kid, I was finger painting and you screamed at me! Just screamed because I got some paint on something. Who knows why? I was just a kid! Hitting me, yelling at me...and now you want us to get along? It doesn't work that way."

Lynn replied, "Stephen, when you were little...I did the best I knew how. That's all I can say. I was an unhappy single mother."

"I'll say!" Stephen interrupted. "You used to always yell at me, 'You're just like your father!' I had to wonder who this awful man was, my father. But you wouldn't tell me, would you? No, but whenever I did something wrong, 'You're just like your father, stubborn! You're just like your father, a wimp!' Everything I did wrong, it was 'You're just like your father!'—apparently, my father was the scum of the earth, and I was his hopeless bum of a son."

Lynn looked down at her lap. "Yes, I was very angry, and I took it out on you. I'm sorry for that, but I tried to raise you right. I took you with me everywhere...but everything good I did, I undid it again with angry words."

"Whatever!" Stephen replied, angrier than ever. "It didn't end when I was a child, though. What about the day I went off to college? All the other students, their parents helped move them into the dorm, but not me. You were too busy attending some society ball to help your own son. You told me to drive myself all alone!"

"You did that?" I asked Lynn.

She sighed, "Bob and I had a social engagement."

"That's no excuse!" Stephen and I yelled, together.

Stephen continued, and now the words fell out of him in a torrent. "You took all your anger out on me! Don't you think I knew it? You looked at me and saw HIM," Stephen said, pointing at me. "And where were you, dear father? All that time, when she was screaming at me and hitting me, all because of you?"

I didn't answer for quite some time. Stephen already knew the story of my divorce from Lynn. He knew that his beloved grandfather had forced us apart, but he still didn't want to face it.. I understood Stephen's anger, yet had grown weary of apologizing. I saw this time as a rebuilding phase, but Stephen wanted to endlessly review the sins of the past.

Finally, I said, "That's it. Enough. I'm sick of this. You, Stephen, have had the best of all possible worlds. Your grandparents helped to raise you and showered you with love. You have a mother and adoptive father who love you and raised you with love, and now your natural parents are together again. You are the luckiest man in the world. You have it all!"

"Oh, really?" Stephen shouted, standing over me. "Then where have you been my whole life?"

I stood to face him and spoke very quietly when I said, "I'm here now, and I'm going to be here for a very long time."

We looked at each other, it seemed, for years. Then Stephen broke down sobbing, I held him in my arms, and Lynn put her arms around us both.

A few weeks later, Stephen invited me to lunch at a seafood place, where we sat on a deck by the bay; munching fish and chips and watching seagulls ride the wind.

"Do you remember," Stephen asked, "The day we met?"

"Of course."

"As I drove out of the airport parking lot, you said, 'How's your mother?'"

"Yes, I did, and you said, 'She's fine. They call her The Silver Fox,' and I laughed."

"That's right," Stephen replied. "When you asked me that, I knew you still loved her. I absolutely knew it, instantly, just from the tone in your voice. Then, when I told Mom about meeting you and she broke down in tears. I knew she still loved you. I thought, my God, what have I done? And now, my parents are getting divorced, and it's all because of the fact that I brought you into our lives! All because of me, but also because of you. You could have been more prudent. You didn't have to ever contact Mom and break up our home."

"That's true. I chose to contact her, but she wanted it, too."

"I'm angry that my wanting to meet my father, something that should have been my birthright, has resulted in my world falling apart, and other peoples' worlds falling apart—not to mention your other children, your ex-wife, all those people have been affected. When I think of all the people whose lives were turned upside down by the fact I wrote one letter...I feel so guilty, just awful. But I'm also angry at you for not controlling all the fallout." He slouched back in his chair, exhausted by his confession.

"Stephen," I said. "Do you really think any force on this earth could have kept your mother and me apart much longer, whether or not you wrote that letter?"

"But I'm the one that brought you together. If I hadn't written that letter..."

"I would have written you."

"You would have?"

"Without a doubt. Stephen. I was waiting until you turned twenty-one. I've been thinking about you and your mother every day of my life for all these years. Is that your fault?"

"No."

"And it isn't your fault your mother and I divorced in the first place, nor is it your fault your mother married Bob, or that she created this mystery around who your father was while you were growing up. All you did was react normally to the difficult position Lynn and I put you in. And I thank you...again...for having the courage to do that."

"I hadn't thought of it that way."

"Don't imagine you're so important, Stephen. There are forces in this world far more powerful than you, or me, or any of us."

We listened to the cries of birds and the lapping of the waves upon the dock supports. Finally, Stephen said, "You know, that wasn't even what I wanted to talk about when I asked you out to lunch."

"It wasn't?"

"No. I wanted to ask you...I don't exactly know how to say this," he said. "But...I'd like to start calling you Dad."

I smiled, and a tear dropped into my tartar sauce. In an instant, Stephen gave me one of the happiest memories of my life.

35

"What are you marrying her, for?" asked my corporate attorney, Paul, combing his hair in one of the many mirrors in his office.

I stopped by Paul's office to take care of the financial arrangements around Lynn's and my impending re-marriage. Only a year previous, I had fought like the devil to place what little remained of my assets into my name only, and now I wanted half of everything transferred to Lynn. Paul—a sad-eyed cynic who had never been in love—tried to warn me of the danger of my actions, though he freely mixed personal opinions with legal advice.

"Lynn's not the woman you want for a third wife. This is the time in a man's life he needs a younger woman," Paul insisted. "Lynn is nearly your age. A man like you can do better."

I smiled. "She's the woman I love," I said. "The woman I have always..."

"What difference does it make?" he interrupted. "One woman is as good as another!"

I laughed uncomfortably, hoping Paul would drop the subject and get down to business.

"Okay, do what you want, Marty," said Paul. "But I'm serious—this time you need a pre-nup, otherwise the bitch is going to take you for everything, just like Barbara."

"No, Paul. I trust her."

"This isn't about trust! It's just good sense. In case this thing doesn't work out, and God knows you divorced this woman once before, didn't you? Do you want to repeat what you just went through with Barbara? How many times do you think you can build back your fortune? You're not invincible Marty. And knowing you, it'll be a woman who takes you down once and for all. That's what they do. They take you for all they can get!"

Paul became passionate as he spoke, spittle flying with each emphatic word. "I've seen it happen too many times before!" he protested. "'We're in love,'" he whined. "'We don't need a pre-nup!' And a couple of years later, what happens? Everyone's scrambling for whatever they can get. Divorce turns couples that 'just couldn't make it work' into couples that hate each other. Stress like that will give you a stroke or cancer or some shit. You want that? Suit yourself."

"I know about that hate," I said. "But this time, it's different."

"Sure it's different. Whatever you say," replied Paul. "I'm just a corporate attorney anyway, I can't do a pre-nup for you, but talk to your divorce attorney, Marcia. Have her prepare a standard contract. All you have to do is fill in the blanks. Numbers for you, numbers for Lynn, everything spelled out. It's easy, and then you go to lunch and forget about it. Trust me, Marty. Fool you once, shame on me... Or however that goes."

I shook my head no, but Paul called me the next day, and the next, pushing the pre-nup idea, admonishing me for making a big mistake. Finally, he got to me. After I had waited decades for her, sworn my undying love to her, turned my life upside down to get her back, I let a man I barely knew convince me to stop trusting Lynn. I still couldn't stand up for her. I still wasn't a man.

I asked Lynn to meet me in the middle of my workday, at our old Italian Restaurant, the one where we had made the pact.

At the table, I said, "I want to talk about a pre-nup."

"You don't trust me?" she asked, straightening up tall in her seat.

"Of course, I do," I said. "This is just a sensible thing to do. You saw what I went through with Barbara."

"You're comparing me to Barbara?"

"Darling, no. Never say that! It's just something you do before getting married, that's all. It's what sensible people do."

"It's what people who don't trust each other do."

"It's a formality, and we'll never look at it again. Please, Sweetheart. My lawyer advised it very strongly, for both our sakes."

Lynn sighed. "I'll have to hire a lawyer to do it. I'm not getting involved."

"Perfect," I said. "Let's have our lawyers prepare the document and keep us out of it as much as possible."

Lynn and I resumed our meal, but things felt different, awkward. Later, when we returned to our cars, we didn't hug goodbye, or kiss.

"I feel like you don't trust me," Lynn said. "I don't like this at all."

The wedding date approached, and just like before, our stress level increased day by day. We planned a simple wedding—just our children and us. But we scheduled a reception dinner, to follow, at our favorite four-star restaurant, Mark's. The guest list swelled to 60, then 70 people. She prepared lists of my friends to invite, lists of her own friends, lists of new friends we had made together. She also made lists of ex-friends to be disinvited: those who no longer spoke to her because of "Poor Bob." That's what everyone called her ex-husband these days.

"You know what, Lynn? I think your father should be there," I said, one day. I had grown tired of avoiding Abner.

"Nice thought," she said, "but he'll never come."

"I'm going to call him," I said.

"You're leaving yourself open, that's all I can say."

When I invited him, Abner simply said, "I'll never do that! Goodbye!" But a few hours later, he called me back, saying, "I want to meet you for lunch. You pick the place."

I met him at Mark's, where I felt comfortable, and waited in my car until I saw Abner go inside. I wanted to make sure he sat there waiting for me a little while. After I joined him, Abner nervously played with his silverware, then asked, "So, where have you been?"

"What a family!" I replied. "You all ask me the same question! You know damn well where I've been and why I've been there!"

I didn't need to explicitly bring up the divorce/adoption/never-contact-Lynn contract and the threats that drove me to sign it. Surely, neither of us would ever forget Abner's dirty secret tricks.

By way of response, Abner looked off into the distance for a while, and then asked, "Are you going to order a drink?"

I did order a drink and we engaged in some idle chitchat, but I didn't waste a lot of time on that. Soon, I said, "Abner, Lynn and I are going to get married. It would make both of us, especially Lynn, very happy if you would attend our reception here in this restaurant."

"Yes, I will," he said. Then, to my astonishment, he added, "If you're worried about me getting along with your parents, don't. I'll be very cordial."

I wanted to ask, "Who are you, and what have you done with Abner Konick?" but I didn't. I just thanked God Abner had finally grown up.

Soon afterward, as Lynn and I planned, Lynn arrived with Abner's new lady friend, Charlotte, an extremely wealthy, thrice-divorced, and, as I would soon learn, uncomfortably direct woman. Lynn squeezed my hand under the table as Charlotte slipped into the chair next to Abner. She beamed and kissed him on the cheek.

Lynn filled me in on the behind-the-scenes drama. "You should have heard Charlotte," she said. "She told me that after Abner hung up the phone with you, she said to him, 'You are a stupid, foolish, old man! Your only daughter is moving to Florida to be with the man she loves, and you are going to shut her out of your life? What is wrong with you? And what about Stephen? Now that his parents are back together, you're going to put a wedge between them? You're terrible! Wake up!' Dad listens to her. I can't believe it, but my father actually listens to someone."

Even as Lynn organized the wedding and reception, she also oversaw the renovations on our beautiful home; bossing workers around with complete authority and asserting her artistic and design sense wherever needed. I had only placed one restriction on the project: no permits. When I renovated that Miami Beach house for Barbara, getting all the necessary permits had slowed everything down tremendously. This time, I wanted our project to quietly proceed with off-duty contractors who could do the construction in record time, without drawing any undue attention.

All year, I worked at my clinic, performing surgery after surgery and coming home exhausted but determined to build back my financial portfolio. Occasionally, my attorney Marcia called me with questions as to the specifics of the pre-nuptial agreement. Contrary to what Paul told me, creating a pre-nup involved far more than filling in a few blanks. Rather, the process entailed negotiating a divorce ahead of time. I assumed Lynn's attorney called her with the same questions, but we never spoke of it. Meanwhile, Paul admonished me frequently that Lynn would try to take me for everything I owned. I didn't want to mistrust her, but when Paul called me a fool, it got to me. I was a sucker for criticism.

Three days before the wedding, I came home from work to find Lynn on the phone, pacing the living room. She hung up and demanded, "What the hell have you and Paul been up to?"

"Darling, what are you talking about?"

"You know what my lawyer just told me? He said, 'I wouldn't sign this pre-nup, and not only that, I wouldn't marry the guy, either!'"

"How dare he!"

"How dare you! Paul insists on no alimony, no equitable distribution. You want to divorce me and leave me penniless? Is that what you have in mind? Revenge? I will not sign this thing, and if you insist, I won't marry you. End of discussion." Lynn grabbed her purse and slammed out the door.

"Paul isn't even handling the pre-nup, Marcia is!" I yelled after her, and then dialed Marcia's number.

"You better come down to my office right away," Marcia said.

At Marcia's office, I discovered Paul's "advisory role" had turned into a full-blown take-over. Woman-hating Paul had been calling meetings without informing Marcia in order to manipulate the pre-nup negotiations.

"The way Paul wants it," Marcia explained, placing the current version of the pre-nup between us on the desk, "is that if you and Lynn divorce within five years, there will be no equitable split, no alimony, nothing. Lynn would be on her own. The longer you stay married, the more the numbers start to even out."

"Yes, I did agree to that," I said. "But I can see how it reads as if I suspected Lynn of being a gold-digger."

"It is worded exactly as if you expected that. At the same time, it's fair. If the two of you are only married a year, there's no reason she should receive half of everything you had before you married her."

"The only reason I've got any money at all is because of Lynn and how she helped me through my divorce. I couldn't be building back my portfolio like this if I didn't have Lynn to come home to every day. Everything I have, as far as I'm concerned, is already due to her. It's already hers."

"Well...I think we should call Paul, then," Marcia suggested, though she hesitated to reach for the phone. "He has been taking a very hard stance on the deal, almost as if he had a personal stake in it."

On the phone with Marcia, Paul launched into a diatribe. "Not only does she not get alimony within the first five years, but I want you to write in a clause regarding all gifts. All gifts revert to Marty. Lynn can't go around claiming those as hers! Write it!"

"I don't think Marty wants to do that," replied even-tempered Marcia.

"Marty? He doesn't know what's good for him! He's in love. He's in no position to say. That's why he has me. Don't you know Lynn is exactly the type of woman who wants to take you for everything? Oh yeah, she'll screw him up, down, and sideways. I can see that type a mile away! You can't. You're a woman. You don't see it." Paul yelled so loudly Marcia had to hold the receiver away from her ear. I could hear everything he said.

Finally, I realized that crazy bastard Paul harbored a personal vendetta against women. What started out sounding like a simple formality had turned into a horrible assault on Lynn and also Marcia. I picked up the pre-nup, tore it in half, and then took the phone from Marcia. Paul continued to scream about my incompetence to run my own life.

"Paul, my heart and my brain are both telling me this is a mistake," I said. "I have ripped up the papers. I trust Lynn completely, and there will be no pre-nup."

"You are out of your goddamn mind!" Paul shot back. "Put Marcia on!"

Marcia shook her head, so I said. "Marcia doesn't have anything to add. I'll speak to you some other time," and hung up.

Marcia collapsed into her chair with a huge sigh of relief.

"Thanks for all you've done, Marcia," I said. "But I have to go to Lynn, now. She is distraught."

I raced out the door, but not before stopping to scoop the pieces of the pre-nup into a manila envelope. Back at our apartment, Lynn, thank goodness, had returned. She sat on the bed, crying and talking on the phone to my mother, of all people. Lynn looked at me with hatred and shoved the receiver into my hands.

"Mother?" I said into the phone. "It's Marty. I'm home."

"What is wrong with you?" my mother screamed. "Get some sense in your head!"

"Yes, Mother," I replied. "I hear what you're saying. I'll speak to you later."

Lynn wore the face of a sad tigress—black makeup smears streaked down her wet cheeks into a mottled mask of grief. Curled up like a child now, she sobbed nearly as hysterically as she had that final day in Philadelphia, the day I left her in Abner's incapable hands. Quickly, I brandished the manila envelope, opened it, and poured its contents all over the bed.

"There's our pre-nup," I said. "There isn't one. I want no part of it. Lynn, I'm so deeply sorry from the bottom of my heart for what I have done to you. Trusting Paul was a huge error in judgment. He's a lunatic, and I let myself be guided by him. It took me a while to realize it, but now I know. Lynn, I will never, ever make another important decision without consulting you. We do everything together, from now on."

Lynn continued crying, but now she reached out for me, ready to forgive. I went to her like a condemned man saved from the gallows.

36

My mother and father flew into Miami the next day, and Abner and Charlotte drove down from Palm Beach. Adam came from the University of Pennsylvania, Jonathan took a weekend off from medical school in Philadelphia, Julie came from Philadelphia as well, and of course Elizabeth didn't have to travel at all, she still lived across the bay. Stephen joined us on a break from the jet setting of his travel-agent life, and those of Lynn's friends still on the "in list" flew down from Philadelphia. Even Sheila and Walter came. Two days remained before the wedding, but Lynn had planned several dinners and brunches to entertain the out-of-towners.

That day, we toured everyone through our as-yet-unfinished house, and that night, hosted them for cocktails at our apartment. I watched Abner and my father like a hawk, but they maintained a respectful distance from each other. I also kept my eye on Sheila, who, like Barbara, relished in finding ways to pull focus. Throughout the entire evening, Lynn's propriety and correctness in the face of all hostilities felt like a protective power over me.

Miraculously, no fist fights, shouting matches, or tears sprang up all evening. But at one point, I looked out the sliding glass door and saw Stephen on the balcony, all alone. I joined him, and we looked out over the calm waters of the bay for quite some time.

"How are you doing?" I asked.

"Okay," he replied.

"No, you're not," I said. "What's going on? Talk to me."

"Oh, I was just thinking about how much I missed, not growing up with you," he said. "Just wondering what it would have been like growing up with you from the time I was born. What if you and Mom had stayed together? What if Bob had never come into the picture? What would it have been like to grow up with parents that loved each other as much as you and Mom do? That would have been so different. I understand it's not your fault it didn't happen. It's just weird, and I can't help thinking...what if?"

"Yeah," I said. "I know. I think about that all the time."

"You do?"

"Are you kidding? But I know that even if that had happened, it wouldn't have been all rose petals and rainbows. Today, your mother and I have the maturity to work out our differences. Back then, we didn't. We loved each other, but didn't know how to keep love alive. Now, we do."

"I think she still blames you, a little."

"I know. She also still thinks I'm a wimp. Pop taught her some weird things about what a man is."

"But you love her?"

"Yes, Stephen, I love her now more than ever."

"But, as a family, we're not back at the beginning, are we?"

"No," I said. "We're not. Like you, I've had my own pain, all these years, and nothing is going to erase it. The three of us can't recapture our lost years. Hell, the major players in the drama that caused it are right there in the living room."

"Except Gram."

We looked out over the water, where waves rose intermittently in the moonlight, and I offered up a moment of silence to Mary.

"All I can say," I told Stephen, "is that our family now is bigger than just the three of us. And that's great. We've lived really rich lives and will continue to do so...but you, your mother, and me are a special family within a family, even though, in a way, you and I know each other the least. I'm glad you want to call me Dad, but I want to earn it, too. I want to be there for you and stand beside you in everything that happens in your life. I know some of your anger from your childhood might never go away, but maybe we can reconcile some of it."

"I'm not angry," he said.

"Maybe not now, but it'll come back, and that's okay."

We listened to the gentle lapping of the waves against the sea wall beneath us and felt a breeze on our faces. The water undulated endlessly and effortlessly. Finally, we rejoined the others inside.

Lynn and I and our five grown children assembled in the rabbi's study. In her off-white, Chanel skirt suit, with its long, gossamer jacket, Lynn looked just as radiant as the first time I married her. The rabbi read the same traditional vows we had used before, and we each said, "I do," just like before, but this time, with our children gathered around, I reduced the kissing of the bride to a simple, respectful kiss on the lips. While we stood there, gazing at each other, I realized that Lynn and Marty, the two bright-eyed youngsters who had once marveled at their gift from God—a gift called love—had vanished. In their place stood two different people, grown adults who knew how to fight for love and would never take it for granted again.

In the vestibule afterward, our photographer spent a lot of time getting the children positioned exactly right, but just as he prepared to click the shutter, Julie broke down sobbing.

I whispered to Lynn, "Go to her. Help her."

Lynn grabbed my arm and refused to move or let me move from my place in the photo line-up. "No," she whispered back. "She is going to have to deal with it. Don't encourage her."

That reaction showed Abner's influence on Lynn. She still called me a wimp for wanting to work out every difficulty with the children, and even with her. In this case, since Julie was her daughter, I deferred. The photographer, and all of us, waited nearly half an hour, until Julie wiped away her tears and finally produced a wan smile, then the click of the camera immortalized that moment forever: Lynn's practiced society smile; my furrowed brow; Julie's puffy face. Adam looks away from the camera, as if searching for an exit. Elizabeth's smile appears genuine, but Jonathan's is gigantic and fake, as is Stephen's. My smile looks awkward, though my eyes are brighter than the heavens. Stephen's eyes look empty.

Looking at the photo now, I see Stephen's face contorted in the same artificial grimace I've seen in photos of him with Abner. I wonder what he was trying to cover up that day—was it guilt about bringing us together again, or anger that we ever separated? I realize now that for all five of the children, our humble little marriage ceremony finalized each, Lynn's and my, respective divorce in a way no other event had done. Sure, Stephen could call me Dad and Julie could enjoy weekends with us, but until they heard us say, "I do," the permanence of this change hadn't really hit any of them.

I think Lynn made the right choice in not comforting her daughter: she and I couldn't and wouldn't apologize for anything we had done. Lynn's silence said, "I'm a parent, but I'm a human being, too." No matter what, Lynn and I stood by our right to be happy with one another.

The enormous group of family and friends at Mark's greeted Lynn, me, and the children with tremendous applause. At first, I worried too much to focus on the party. As soon as I entered the restaurant, I turned to my office assistant, Sharon, with furrowed brow, and I think the question in my eyes said it all. I had told her to watch Abner for me, in case he caused trouble. Sharon smiled broadly and gave me a thumbs up sign. Thank God. Abner had been true to his word and behaved cordially toward both my parents. In fact, for the rest of his life, Abner never brought up his old animosity towards my family or me again. I still wouldn't call him a friendly man, but he wiped the slate clean, and that gesture said a lot.

37

Strolling through Madeira, Spain, on our honeymoon, Lynn and I found a strange attraction—a flat-bottomed gondola had been rigged to slide down a narrow, ancient, and very steep cobblestone street. Two men dressed as Venetian gondoliers invited us to step inside the boat. Against strenuous objection, I convinced Lynn to do it. The men ran alongside for a few meters as they pushed the boat, then let go, propelling us down the terrifying slope! Lynn screamed her head off while we careened through the chute of age-worn cobblestones, and I laughed so hard I thought my face would crack open.

After we safely coasted to a stop at the bottom of the street, Lynn embraced me and said, "Only with you, Marty. I would never do such crazy things if it weren't for you."

All the rest of the day, we adventured on the beautiful beach, beside dramatic green mountains dropping straight into the sea. We talked, we kissed, and sometimes we sat in silence. At times, I caught Lynn staring moodily off at the horizon, but I left her to her thoughts.

That night, we dined alfresco at a cliff-top restaurant overlooking the Atlantic. A waiter served us the catch of the day paired perfectly with a dry chardonnay. As soon as he left, Lynn spoke.

"I want a divorce," she said.

"What? What did you say?"

"I want a divorce," she said, again. "This is a mistake."

"I don't believe you, Lynn! Let me remind you of something: we've already done that, and we are never doing it again! What else?"

"Oh, you are rotten!" she said.

"I am not," I said. "I love you. Now, what's going on?"

"I'm afraid!" she admitted.

"It's okay, Lynn. We can be afraid together, okay?"

She stared at the ocean for a while, then looked down at her plate and took a bite of snapper. "Okay," she said. "But I'm still afraid."

I laughed. "A divorce, on our honeymoon! You are too much, Lynn. You are too much!"

Before leaving Miami, Lynn and I let go of our apartment and moved our things into storage, expecting the house to be completely finished when we got home, but we returned to a silent, boarded-up house surrounded by ribbons of yellow, crime-scene tape. Nailed to a palm tree in the yard, a notice informed us the City of Miami Code Enforcement Division had shut down our renovation for lack of building permits.

I kicked the tree, and Lynn burst into tears.

"What are we going to do?" she sobbed. "We have no place to live!"

Standing on the lawn, overlooking piles of bricks, scattered pipes, and a big hole in the roof where the air conditioner should have been, I remembered the cruise on our first honeymoon, when I stayed up all night concocting a romantic tale to tell the cabin steward so we could get a better cabin. I felt this situation required the same level of creativity.

"Don't worry, Gorgeous," I said. "By tomorrow morning, I'll have an idea. For now, let's go check into a hotel."

The next day, I met with the Building Department's chief inspector, a stern little Cuban man with a heavy accent and friendly eyes. He pulled out a thin file containing our paperwork.

"See this?" he said. "You only filed for painting, but I hear it's a lot more than painting going on, and there are no permits for anything else!"

"Oh, my God!" I exclaimed. "I don't believe this!"

"What?" he asked. "What are you talking about?"

"You see, I just got married. It's my third marriage, but I remarried my first wife..." I proceeded to tell him the story of Lynn and me, in a nutshell, and by the end of it, the chief inspector smiled, though still clearly puzzled as to how all this affected the permits. "I'm a dentist, you see," I continued, "and I have a very busy practice, so I told my wife, 'if you want this house you are going to have to take care of all the renovations yourself.' I put the house in her name and everything." Finally, the chief inspector nodded with understanding.

"Oh," he said. "She didn't know what to do!"

"I guess not. I'm so embarrassed!"

Once the chief inspector saw it had all been an innocent mistake by two people so distracted by their whirlwind romance that they couldn't remember to get building permits for their love nest, he said, "Don't worry, don't worry at all. Tell her to come tomorrow and we'll straighten things out."

Back at the house, I told Lynn about my conversation with the chief inspector. "Okay, Lynn. This is what I suggest you do. Are you listening?"

"I'm listening," she answered eagerly, that old mischievous twinkle in her eye.

"You take a bottle of champagne, wrapped up. Keep it concealed when you go in. When you see the chief inspector, pour your heart out to him, give him the champagne. He'll be charmed, you'll see. Everything will be fine."

"But what do I say?"

"Trust your intuition. You'll figure it out."

Bright and early the next morning, Lynn walked into the chief inspector's office and proceeded to tell the man how furiously I yelled at her for her carelessness, and how we now had no place to live. "It's all my fault!" she cried.

"No, no! I don't want you crying," replied the chief inspector. "Let me help you."

He then walked her through the application process, step by step, and she left the office with every single permit we needed. When Lynn came back to our hotel with the story of how she'd spent her day, I laughed so hard I fell off the bed.

"I've never done anything like that in my life!" Lynn exclaimed. Of course not. She hadn't a lying bone in her body, and I loved that about her. But just this once...

Within a couple of months, we finished the house, probably setting a Miami-Dade County record for the speed of such a soup-to-nuts renovation. We restored the house one hundred percent back to its original glory, and Lynn managed the whole thing herself. She learned about electrical systems and plumbing and cabinets and foundations and loved every minute of it. I felt glad we had this in common, now—a love for reviving the glory and spirit of beautiful, abandoned homes. That was us, all right: Lost Causes Incorporated.

During the final renovations, Lynn and I attended an antique show looking for pieces for the house. While she shopped in another booth, I secretly bought something magnificent I'd found—an 18-carat gold, antique key. I picked out an antique doorknob for the front door, then had a locksmith cut the key specially to fit. I even had a jeweler engrave Lynn's name on the key.

The day we finally moved in, I surprised Lynn by picking her up and carrying her over the threshold..

"I have something for you," I said next, and brought out a velvet box. Inside, she found her key and screamed with delight.

"It's a gold key to our house—our first house together," I said.

"I love it, Marty," Lynn said, through tears of joy. "How do you think of these things?"

"Darling," I said, taking her in my arms. "With you, it comes naturally."

I looked around our home at the high ceilings, broad archways, and shining wooden details. I gazed out the windows at a yard Lynn had expertly designed with climbing vines and flowering shrubs that already looked at ease, as if they had been growing there for decades. Our single bayside acre bloomed joyously, like a barely tamed wild thing, reminding me of my astrologer Ginger's magnificent garden.

What had Ginger told me so long ago, I wondered, during my dark days with Barbara? "You will marry again," I remembered, "but to the same person." To think how crazy that had seemed at the time. Against all the odds, though, it came true. But I remembered Ginger also warned me about a pattern: I find Lynn in every lifetime, and then I leave her. Sure enough, I'd left her decades ago, but this time, I got her back. I ended the pattern. Now, Lynn and I could complete the unfinished business of living out our love forever and ever, unto death. All I had to do was never leave her again.

38

"Are you ready?" I asked Lynn one evening as I selected a shirt and tie, preparing to head out for dinner and a symphony concert. Our marriage held strong, so far, for almost exactly a year.

"What do you mean? We have an hour," she replied, still in her jeans.

"Darling, our reservations are at six."

"No, they're at seven."

"Sweetheart, they're at six."

"How can you be so sure of yourself?" she asked, turning red. "You always think you're right! They're at seven!"

"Because I'm always right, that's why," I joked, but my joke only made her angry, so I added, "I remember making them at six, because the symphony starts at eight thirty."

"And I remember telling you we don't need two and a half hours to eat, for God's sakes!"

"We don't need to scream at each other, Lynn. Six or seven, who cares? It's just dinner."

"You think you're so smart. You always get everything right, don't you?"

"I am smart, but why does it piss you off so much? Let's just keep it simple: from now on, I get two votes and you get one. There'll be no more arguments, okay?" I could never resist teasing her at the exact wrong moment.

Lynn screamed in rage. "I've had enough!" she shouted. I followed her into the kitchen with my shirt still unbuttoned and a tie in my hand, but she strode back into the bedroom and emerged with an overnight bag. "I can't take this anymore! How did I ever get talked into marrying you?" she shouted as she slammed out the front door. I heard her car peel out of the driveway.

She didn't return all night, and I didn't sleep.

After a little snooping around, I discovered Lynn had left behind her make-up kit and even her wallet. I don't know what she packed in that case, but it wouldn't get her very far. She could have stayed overnight at any number of friend's houses, but I knew Lynn would grow furious if I called around asking for her, so I summoned patience and waited.

Lynn and I fought often, just like in our first marriage. I still mouthed off like the smart aleck and control freak I was, and she still excavated every nook and cranny of a conversation for slights against her. So far, we always worked things out, though. Our fights never progressed to the point of either of us leaving overnight, or even going to bed angry. Until that day.

The next morning, I decided not to go into work and resolved to wait around the house until Lynn came back, even if it took days, but she didn't hold out that long. I was still sipping my morning coffee when I heard the door open.

"Oh!" she said. "I thought you'd be at work."

"I took the day off. I thought we could spend some time together."

"I'm sorry I flew off the handle," she said, putting down her bag. "Do you forgive me?"

"Of course, Sweetheart. I love you. But let's talk about what's bothering you."

"Okay. Can we go to Key Biscayne?" she asked, with a girlish smile.

Soon, we curled our toes into the sand beneath an avenue of palms, before a bright ocean. "Okay," I said. "Maybe the reservations were at seven."

"Who cares about the reservations," she said. "It's just your attitude. So sure of yourself all the time. Can't you once in a while say, 'Gee, maybe you're right. I could be wrong. There is an outside chance that maybe in a hundred years I could be wrong!'"

"Maybe I could be wrong. Maybe I could be wrong. Maybe I could be wrong," I repeated experimentally. "Nope. Don't like the taste of it in my mouth. Feels prickly."

"I swear, you're impossible," she said, but her anger had abated. "And Stephen's just like you. Always making a joke out of everything. Drives me crazy."

"But I love you," I said. "And that's no joke."

Lynn sighed. "That's another part of the problem," she said. "I feel like you don't know me. You love me, but it isn't real, because you don't know me. Not really."

212

"How can you say that?" I asked, reeling at the notion. I felt I knew Lynn like a part of my own body.

"Do you remember when we first met again, in New York, at the Park Lane, and I told you about my affairs when I was married to Bob?"

"Don't remind me of that. I don't want to know about you being with other men. Some things you can keep to yourself!"

"That's just it, Marty. There are a lot of things about me that aren't nice and that I'm ashamed of. But I'm tired of keeping secrets and feeling like this marriage will be over when you find out about my family, everything, and me. I can keep up appearances in public, Marty, but not with you, not in private. I want you to know the truth, even if it's the end."

Her words seemed to propel Lynn into the ocean. She ran away from them, and me, and soon stood in the water, up to the rolled-up hems of her jeans. Then she walked further in, all the way up to her knees. The open collar of her linen shirt fell to one side, and Lynn looked back at me over a bare, freckled shoulder.

I waded out to meet my wife and held her in my arms. A school of tiny fish whooshed around our ankles and away. "Tell me, then," I said. "Tell me everything."

"It starts with my father," she said. "He beat us, you know. We never spoke of it, but at the least provocation he would make me or my brothers lie spread-eagled and beat us with a belt. Me, especially. Thank God he was gone all week in Delaware, because when he used to come home on the weekends, he just beat us and yelled at me and my brothers and my mom. Frequently, he left us bleeding. We kept it a secret."

"Darling, I'm so sorry."

"What's most disturbing is that he really enjoyed beating us. It put a smile on his face. Over the years, I've worked on forgiving him, but it isn't easy. Of course, everything had to look good to the public. My mother was determined to keep up the façade of a happy family, so we always pretended everything was normal. Oh, she acted dignified, like she had some power, but Mother had nothing. We were all completely controlled by my father. Even when he wasn't home, he controlled us, because if a single thing was out of order when Dad got back, we'd all have hell to pay."

Lynn locked eyes with me. A wave gently washed up and wetted us to the thighs, but we didn't move. "This went on practically up until the day I met you," she said. "When I started dating, I guess he decided I was too old to beat. I don't know. Or when they saw you, I guess Mom and Dad decided I was worth something after all."

I held her tighter, not knowing what to say. I wasn't surprised to hear these things about Abner, but I never imagined how much darkness lay beneath the surface of the Konick household.

"My mother followed suit," Lynn continued. "When no one else was around, she treated my brothers and me like garbage. You want to know what kind of mother Mary was? One time when I was a kid, I was sick, but she made me come down to dinner anyway. I tried to eat but vomited right there at the table. You know what she did? She spooned up my puke and made me eat it, shouting at me all the while. That's how it was in our house."

With Lynn holding tightly to my t-shirt, we turned back toward shore and slogged gracelessly through the knee-deep water, but the ocean sent in another wave to throw us off-balance. While we steadied ourselves, Lynn didn't gasp or complain, just clung to me even more tightly, and shouted over the wave's thunder. "After our divorce, my mother and father wouldn't give me a penny! Not one penny of support or help, with all the money they had! Once Stephen was born, Dad kicked me out of the house on my own—to punish me for not holding onto my husband!"

"But your father didn't want you to hold onto me. He kicked me out of the house, first!" I replied. We took advantage of the receding waterline and dashed for dry land.

"All the same," gasped Lynn, as she sat, exhausted, on the sand. "Dad said the divorce was all my fault and I had to be punished. Mom seemed to think so, too, or else she just went along with it, like always. They bought Stephen whatever he wanted and took care of him while I was at work. They adored him. In the meantime, they never spoke to me. Never. My mother picked up Stephen from my apartment every weekday morning, before I went to work. She just showed up and took him from me silently. At the end of the day, she silently gave him back, as if I were nothing but an overnight wet-nurse. That was our interaction for many years, until they moved to Florida."

"Oh God, Oh God," I muttered, my head in my hands, tortured by the thought of Lynn going through such isolation while I lived only hours away, longing for her and Stephen with every breath in my body.

Lynn picked up a seashell and flung it into the water. "As you've noticed, my father and Stephen became very close over the years," she said. "That worked out well for Dad. He rejected me, who he considered a useless daughter, and gained a wonderful grandson. I bet he thought it was a great trade. Stephen's smart, good-looking, affable—everything you are, too. It was like Dad finally got to have a version of you he could control. In fact, at Mom's funeral, afterwards, when everyone gathered at the house, Dad told everyone Stephen was the son he had always wanted. He said that right in front of my brothers."

I shook my head, realizing my assessment of Abner as a very sick man hadn't been off the mark.

"My brothers and I never measured up," Lynn added, contemplatively. She reached between her bent knees to dig a hole in the wet sand. A wave quickly washed in, filled the hole, and got us even wetter, but we both just sat there, at the mercy of the sea. Lynn added, "We were completely unloved, you know, until you came along and my mother started trying to live vicariously through us. The European honeymoon and all that. Oh God, you know what else my father said at my mother's funeral?" Lynn dug her hole deeper, deeper, as if a solution to Abner's cruelty lay buried there. "Of course, he was drunk. He stood up in the living room surrounded by our family and friends, and said, 'My wife, she had the tightest pussy there was!'"

"Good God!"

"I'm not kidding. That's all the value he saw in her. Not a wonderful wife and mother, not a caring person, not her elegance and grace and style—just a tight pussy. And he thought it was a compliment! But my father loves Stephen. Oh, boy. Everything else aside, when Stephen was born, Dad became grandfather of the year. I couldn't complain. I needed the help."

Lynn stopped digging, looked into my eyes, and held me tightly. I wrapped my arms around her and felt her skin's warmth beneath the chill of the sea spray. "Of course," she went on. "My father brainwashed Stephen against you throughout his childhood. Though I wasn't much better, to be honest. I was very angry."

"I know. I understand, now."

"I'm sorry," Lynn said. "But there's more."

"Go ahead," I said.

"After Dad kicked me out, I became a paralegal. It's just a secretary. I had no education to speak of. I dated a lot of lawyers but always took Stephen on my dates. If we went out to dinner, it was the three of us. I told the guys we were a package deal from the start. Most of them didn't want to put up with that." She buried her face in my neck as she continued the story, muffling her words. "But there was one guy who acted like he didn't mind," she said. "A lawyer. He seemed very sweet at dinner. Well, he invited me to a weekend skiing in Vermont, so I left Stephen with my parents that time and I went. Somehow, while we were there, he drugged me. It must have been during dinner. That night, while I was unconscious, he raped me, sodomized me, everything you can imagine. I woke up later, all alone, in horrible pain, in this hotel room." She began to cry, and I held her tighter. "I was all by myself, with no way back. I got myself to the hospital."

I let go of her, then, because my stomach cramped. I had to curl up in a ball, my head on my knees, and weep. "Lynn," I whispered. "Lynn, Lynn, Lynn..." I continued saying her name, as if by claiming her I could take away the past. Despite the troubles I had had in my life, I maintained a sense of myself as always in control, taking care of others, capable, but in that moment I realized how I really floundered in the world, small and helpless. I couldn't go back in time and take care of Lynn, couldn't make her memories go away, but had to face all that had happened after I left her. I became a helpless child in the face of it.

"There were a lot of bad incidents," she said. "But that was the worst. I dated a lot of assholes."

We sat in silence a long time, and the tide slowly went out. My stomach cramp eased with it.

"Guess what?" I asked.

"What?"

"I still love you. More than ever, in fact."

"Good," Lynn said. "I feel a lot better, now."

"You can tell me anything you need to, Lynn," I said, wiping sand off her cheek. "I don't want you to feel like there's any part of your life that could take my love for you away. I will love you until I die. I promise you that before God."

"I will love you until I die, too," she said. "Forever."

"Prove it," I said, standing and pulling her up with me. "Match me. I say, 'You're my girl,' what do you say to that?"

"You're my guy," she answered, finally smiling.

"I love you with all my heart," I said.

"I love you with all my soul," she replied. "But sometimes I hate you, too, when you're bossy."

"Sometimes we hate each other," I said, kissing her. "So what?"

"You know what's weird?" she asked, as we strolled along the shoreline once more. "Whenever I feel bad, I like to come to the beach with you. It's my favorite thing."

"What's weird about that?"

"Because sometimes you're the reason I'm feeling bad. But I still want to come here with you."

I put my hand up under her shirt's thin fabric and squeezed Lynn around the waist. "I'm glad," I said. I tried to hold her close, but she jumped up and broke away, suddenly exuberant.

"You know what, Marty?" she exclaimed. "I'm happy!"

"Already?"

"Yes! I want to run!"

"Go for it!" I replied.

As Lynn dashed away from me, her heels kicked sand every which way. She reached skyward, like a bird about to take to the air, and let her hands flop around at the ends of her arms. I heard the clatter of her wooden bracelets, like witch doctors' rattles. Then, without breaking momentum, she pivoted and ran back toward me, now pumping her arms, setting a determined stride. She wasn't just running free anymore; she had something in mind.

"Lynn? No! No, don't!"

"I am!" she screamed, and then leapt into my arms—legs thrown up, head thrown back, full of trust.

I caught her, and we fell back into the sand just as a wave washed up and drenched us both. She shrieked with joy and I laughed, relieved that our day had come to this.

I kissed her sandy lips and said, "You're my gal, Lynn. No matter what."

Her arms, tight around my neck, silently matched me.

I had done it, finally, I thought to myself. It had taken so very many years but I had done it. I had become the man she wanted me to be. She no longer needed her father to turn to. I was the man she needed. This confessional proved it. And I felt that we were finally the unit we were meant to be, Lynn and Marty, stronger than the sum of their parts. I simply held the her close...the man in her life.

39

"Marty, this is Dr. Gutierrez," said the man on the phone. I already didn't like his tone. "Are you sitting down?"

"What difference does that make? Do you have the cytology report?" I asked, pacing the living room.

"Yes, I do. It's bad news," he replied. "That little lump in your neck is no pea, it's a melanoma. I'm not going to sugar coat this, Marty. It's the deadliest cancer you can get."

When I first heard the diagnosis there was not only a literal lump in my throat but also a metaphorical lump. How could this be happening? How could I, we, be being punished like this? Had we had two bites of the forbidden fruit and this was just too much for the fates to allow? I thought of Ginger, the astrologer. Had I heard her wrong? Had she talked about my and Lynn's love being once again destined to be unfulfilled? Was I to be leaving her once again? The doctor repeated himself "the deadliest cancer you can get" and then Ginger's words rang cacophonous in my ears. In every lifetime, you always find her...but you leave her in the end.

Once again, I swore it wouldn't happen.

By 2005, Lynn and I had enjoyed trips around the world, renovated and decorated numerous houses, buried both my parents, seen all our children married, and become grandparents seven times over. I had recently retired due to cervical radiculitis, a genetic disorder that came upon me very suddenly. The disease caused uncontrollable tremors in my hands. I hated the tremors, but loved retirement and the chance to spend more time with Lynn. To celebrate this new phase of life, we moved to Santa Fe, New Mexico, a beautiful, high desert town where we could immerse ourselves in art, opera, theater, and the symphony to our hearts' content. Living there felt like paradise. I thought life couldn't be more perfect. Now, this.

Lynn had gone downtown to run errands that day, but I needed to see her right away. This being the age of cell phones, I called her, asking, "Where are you right now?"

Puzzled and clearly alarmed by the desperate tone in my voice, she told me she was driving to visit one of our friends. "Do you want to meet me there?" she asked.

"Not inside," I answered. "Outside on the sidewalk."

I jumped in the car and raced through winding lanes to Santa Fe's quaint Acequia Madre district, where fallen yellow leaves spotted the ground in front of tiny, 200-year-old adobe homes, and a stream trickled through a rock-lined chute, bringing life to the desert. As promised, Lynn waited in front of our friend's garden gate, bundled up in an overcoat. I skidded the car to a stop on the narrow street, and when I got out, realized I had forgotten a coat and even my boots. I faced Lynn, standing in my house slippers in the cold and wet.

"The lump," I said. "It's a melanoma. It's practically a death sentence."

Lynn burst into tears, as did I. While I held her, I swore, "I won't die. I won't leave you alone. I refuse. I will fight this. I swear I won't leave you."

I simply didn't think Lynn could go on living without me, not with any modicum of happiness. Our souls and lives had twined together completely by now.

The very next day, we flew to the John Wayne Cancer Institute in Santa Monica, California. There, I underwent a neck resection, but the cancer spread. In late October, we returned for more surgery, then again in November.

In late December, we returned to California for more surgery on New Year's eve, 2006, Lynn snuck me out of the hospital so I could take her to dinner. I couldn't keep down a thing, but we tried to pretend to dine like it was the old days, knowing this might be our last outing, ever.

"Remember that pact we made?" I asked. "Love unto death?"

"Sure I do, but it doesn't matter, because you're not going to die," Lynn replied matter-of-factly, as if she were describing the color of the walls.

Within the next couple of months, I returned to the hospital for a fifth surgery, then a sixth. Each time the treatment failed, I asked the doctors, "Okay, what do we do next?" Luckily, the doctors always provided a next option, another thing to try, even though each "next" escalated into a more painful, risky, and invasive procedure than the last. I never considered giving up, though. I had to survive for Lynn. We lived as one heart, one soul.

As the treatment progressed, our five children rallied around us, visiting often, helping to change my dressings, and doing everything they could. To my oncologists, I chanted, "What's next? What's next?" like a mantra, month in and month out.

Lynn took on the same warrior role she had used to encourage me during my divorce from Barbara—always cheerful and smiling. After that day on the sidewalk, I never saw her cry. Every time I came out of surgery, I viewed Lynn's beautiful face before anything else and felt her kiss. When our out-of-pocket expenses piled up, Lynn sold the securities from our portfolio. Just like when she renovated that termite-riddled house in Miami, she took control, managed everything, and never entertained the notion that this endeavor could be a lost cause.

She mothered me, too, in the same strict but loving way I had seen her act with the children. "You have to get up and walk," Lynn told me, many times. "You need your exercise." Then she would swing my legs over the side of the bed, put her arm around my back, and say, "Up we go. No arguments." Lynn continually found new ways to cheer me up. She combed my hair, manicured my nails, and when she helped me into the shower, she disrobed and got in there with me, "to make sure I didn't fall." Florence Nightingale had nothing on my wife.

During the ensuing months and my seventh, and eighth surgeries, Lynn morphed into a beautiful head nurse who changed my surgical drains, checked my dressings, examined every diagnostic report with the aplomb of a seasoned physician, and advocated for me endlessly. If my lunch arrived late, Lynn put out an alert. If a doctor visited with less than complete test results, Lynn sent him marching to fetch the information we needed. Lynn inspired both love and fear up and down the halls of that hospital every time we came for one of our "visits."

And before each surgery, Lynn held my hand while I recited my prayer:

Holy Spirit, lord of life, from thy clear celestial height, please hear my voice. Let your pure beaming radiance shine upon Lynn and me, and let the warmth of your healing light penetrate within me.

Each time I survived another surgery, my doctors shook their heads with amazement. The cancer kept on spreading, but somehow I stayed alive. I had to, for Lynn. I quickly lost my good looks, what with all the carving away at my neck, but Lynn never noticed. "Look at you, you're going to be fine!" she would say. "The pink is coming back into your cheeks!" Lynn told the doctors, "He won't die. He wouldn't dare leave me."

She seemed completely confident, but I thought deep down, Lynn must know it's over. I hoped beneath all the optimism and cheerleading, she also prepared herself, emotionally, for my inevitable death.

I later learned that, as the bills for Lynn's hotel rooms and miscellaneous expenses piled up, she sold off our artwork and her jewelry. These were just things, of course, but we had acquired them for each other through our travels over the past decade and a half. Each item was a heartfelt gift from one of us to the other—a memento of some special moment. If I had known, I would have been heartbroken over these losses, but Lynn took care of everything quietly, ensuring I could continue to stay in the best hotels, get the best care, and not think about finances.

Julie flew out to sit with Lynn during many of my surgeries, none of which lasted fewer than seven hours. She told me much later that despite the smiles Lynn showed me before and after, Lynn cried hysterically every time they rolled me into that operating room. But around me, Lynn sparkled like a font of optimism. I guess all Mary's training in "keeping up appearances" had some value after all, because Lynn's bright attitude kept me fighting.

Finally, Lynn sold a painting from our living room—one she knew I would miss. She checked that sale with me, first.

"My love," I said. "You don't have to do this. After I die, there will be plenty of money, and you'll be okay." I had already calculated that with my life insurance, I carried more value dead than alive.

"Marty! Stop that talk!" she reprimanded. "You're not going to die. Do you hear me? You are the strongest willed and most stubborn person I have ever met. Nothing can defeat you, and you're not going anywhere until you are ready to go. Got it? Now, I don't want to hear any more of this because it upsets me."

I smiled. "I guess you really do like me," I said.

"Marty, this is a very serious conversation," she replied. "You're going to be sixty-eight years old, and when are you going to grow up?"

"This is as grown up as I'm going to get. I'm happy this way. I hope you're not still trying to remake me," I replied. The conversation had drained my feeble energy reserves, but I added, "What you see is what you got, Lynn. I love you, though."

Then, in August of 2006, eleven months after the whole ordeal began, I received a lucky break by qualifying as a candidate for a phase-three, clinical-trial antibody: an experimental drug still in the pipeline for FDA approval. Bristol-Meyers only accepted one-hundred-and-fifty people worldwide to receive this antibody; but the doctors warned me if it did save my life, the antibody would leave me with potentially life-threatening side effects.

I said, "Let's do it!"

I harbored no fantasies about letting go and accepting a peaceful death. I wanted to live under any circumstances whatsoever, for Lynn. I couldn't face her living the rest of her life with a broken heart.

The drug eradicated the melanoma from every area of my body except my left lung. I also ended up with ulcerative colitis, one of the predicted side effects of the drug, so I had to stay in the hospital through January, when we finally scheduled a ninth surgery, where the doctors planned to remove the lung. While we awaited the date, Abner, back in Palm Beach, died from leukemia. Although I encouraged her to go, Lynn skipped the funeral. She didn't want to leave my side.

Ten days later, they removed my left lung. That very week, I called a meeting in my hospital room and said, "I'm checking out!" While my thoracic surgeon gasped, my primary oncologist, who knew me well, laughed his head off. They agreed I could recuperate for another week in a wonderful hotel, Casa del Mar, which was right on the ocean. Relieved to be out of the hospital, Lynn and I took rejuvenating walks along the beach before finally returning home.

Every three months afterward, Lynn and I returned to Santa Monica for three days of hours-long tests including blood draws, CAT scans, MRIs, eye exams, and everything else imaginable. I had become an old man overnight, and the stress of these tests brought me to the brink of collapse, but Lynn, still a spry young woman of sixty-three, ushered me through each one with verve.

She always said, "Marty, it's going to be okay. It'll all be over in a couple of hours. They won't find anything."

"Promise?" I'd ask.

"I promise!" she used to reply with a smile. Oh God, I remember looking at her radiant smile, thinking how can Lynn be more gorgeous now than ever before? She grew more beautiful every day, as if by some enchanted spell.

Each grueling day of tests began at seven a.m. and went on until the afternoon. Tension always remained high until the afternoon of the third day, when Lynn sat, holding my hand, in the same oncologist's office where once upon a time we heard, "Well...we've had a setback," time and time again. But with each three-month check-up, miraculously, the doctor now told me, "Marty, your scans are great. Everything is fine!" I still stayed at the hospital though, sometimes for weeks, because of the colitis. It twisted me in knots, but, as unpleasant as it was, colitis wouldn't kill me, so I felt I could bear it.

Lynn and I decided to do everything we wanted to do before the cancer returned, so we booked passage on cruises all over the world, returning every three months to Santa Monica for that awful battery of tests. After a year, the doctors reset the tests to six-month intervals, so Lynn and I got to have even more fun during the in-between times. On our cruises, we talked about my death a lot. When the cancer returned, my doctors would not find much tissue left to carve out of me, so that would be the end. I wanted to discuss every issue—financial, emotional, legal, and spiritual—so I could rest assured about Lynn's future happiness.

One morning Lynn and I lounged by the pool, enjoying the sunrise. "You know," she said, "in all our discussions, you've never told me where you want to be buried."

"Buried? Who cares? Oh God, I'm tired of talking about me all the time and my death. Let's talk about you. Where do you want to be buried?"

"What are you talking about? I'm healthy as a horse."

"Okay, but when you die, what do you want?"

"Well, I don't want to be buried near your parents!" she replied, spicy as ever.

"I understand that," I said. "Neither do I, actually."

"I want to be cremated," she added. "But if you want to be buried with your parents and family, that's okay with me."

"No," I said. "I want to be with you...Lynn, does anyone know about this? Your wishes?"

"Oh, Stephen will take care of it," she said.

"Have you ever discussed it with him?" I asked, and she admitted she hadn't. "I want you to write these things down. I won't be here when you die, so somebody has to know what to do. What about a funeral?"

"I don't want to talk about this!"

"Please, Lynn. What do you want?"

She sighed, leaned back in the chair so the morning sun could fall on her lightly freckled shoulders, and answered. "I don't want any kind of big deal. I want poetry and our favorite music played. That's all."

"Put it in writing. Please do that so I know you'll be taken care of to the end." Then I added, "You know what I want? I want my ashes mixed with yours and we'll give Stephen instructions on where to scatter them."

"Okay," she replied, "Whatever you want. Now, can we talk about something else?"

"Sure."

"Wait," she added suddenly. "I have an idea. You know what I want when I die? I want a memorial fund set up that contributes to the arts. Something that would let children see shows and concerts at a really great theater. To nurture the next generation of artists."

"That's nice. That's a great thought. Put it in writing, okay?"

"Okay, I will...later," Lynn replied as she slathered on sunscreen, picked a mimosa from a waiter's tray, then took out a book to enjoy another perfect day—each sunrise, more than ever now, a gift.

40

March 2011

"You always told me I wrote you such great letters," I told her. "Well I have a gift for you."

"What is it?" she asked, as if the trip was not gift enough.

After all the efforts the doctors had put in, the experimental medications, the numerous operations to keep the cancer at bay and tireless support of Lynn, I was finally feeling as if I may just beat this thing or, at least, keep it at bay for some time to come. As a result of these monumental efforts to reach this stage, both Lynn and I were exhausted and needed a break. We decided we would take a trip. Not just any trip but the journey of a lifetime. We settled on a safari. I immediately saw the irony in the fact that we were about to enter a new stage in our own lives by traveling to an old world and I had an epiphany—that this may just be the last of our physical journeys and the start of a new adventure, a more spiritual journey. And I wanted to express this sudden and newfound understanding in the best way possible, the written word. So I sat down and wrote Lynn a letter and mailed it for her to receive once we returned home—a sort of punctuation after this trip of a lifetime.

"So what is this gift?" she pushed.

"Well, it is a letter. But I have mailed it to you and you won't get it until after we get home. I think it expresses my new lease on life and the way I want us to move forward from the point when we get home on through for the rest of our lives. For the first time in a long time, I believe we have a lot of life to live."

Dearest Lynn,

When you read this letter, I believe we will be at the end of one journey and the beginning of a new one. Most recently, we will have crossed the Equator, come face to face with beasts both wild and endangered; engaged with foreigners, strangers and met new friends;

crossed arid sands, lush gardens, mighty seas and tranquil waters. Because of this and journeys past, we will have seen the world...but moreover, found our place in it. And that place is right here, where we stand, side by side, with each other. I truly have enjoyed our travels but both of us know they have included times of avoidance as well as the desperate search for the fountain of youth. Well, while I appreciate a vacation here and there and the occasional trip to far off lands...I believe we can stop searching. For we have found what we have been looking for—the love of one another.

Yes, you could say we found that love some decades ago buried within the lust of youth. Ours was a pure love—like none I'd seen then nor none I've seen since. I truly believe you love—really love—but once. And you are mine. Ours was meant to be. But ours was set up to fail by the very people we turned to for support. Our only mistake back then was naiveté. How were we to know that the only examples of family foundation were fundamentally flawed—that their idea of love wasn't love but loyalty and obligation, fealty and servitude. There was no feeling and emotion but rather a bitter cycle of resentment and anger.

I was told I wasn't a man, back then, and as such I didn't deserve the love of my life. And, truth be told, I wasn't a man. A real man would have stood and fought or died trying. When my love was ripped from me, both wife and child, I didn't fight. I didn't deserve the love that was meant to be, that was fated in the astrological stars. Instead, I retreated to the cyclical world I had grown up in, the very world that had just ripped the love from my arms and heart—an emotionless, empty world in which I was allowed to function but not flourish. For 21 years I lived in that world, never forgetting what I had given up and the price I paid for doing so.

I mentioned a second journey, my dearest Lynn, and that begins now. For what stands before you is the man you always wanted and the man I was meant to be. And what stands before me is the completed woman—confident and strong, no longer "daddy's little girl" unable to speak for herself...in fact, under no man's control...not even me! But moreover, we are a whole stronger than the sum of our parts. No one gets a second chance...or so they say. But we, it seems, have won some cosmic lottery—the same lottery that brought us together all those years ago across a college campus. We have been given that second chance. And it is what we do with it that matters most.

These past twenty plus years together have been magical, a honeymoon to rival our first. But there must be more to this almost unbelievable, inconceivable coming together of two hearts. We have children—one together and several apart—but we did not do our duty to them. We did not break the cycle of being raised in loveless atmospheres with flawed parents. And for that, I will always be sorry. For the chain has not been broken...until now.

I have had an epiphany. We have found a rare and fundamental love and love needs to lead by example. Not only can we be better, more loving and understanding parents, unlike the parents we have, but also we can spread this love to others. By the time you read this letter, we will be back from this latest adventure. And it will be time start a new adventure based not on the love we've shared between us but the love we can share with others. It is time we spend our money, time and energy giving back for the gifts we have been given. I once said to you before we were married that maybe we had to go through our worlds to make the world a better place. Well the time is now. You have often spoken about supporting the local arts and, especially, encouraging, youth in the arts...well that is a start. What better way to be both a mother and a lover than the support of youth in the arts?

Oh, my dear Lynn, I feel life a new just thinking about the possibilities of what we have ahead—no longer prematurely mourning the loss we thought we'd face but rather celebrating so much living we have ahead. Yes, ours will eventually be a story that comes to an end. But I am determined that ours, above all others, will be the story with the happiest of endings.

Your loving partner in life,
Marty

41

I clutched Lynn's hand for dear life as the tiny, tin can of an airplane buzzed away from Johannesburg, over South Africa's vast green and gold landscape, and finally to a dirt airstrip set in the middle of a vast savannah. Our private plane touched down, and when we stepped outside, Lynn and I gasped at the oppressive heat. Dylan, our safari guide, and Andrew, our tracker, emerged from a hut to meet us. Then, we all climbed into a Range Rover and headed for the a safari camp in the northeast corner of Kruger Park.

Lynn and I clamped our lips shut, trying as hard as we could to remain quiet and still as Andrew insisted, but when a herd of giraffe crossed our path, we couldn't help but cry out in delight. Never did we imagine we'd actually be here, on safari, viewing these near-mythical creatures in the wild. Later on that ride, seeing Lynn's eyes get round as tennis balls, and when I looked where she pointed, a mother lion suckled her cub mere meters away. By the time we reached the safari camp itself, we had already spotted Africa's big five game animals.

While Andrew helped me out of the vehicle, he shook his head in disbelief. "You two are very lucky. Some people spend weeks here and might be lucky if they see one large cat the entire time. I can't believe the trip we just had. It's not always like that, not at all."

Andrew deposited Lynn and me at the resort's main clubhouse, a steel-and-glass marvel of modern engineering designed to keep us safe and comfortable in Africa's 100-plus degree weather. There, from a tree-shaded, open-air pavilion, we ordered drinks from a friendly hostess who informed us that, situated on a 50,000-acre reserve, the safari camp stood hundreds of miles from anything remotely resembling civilization, yet the bar and restaurant offered everything our hearts could desire.

Our villa, like the others, perched cantilevered over the side of a large hill. At the base of the hill, a watering hole welcomed elephants, giraffes, monkeys, lions…an endless stream of wildlife we could watch from a wall of windows. I have never seen anything like this house, before or since. It contained every modern, luxurious, and sleek design element, while standing way out there, among the monkeys and the zebras, looking completely incongruous. Mosquito netting shrouded the bed and sofa, and outdoors, the netting also encompassed a day bed. We could even sleep on the porch if we wanted, in the open air, because of how high the house stood off the ground. The notion that, even at this stage of my life, I could still enjoy an African safari in so much safety and comfort—made me so happy.

One could not leave the buildings at night. When ready for dinner, Lynn and I called the clubhouse and someone came to get us in a Range Rover. Our guide Andrew emphasized several times the importance of following this and all the rules of the lodge.

"People who don't follow these rules can and do get attacked by predator animals," he told us. "It's not just a precaution. There is serious danger, here. On other safaris, not here, but where the resort rules are more lax, it has happened that a tourist will disappear, never to be seen again."

Andrew tried to warn us about every potential danger, but in truth he didn't know every danger. In a place like that, no one can know everything that lurks in the bush.

Our guide's keen eye and tracker's expert skills ensured Lynn and I enjoyed several magnificent outings, both in the early morning and late afternoon. Then, at night, as we watched from our deck, the eyes of unknown animals gleamed in the darkness—now appearing, now disappearing—while a vast panorama of stars stretched out above us. The tiny suns seemed to look down upon Lynn and I, watching over us like the eyes of beneficent gods. I never saw the smile leave Lynn's face.

On one of our safaris, we spotted a family of leopards—a snoozing mother and two little cubs playing in the tall grass. Andrew whispered, "Don't talk or stand up. They could attack."

During another trip, a pride of lions that had just taken down a giraffe gathered around its carcass. Lion cubs jumped happily around the kill, females ripped the animal limb from limb, and the papa lion—he couldn't have cared less. He slept through it all.

230

After three unforgettable days in Kruger Park, Lynn and I returned to Cape Town, full of wonder and stories we couldn't wait to tell our children. In a store in Cape Town, Lynn noticed a shopkeeper avidly watching a tiny television behind the counter. "You look concerned," she commented.

"Oh, I'm just watching the tsunami news," said the woman. Indeed, while we had hid ourselves away at Kruger Park, the famous 2011 tsunami had struck Japan and destroyed a nuclear reactor. Lynn called Julie right away, concerned about her living in a house on the California coast, but Julie told her not to worry, so we embarked upon the last leg of our journey—a cruise that sailed up Africa's Atlantic coast and ended at the Canary Islands.

The first evening aboard, we cruised around the tip of Africa. Despite brain-melting heat, Lynn and I couldn't pull ourselves away from the rail.

I was pointing and saying, "Look at that, Sweetie. The Cape of Good Hope!"

Lynn hugged me tightly as we stood in the sunshine, not wanting to miss a moment of our extraordinary lives. The next evening, the ship's crew threw a formal dinner to kick off two and a half days of entertainment designed to keep us occupied while we sailed up to Namibia. Lynn looked as beautiful as ever when she slipped into her gown, but when I prepared to fasten her necklace, as I always had, no necklace appeared. She had sold them all to pay my expenses during the cancer treatments.

"Oh Marty, look at everything we have," she said. "This wonderful life! Who needs jewelry? A bare neck is the most beautiful thing a woman can show." One thing about Lynn, she never looked back.

The next day, the ship offered educational and historical lectures about Namibia, so we attended those, preparing for our next cultural experience, but when we finally docked in Namibia, Lynn felt tired.

"I'm just dragging," she said. "I don't know why."

We skipped the sightseeing in Namibia so Lynn could nap, which suited me as well, because I wanted to rest up for that evening's entertainment. It turned out to be the most elegant night of both our lives.

Namibia boasts some of the most famous sand dunes south of the Sahara so the cruise line set up a spectacular evening in this incredible environment, the details of which the organizers kept secret. Lynn and I boarded a Jeep for an hour-long ride that bounced us around the outback until we reached those great, bare heaps of sand, which rose suddenly, voluptuously out of the ground. Our driver eased between two bare, sandy mountains, as if finding a secret passage, then we disembarked in an open space nestled amongst sky-scraper-like dunes. On both sides, walls of gleaming white rose to the clouds, and in the middle, a beautiful white tent sheltered tables set with crystal, silver, candles, the works. From the tent's ceiling, sparkling chandeliers hung, and all around the clearing stood the camels that had carried these riches into our secret oasis.

"Now, that's what I call dining!" I told Lynn.

She laughed and bent down to remove her high heels, useless in the sand. Barefoot in her black evening gown, Lynn looked like the world's most elegant thrill-seeker. I loved her a little bit extra in that moment.

At the entrance to the tent, a column of Namibians in native dress—some playing exotic musical instruments, others serving cocktails—greeted us warmly. While we ate dinner, I didn't know where to look first. Each mountain surrounding us rose more magnificently than the last. As evening wore on, many of the other passengers climbed up through the sand and cried out in amazement at the views from various heights.

Lynn said, "Marty, I want to do it. I want to climb that dune!"

"I don't know if I can, with my one lung," I said.

"You do as much as you can," she answered, then took off, running up the sand as fleet-footed as a gazelle.

I chugged along behind Lynn, determined as ever, taking my time to stop and enjoy the view, and I finally did join her at the top. As the sun began to set, it cast its colors over the sand. Together, the sky and the dunes turned coral and pink and violet—just like at home in Santa Fe, really, only different in some grand, immeasurable, African way. Everything about that place looms in my memories as magical.

The perma-grin Lynn had worn since the safari didn't fade with the sunset. While I trudged, and she glided, down the mountain, she said, "Give me your camera!" and Lynn took photo after photo of every beautiful thing there. The sensuous, shifting sands; the glamorous tent; and all the frolicking people. I saw someone take a picture of Lynn, too. With her boundless enthusiasm and her sleek, black gown, Lynn looked like some kind of sand nymph. It turned out to be the ship's captain who took that photo. He sent me a copy, later. I had it framed, but I can't look at it now. It makes me too sad.

Back onboard ship that evening, Lynn and I fell into bed, dead tired. I'm sure the other passengers remember us as the oldest, yet most enthusiastic couple among those who climbed to the top. I hit the pillow hard, but Lynn sat up in bed with a worried look.

"What's the matter, Gorgeous?" I mumbled, trying to drag her down into the bed with me.

Lynn put her hands on her abdomen. "I'm just not myself," she said. "It's the same thing as this afternoon. I don't know what it is."

The next morning, Lynn ran a fever, so I convinced her to walk down to the ship's infirmary, still in her dressing gown. They gave her Tylenol and an IV drip of saline for dehydration. After a half hour, the fever broke, so the ship's doctor prescribed an antibiotic and told Lynn to eat bland foods. We spent the next two hours in our room, then boom, Lynn grew feverish again. We returned to the infirmary for more IV saline and cold compresses on her neck and forehead. Her temperature dropped again, but this time Lynn complained of chills. The doctor covered her with a blanket, and after a little while, Lynn felt fine again.

"I'm going to put you on a second antibiotic," said the doctor, a forty-something Turkish woman. "I'm worried about a tropical disease, though with these symptoms it could be a lot of things...or just a common cold."

For the next twenty-four hours, Lynn and I shuttled back and forth to the infirmary. She felt better, then worse, then better, then hot, then cold. But eventually, Lynn said she felt significantly better.

"I want to get dressed, go to the dining room to eat, and attend that lecture about Sao Tome et Principe, tonight," she said. It would take four or five days for the ship to pass Angola, The Congo, and Gabon, in order to dock at the tiny two-island nation of Sao Tome et Principe. In the meantime, Lynn didn't want to miss the gourmet dinners and educational lectures. We did as she requested, but by fifteen minutes into the lecture, Lynn whispered, "I'm so cold, I'm shaking. I can't control it."

I felt her, and Lynn's skin burned hot as the African sun.

Over the next couple of days, we returned to the infirmary multiple times. Lynn's condition continued to vacillate, but finally, things improved again, so we headed back to our suite and settled down to listen to one of Lynn's favorite symphonies. Each little detail of the next few hours played out as if time chopped itself up into dice-sized moments that could be spilled out on a table, rearranged, and examined.

Lynn did a crossword puzzle while I watched the tsunami news on television. I suggested we watch the sun set over the ocean, so we walked out on the terrace. She said she wanted to read in bed. I said I would stay up and wake her when it came time for her medication, which I did. I climbed into bed beside her, and she returned to sleep. In the middle of the night, Lynn got up and used the bathroom. I turned on the light so she wouldn't trip. She came back and fell asleep in my arms.

In the morning, I got up and let in room service, which brought our breakfast, but Lynn said, "I want to sleep a little more."

I said, "I'll keep the food covered and wait a half an hour for you."

A little while later, I wandered into the bedroom to check on Lynn and found her half on the bed, half off. One arm reached for the wall in front of her, and she grunted, unable to talk, but clearly trying to cry out for help.

I lifted her back onto the bed, only to discover Lynn burned with fever again. Worse yet, she lay in a pool of her own excrement.

I called the doctor, who came running with a nurse and a wheelchair. They took her to the infirmary, cleaned her up, and installed another IV drip, as well as oxygen. Lynn moaned, moaned, and moaned, unable to talk. Her eyes darted here and there, so frightened. I held her hand and tried to smile reassuringly, like Lynn would have done for me.

I said, "Darling, I'm here for you. We're going to fix this. I'm here."

"I think this is malaria," the doctor told me. "I don't have much medication for it. I can't even test her for it onboard ship, but I can give her some quinine."

The doctor put a quinine pill on Lynn's tongue and encouraged her to sip some water, but Lynn spit it out. I crushed the pill and mashed it up in the water, then helped Lynn drink it, holding her lips into shape, ensuring the water went down the right pipe, coaxing her along. Then, the phone in the infirmary rang. Over the line, the ship's captain asked to meet with the doctor and me.

Reluctantly, I left Lynn's side for the meeting. In the captain's office, I met the captain as well as the guest relations manager and purser.

"I'm sorry," said the captain, as soon as I sat down. "But you're going to have to get off at the next port."

42

"Lynn needs more care than we can give her, here," said the captain, leaning back in his chair and tenting his fingers, as if this were a casual conversation. The guest relations manager, purser, and ship's doctor watched me, stealthy as leopards, their eyes betraying nothing.

"What's at the next port?" I asked.

"Well," continued the captain. He paused before continuing, as if this difficult question required a complicated answer. "Sao Tome et Principe is a former Portuguese colony. There's a hospital there," he finally replied, with a confident nod of the head.

"Don't forget, Captain, I attended one of the lectures," I said. "You are talking about the poorest country in the whole world."

The captain looked at his hands. The others looked away, too. It felt like a sick game of peek-a-boo: like children, the four of them seemed to believe if they didn't look at me, I couldn't see them casually turn my wife into a piece of expendable cargo.

"I'm not getting off," I told them, looking each person in turn, right in the eyes.

"You have to get off. You can't stay here," shot back the captain.

"Really? Tell me about this hospital supposedly out in the middle of God-forsaken nowhere."

"There is a hospital," he said. The others nodded and mumbled agreement.

"Everybody's so sure of that," I replied with dark sarcasm.

"I have never been spoken to like this," said the doctor, slitting her eyes at me.

"Get over it," I replied. "I'm concerned about my wife, not your pride." I added, "Captain, you have a computer in front of you. I want you to go to the search engine and type in 'medical care Sao Tome et Principe.'"

"That's not necessary," replied the captain, unmoving.

"For me, it's necessary. Please check it."

The others looked over the captain's shoulder while he typed on his laptop. I sat across the desk from them with zero curiosity, knowing full well the results he would pull up. When I could see from his eyes that the captain had hit upon a web page, I asked, "Please read what it says aloud, so we can all hear it."

The captain cleared his throat and read: "Medical care and facilities Sao Tome et Principe: poor to inadequate."

"God damn it! This is where you want to dump us? Not a chance in hell!" I stormed out of the cabin, but making my way down the hallway, I nearly collapsed, then remembered my body couldn't stomp around like that anymore. I had to take it easy. Leaning against the wall, catching my breath, I understood no one on this boat could help us. I had to transport Lynn off the ship, not to Sao Tome et Principe, but to a real hospital.

Returning to our suite, I called a friend in America, a former client, who occupied a high government position. I had never, ever tried to take advantage of this connection before, but if ever a time had come, this was it. Trained to be completely professional in any emergency, he suggested hiring a medical evacuation jet from a French hospital. Spain's location made it the closest European country to the ship's location, but I spoke French and not Spanish, so we agreed a French jet would be best.

"I'll arrange everything," he said. "Just remain calm and tell Lynn to stay strong."

Soon, my friend called back and told me a private jet would meet us at the Sao Tome at Principe airport. Doctors at the American hospital in Paris prepared to receive us. I called the captain, told him of my plan, then returned to Lynn, in the infirmary, and said, "Sweetheart, keep fighting. You're going to be fine. I have a surprise! We're leaving on a jet, and they're going to take us to Paris! Hey, you wanted to go to Paris after the cruise, anyway."

"Out of here, out of here..." Lynn replied, between grunts.

"Yes, I know," I said, taking her hand in mine. "Just be strong. Keep fighting. You are going to be just fine. Lynnie, I love you so much."

She tried to reply, to say she loved me, too, but by now she could only grunt.

"I know," I told her. "I know."

I left Lynn's side to go pack our things and make some final calls, but dashed back five minutes later, afraid to leave her alone, and for good reason. Those five minutes had worsened her condition. I ran back to the suite and threw all the medicines I now needed for survival in a small case. I ran back to Lynn, reassured her, then returned to the suite, trying to find things that could help Lynn—her unfinished book, her iPod, some Tylenol. I had no idea what to do, just ran back and forth, trying to somehow prepare for our next step.

Each time I saw Lynn, her condition declined. She lost the ability even to grunt, and soon, to my horror, her eyes fixed in a hard stare while her temperature rose hotter and hotter. Soon afterward, she lost control of her legs, arms, and even fingers. When I squeezed her hand, it lay there, unresponsive as a dishrag.

I prayed out loud, "Oh God, we've got to get out of here. Please get us out of here."

As night fell, the captain increased the ship's speed to maximum. I'm sure he crossed his fingers and hoped the passengers wouldn't notice our sudden breakneck speed. Goodness knows, like us, they had paid a lot of money for a trouble-free cruise.

We arrived at Sao Tome et Principe six hours before expected. Since no dock existed there, the ship's doctor, captain, purser, guest relations manager, Lynn on a stretcher, and I all disembarked via a small boat, called a tender, that sailed out to meet us. On the tender, we met a port agent, a young man who would serve as our translator. On land, we found a rudimentary ambulance waiting near a dirt airstrip similar to the one in Kruger Park, but no jet.

"The plane has not arrived yet," said the ambulance driver, with a shrug.

"We'll wait," I said.

"No." The doctor shook her head. "We can't let Lynn sit in this ambulance, in this heat. We're going to have to go to the hospital. They'll be able to do more for her there."

I had to agree. While the ambulance drove through town, my heart fell at the poverty I saw. Every brick and board of the town looked broken down, neglected. Paint peeled from cracked walls. Broken windows outnumbered unbroken ones. The once-paved street, with its ruts and potholes too numerous to count, jostled us endlessly. Meanwhile, wild dogs, pigs, and chickens roamed the streets, along with people dressed, essentially, in rags. A jungle surrounded the whole place and seemed eager to envelop the town any minute. Forget the third world. If there is a fourth world, I thought, this place is it.

The ambulance ascended a hill to the hospital—a group of one-story buildings in the same state of rapid decline as everything else on the island. Orderlies took Lynn, on her stretcher, into the emergency room, with its crumbling walls, filthy floors, and peeling paint. I immediately noticed the absence of a sink for washing hands. The room offered no windows, no fans, and no air circulation at all, and certainly no air conditioning in the 100-plus degree heat.

Hospital personnel flooded into the room, followed by a doctor who stood tall and midnight black in an incongruously clean, white smock. He only spoke Portuguese, so while the ship's doctor explained Lynn's symptoms in English, the port agent translated everything she said for the doctor.

The island doctor took a finger-puncture of blood from Lynn and placed it on a slide, then under a microscope. When he stood up from his seat at the microscope, the doctor held his mouth fixed, unsmiling. He said, "malaria falciparum" to the port agent, who said, "it's malaria falciparum" to the ship's doctor. The same in any language. The ship's doctor's face fell.

"What does that mean?" I asked.

"Malaria Falciparum is the most violent and deadly form of malaria known," she replied.

The island doctor injected Lynn with a concoction of medicine I didn't dare question and attached an oxygen mask and EKG monitor to her with quick but gentle hands. I knew then that despite the filth and poverty here, we had brought her to the right place. Few hospitals in the world would be prepared to treat this rare strain of malaria with such immediacy, but the island doctor, clearly, had seen it before.

A few minutes after the injection, a nurse discovered the tank had run out of oxygen, so nurses and orderlies dashed up and down the hospital halls looking for another tank. Someone finally pulled one out of the ambulance. Meanwhile, Lynn didn't move. Her eyes remained open in that glassy stare. I looked at her feet and hands and noticed them tinged with blue. I touched the doctor's shoulder and pointed at her hands. He nodded. My eyes darted between the doctor, Lynn's face, and Lynn's heart rate on the EKG monitor.

"Lynn," I said. "I'm right here. Keep fighting, Darling. Everybody here is helping you. Keep fighting. Keep fighting!"

Then the EKG monitor went flat.

The doctor grabbed paddles and jolted Lynn, but nothing happened. He began the chest compressions for CPR. I pointed to my mouth, and the doctor nodded yes, so I began mouth-to-mouth resuscitation. The doctor compressed her chest alternately with my mouth breathing, but Lynn didn't respond.

Eventually, the doctor stopped his compressions, but I wouldn't. I kept breathing into her mouth. By now, I had lost track of the rhythm I knew to use, the correct number of breaths per chest compression. I just breathed into her again, and again, and again, and again.

Finally, I felt a hand on my shoulder.

"No!" I screamed, "It wasn't supposed to be you! It should have been me!" I remember climbing up on the gurney, lying down next to Lynn, and holding her still-warm body in my arms, whispering, "Wait for me, Lynn. Wait for me."

I remember feeling the cruel rapidity with which her body's warmth faded away, and I remember sounds coming out of me, too, but they weren't words, just sounds, urgent appeals to God from some animal place in me.

Eventually, someone pulled me off the gurney. I watched nurses remove Lynn's oxygen mask, take out the IV, and disconnect the EKG. Returning to Lynn's side, I saw a strangely peaceful look on her face. Her eyes had relaxed, and her mouth wore what might almost have been a smile.

I closed Lynn's eyes.

Someone covered her with a sheet.

I collapsed, sobbing and screaming her name, against the dirty wall.

43

At some point, the port agent put his arm around my back and guided me outdoors. There, I met the French physician, nurse, medical assistant, pilot, and crew of the medical jet that had finally arrived. Their white faces, atop crisp, white uniforms, quickly reddened as they stood, unshaded, in the morning sun. Wild pigs grunted and sniffed at their immaculate shoes.

I felt nothing upon seeing these people. To the extent that I knew anything at that point, I knew they couldn't have saved Lynn. Along with the port agent, ship's doctor, purser, and guest-relations manager (the captain had returned to the ship), we all walked into a shaded clearing at the edge of the encroaching jungle.

In English, the pilot told me, "Dr. Kraidin, we have to go, now."

"Go?" I asked. "Where?"

"We're going to take you to Paris," he said.

"We've got to get my wife, first," I replied, feeling uncomfortable having left her side at all.

"No," the pilot said. "We can't take her. Only you."

He went on to explain that the jet's flight path would take them through a refueling stop in a country, I don't remember which one, where we would have to declare everything on board, including Lynn's body. By law, officials would have to remove and examine her.

"I don't know the people there, what kind of conditions they have in that country. You could be stuck there for days, and her body would be out of your hands," the pilot said. "My recommendation is that you fly to Paris with us, and we send another plane in a few days' time to pick up your wife and take her on a different flight path, to avoid the hassle."

"No," I replied. "Either my wife goes with me, or we don't go." The thought of Lynn taking a separate airplane, all by herself, didn't sit well with me. She'd be lonely, I thought. She remained my wife, and I certainly didn't plan to leave her all alone in this rotting backwater of the world. The fact that the pilot expected me to suddenly treat Lynn as a thing, not a person, just because she had died, made no sense to me.

"Then you'll have to stay here until we can get another plane to take you both out," the pilot replied.

"And what am I supposed to do in the meantime?"

"Well, you'll check into the hotel."

"Is the hotel just like the hospital?" I replied in a panic. In my condition, I felt quite sure in a few days' time they would have two bodies to transport, not one. "Did you see a hotel on the way here?" I asked everyone. "I didn't see a hotel."

"Oh," said the ship's doctor, "There has to be a hotel!"

"Yeah, just like, 'there has to be a hospital?'" I spat back at her, and then tried to calm down, but my head wanted to explode. None of our friends or children knew where we were. Lynn and I could disappear forever here, quite easily.

"I don't speak the language," I said. "None of them speak English, and you're asking me to stay here, all alone…no translator, no way of communicating if the jet doesn't arrive, if we're in danger…" I looked at the ship's doctor steadily, and my eyes asked her to see me—a man with a crater carved out of his neck, violently shaking hands, and the grief of lifetimes in his eyes, but not a fool. "Let me tell you something," I said. "You have one dead passenger right now. And I'm a passenger, too. And I'm still alive. Now you're trying for two dead passengers? Like hell you will!" The ship's doctor opened her mouth to protest, but I added in the strongest voice I could muster, "I am still a live passenger of record, and either I go on board that ship with my wife, or I sit right here. And if I have to sit here in this jungle, you don't leave, either. If you think you are going to abandon me here, I am fully capable of creating an international incident. You got it? Now, tell that to the captain."

The ship's doctor shrugged her shoulders, walked into the hospital to call the captain, and came back saying we would have to wait for a response. No one had the guts to walk out on me, so the entire group sat there, in broken plastic chairs and on fallen logs, in the shade inside the edge of the jungle. The sun rose high and the air became suffocatingly hot, but I refused to move. Pregnant dogs, starving goats, and stinking pigs roamed the area. Trash blew around on a hot wind. Still, I sat. A spot of sun burned my cheek, but I didn't move deeper into the shade. A waft of animal excrement assailed my nostrils, but I didn't put a handkerchief to my nose. I just sat, on strike from life.

The others thought I awaited the captain's permission to board the ship, and I did, but my stillness really represented a sit-in for Lynn's life. My stillness said no, I don't accept this, any of this. My silence said, I want Lynn alive, and I want her now. Lynn always complained I had to have everything my way...well, I wanted my way again. I rebelled against everyone, against God. I tried, with sheer force of willpower, to awaken myself from this nightmare.

I wanted to pull the trees out by their roots, wipe this island off the face of the earth, tear the blue right off the blazing sky and the waves off the ocean itself. But with no food in my belly and no baggage but a satchel full of medicine, I slouched in my chair, weak as a babe in arms. No longer the young man who had battled Abner for independence, the ardent lover who had trysted with Lynn in secret, the warrior who had stood up for his love against Barbara and five children, or the sacrificial lamb who had given parts of his body to keep his soul united with Lynn's, this world had reduced me to a husk of a man, with stillness the only power left to me. So I sat, trying to breathe more air into Lynn with my mind.

Lost inside my own world, I became completely unaware of the others. I must have cried a great deal. I don't recall the tears, only the dryness of my eyes when I became so dehydrated no more water would flow from me. At one point, the medical jet physician offered me a glass of water and checked my blood pressure. He found it high and steadily rising. Still, I sat.

The ship's doctor, purser, guest relations manager, medical jet physician, nurse, pilot, and crew—they sat, too. Six hours later, a call came in.

"The captain has agreed to take you and Lynn back onboard ship," the ship's doctor said.

Her words meant food, water, air conditioning, cleanliness, safety, and that I wouldn't die of exposure here and now on the edge of the jungle. I wouldn't join Lynn on the other side, not today.

I felt vaguely disappointed.

44

"Come on, Dr. Kraidin," said the ship's doctor, extending her hand through the jungle's dappled shade to help me up from my chair. "We have to go, now."

"Wait a minute," I said. "Where's my wife? She's coming with me."

"No," said the doctor, shaking her head. "She can't go with you. We have to do this quietly. We don't want to arouse and upset the passengers, so we'll take you onboard first, and she'll come in a separate tender."

"Okay," I replied. "But I want to see her, first. Where is she?"

"They put her in the morgue. It's that building over there." The doctor pointed to a cinderblock bungalow with a pitched roof.

Entourage in tow, I walked to the morgue—nothing but a large, empty room with a table in the middle. Upon the table lay a body draped in sheets. The others stood in the doorway, maintaining a polite distance, while I walked to the shrouded form. I placed one hand on the chest, the other on the forehead, of the body.

I said a prayer, then told Lynn, "Darling, my beautiful Lynn. I love you so much. I will always be with you. My heart is yours forever. Even death can't keep us apart."

Even as I spoke, I sensed something amiss; so finally, I pulled the sheet away to look at Lynn's face. A black man in an advanced state of decomposition stared back at me. I screamed and ripped the sheet off the body.

Everyone standing in the doorway screamed and shouted, "My God! My God!" in their French, Moroccan, and Portuguese accents.

"God has nothing to do with this, damn you," I bellowed. "Find my wife!"

Everyone ran out of the building and in different directions, except the ship's doctor, who walked outside with me.

"And this is who you were going to bring on board!" I yelled at her, my admonishment a clear accusation of incompetence, so desperately did I desire to find someone to blame for all of this.

"I'm so sorry, Dr. Kraidin. We'll find your wife," she assured me, and then ran off to join in the search.

I heard shouts of, "Where's the blonde?" and "Find the white woman!" while I leaned against the wall of the morgue, trying to reduce my body's violent shaking. The dead man's mocking gaze seared itself into my brain. "One body is not just like another," I wanted to scream at these people. "I want my wife!"

But inside, something in me recognized God had found a way to tell me just the opposite, to tell me Lynn is dead now, just like any other corpse, and her body doesn't contain her. Only my heart contains her, now. I couldn't hear that message yet, though. To me, she still inhabited her body, and Lynn had disappeared somewhere on the campus of this hospital just as if she'd carelessly wandered off without a map.

Finally, someone guided me to another building, where I found Lynn and repeated my prayers.

After boarding the ship, I breathlessly endured the hour-long wait until Lynn's body followed. Then, I watched the doctor slide my wife into the refrigerated oblivion of a morgue drawer. Finally, I shuffled to the computer center, where I pulled up our email list of family and friends and wrote:

> Lynn died this morning March 19, 2011 from virulent malaria. I am onboard the Silver WIND with her trying to get us both back to the U.S. together. My heart is broken. I will contact you with further information.

> Marty

Each day, the doctor permitted me to see Lynn for less than a minute. I knelt down to the drawer and kissed her cold lips, her cheeks. I smoothed her hair and spoke lovingly to my darling, my gorgeous Lynn. As the ship sailed on—through endless, sleepless days and nights—I lived for those few seconds alone with my wife.

One day, I brought Lynn's cosmetics along and asked the doctor to put some lipstick on Lynn after I left. I didn't think it a strange request. The doctor held the small, pink bag in her hands like some barnacled thing I'd pulled up from the bottom of the sea. She gazed at it for quite some time, and when she looked up, her face had reddened, her eyes filled with tears. The tension in her expression showed how hard she worked to keep her emotions in check.

"Yes," she said. "I'll do it."

Lynn's voice rang in my ears, saying, "Always keep your chin up and be dignified."

I knew the last thing she'd want at a time like this would be to look dead.

45

March 2011

"I'm so sorry, Mom. I've been so stupid," sobbed Stephen, collapsing upon the open casket. I had arranged for him and Julie to sit for a few minutes with Lynn's body, just before the memorial. Julie declined, but Stephen desperately wanted to see her. "I want to do it all over, Mom. I wish I could..."

"Stephen, don't," I said.

"No, Dad, I have to. I have to tell her I'm sorry. I was so angry with both of you. I was going to really show you, you know, because it was all about me, me, me."

"I know that. So did Mom. It was something you had to work out for yourself. She knew that."

My words provided little comfort to Stephen, who continued to sob and apologize to his mother. Finally, still shaking and crying, he stood and put his head on my shoulder. I held my son, my last remaining link to Lynn, as close as I could, my arms steady now, my heart prepared to survive this loss, having vowed to honor Lynn's memory in every aspect of the life that remained to me.

Finally, Stephen fell into a chair, exhausted. I kissed Lynn's lips, arranged her washed and curled hair just so around her ears, and said, "I love you, Lynn. I'll see you, soon. Wait for me, Darling." With that I tucked her unopened letter into the casket beside her. I had found the letter in our mail a few days after we got back from the trip and couldn't bare to reread it or even open it. It was my gift to her, my final words and they were sacred. They belonged to her and with her.

Though a funeral director stood by, prepared to do his job, I took hold of the casket lid myself, and gently closed it.

Following Lynn's memorial—a beautiful ceremony I arranged myself, which attracted more than 500 old friends from all parts of the country—I had her body cremated, as she requested. Then I traveled to Florida, to spend the summer with Stephen. Divorced by this time, he enjoyed part-time custody of my wonderful 12-year-old granddaughter. Each day, Lynn's absence felt palpable to all three of us.

Walking on the beach, I remembered the first time Lynn jumped into my arms that day on Lewes Beach. I collapsed on the sand, not crying, just wanting to replay the memory over and over with complete concentration, like the carefully memorized lyrics of a favorite song.

Playing with my granddaughter on the floor of Stephen's boat, I recalled finding Lynn huddled on the floor of our apartment with then-college-age Jonathan, talking quietly and earnestly, and how she said, "This is a private conversation." She respected intimacy, Lynn did. She listened to people.

In a café one morning, I looked down into my coffee cup, as if into a crystal ball, and there I saw the cup of coffee I had been drinking when Lynn returned from the only night she ever spent away from me since our remarriage. I remembered how we had driven to Key Biscayne and she'd told me her secrets, her defects, her mistakes. How important it had been to her that I love the real Lynn, not an idealized image.

Strolling down the street, I saw a beautiful old house for sale and remembered—and this time tears did streak my cheeks—how Lynn had managed the Miami house renovation like she'd been born to it. And then our shenanigans later, with the chief inspector...oh, she wrapped him around her little finger, didn't she? We had so much fun together, Lynn and I.

The unusual calm of my life with Stephen and his daughter felt odd, though, and uncomfortable. Prone to frequent rages and sullen moods, Lynn had seldom remained placid for long. Not a week went by without Lynn perceiving some dreadful offense against her, especially from one of the children.

Her frequent refrain, "He should know better!" Always made me shake my head. I used to ask her, "Why? Why should Stephen automatically know how to behave? The boy wasn't born knowing everything!" Lynn thought she had set a good example, one that need only be emulated to achieve perfect social correctness, but she conveniently forgot some of the less-ideal moments in her parenting history.

From afar, one day, I spied a wedding taking place at a quaint seaside chapel, and I remembered both my weddings to Lynn, as different as they had been—the first an ecstatic romp; the second, a careful, determined undertaking. All five of our children's weddings had, for us, been tense, exercises in negotiating the role of the stepparent in the ceremony. Of course, three of the weddings enabled Barbara to publicly exhibit her disgust with Lynn and me. And the other two—Stephen and Julie's—required Lynn and I to exchange words with Bob. With Lynn's coaching, I behaved like a player at "decorum" as an Olympic event. Even after our remarriage, Lynn and I still had to fight, fight, fight at every family event, to gain acceptance from those we loved the most.

I'll never forget Lynn's vehemence when she objected to Elizabeth's wedding plans: "I will not wear a formal gown on a Sunday afternoon!" Lynn could be inflexible, stubborn and rule-bound, just like me, but about completely different things.

"I hate to say this," said Stephen one day, as we boarded his boat in the Palm Beach Marina. "I miss Mom a lot, but things between you and me are a lot easier now, in a way."

I knew what he meant, and laughed a little. "She was always offended about something," I said, stepping over the gunwale.

"If she wasn't not-speaking to me, she'd be not-speaking to Julie," Stephen added, with a good-natured chuckle. "It was always something, with Mom."

"And she never wanted us to talk things out. Oh, she hated when I wanted to sit down with you and discuss whatever was wrong. She would forbid it!"

"It's weird," said Stephen, "but I kind of feel like you and I have grown closer this summer than we've ever been." He unwound the rope from the bollard that kept us shore-bound.

I couldn't deny the truth of this observation. Thinking about everything Stephen and Lynn had endured during his childhood—their anger, confusion, and loneliness—I wished I could have been there for the two of them, counteracting Lynn's Abner-like stubbornness with my "wimpy" hugs and kisses. But I'd felt that regret before. Didn't want to feel it again. Life had taught me to leave the past alone and look ahead, chanting only, "What's next? What's next? What's next?"

I fell silent a moment. "I think this, our relationship, is her final gift to us," I said.

Stephen took the wheel, powered up the motor, and guided his boat clear of the marina. "Maybe it is," he said, as we cut through the open water, out to sea, and into the blue unknown. "Maybe it is, at that."

Epilogue

After Lynn's death, every time I asked myself, "What's next?" My thoughts led me toward fulfilling Lynn's wish to let her legacy live on as an arts endowment for children. Lynn had mentioned Santa Fe's Lensic Performing Arts Center as the best place to create some kind of special fund in her memory. As Santa Fe's premier venue for everything from concerts to plays to live opera simulcasts from the Met, this elegant Spanish Renaissance theater provided Lynn with the chance to become a patron of the arts and be actively involved in programming. Through the Lensic, Lynn helped bring world-class performances to the little mountain town of Santa Fe.

Now, the Lynn Kraidin Memorial Foundation underwrites a program that busses children from all socio-economic levels to the Lensic, in downtown Santa Fe, to see incredible live performances, many of which are concerts by prodigy musicians who are themselves children.

I know each child will come away from the performances with something different, but I dare to hope that all those children will emerge with something of Lynn's life. Above all, I want the children to hear the soul-stirring unity of a beautiful symphony and realize that, together, we can create something far greater than any of us could ever make alone.

www.ingramcontent.com/pod-product-compliance
Lightning Source LLC
Chambersburg PA
CBHW031057020726
47495CB00007B/1930